T0129413

1 DOWN: A PERSON OF INTEREST

Quinn Carr has been quietly creating crosswords for the *Chestnut Station Chronicle* in her small Colorado town since she was in high school, but she has yet to solve the puzzle of how to make a living from her passion. So she lives with her parents and works at the local diner, catering to regulars like The Retireds, a charming if cantankerous crew of elderly men. The most recent member to join the group is a recently retired tailor, the unfortunately named Hugh Pugh.

4-LETTER WORD FOR "IMPALE"

But Hugh's misfortune dramatically increases when he's arrested for stabbing his husband with a pair of fabric shears. With a cryptic crossword clue left at the crime scene, Quinn seems tailor-made for solving this murder. The local police may be determined to pin the crime on the kindly tailor, but Quinn will use her penchant for puzzles and what her therapist calls her "obsessive coping mechanism" to get the clues to line up and catch the real culprit—before the killer boxes her in. . . .

By Becky Clark

Puzzling Ink
Punning with Scissors

Punning with Scissors

Becky Clark

LYRICAL UNDERGROUND
Kensington Publishing Corp.
www.kensingtonbooks.com

LYRICAL PRESS BOOKS are published by
Kensington Publishing Corp.
119 West 40th Street
New York, NY 10018

All Kensington titles, imprints, and distributed lines are available at special quantity discounts for bulk purchases for sales promotion, premiums, fund-raising, educational, or institutional use.

Special book excerpts or customized printings can also be created to fit specific needs. For details, write or phone the office of the Kensington Sales Manager: Kensington Publishing Corp., 119 West 40th Street, New York, NY 10018. Attn. Sales Department. Phone: 1-800-221-2647.

First Electronic Edition: May 2021
ISBN-13: 978-1-5161-1064-3 (ebook)
ISBN-10: 1-5161-1064-1 (ebook)

First Print Edition: May 2021
ISBN-13: 978-1-5161-1067-4
ISBN-10: 1-5161-1067-6

Printed in the United States of America

Chapter 1

Quinn Carr unlocked the door to the Chestnut Station Diner to let Jethro and the Retireds in. They all tried to push past her, drooling, scratching their butts, and sniffing the air. All except the dog, of course.

Jethro made his rounds, nose, jowls, and long bloodhound ears brushing the linoleum as he checked the entire diner for anything amiss, ending at the kitchen doorway to accept his slice of bacon. Normally he got it from Jake Szabo, the owner and cook, but today Quinn had to handle the diner alone.

The Retireds kept their jowls and long ears off the floor as they shuffled their way to their regular table, joking, complaining, and teasing each other with the ease and privilege bestowed upon old men who'd known each other for decades. This was their domain. The diner afforded them their modern-day fiefdom. They presumed they had dominion over all they could see, and sometimes they did, but only when Quinn allowed them to keep a precious coffeepot on their table.

Quinn followed Jethro to the kitchen, where she stepped around him and offered a crunchy strip of bacon already waiting for him.

She'd only been at the diner a few months since she'd boomeranged back home under less-than-ideal circumstances, but learned almost immediately that the key to working there—and the key to her entire life—was her overzealous attention to organization. Making sure bacon was ready for Jethro first thing. Table condiments perfectly filled and centered. Floor spotless and ready to be trod upon by today's diners. Pantry items stacked together with like items. Spices alphabetized. She even took it upon herself to color-code the plastic bins for food prep, bringing in her label-maker when she realized with horror that Jake didn't even own one.

Her therapist believed this to be an "obsessive coping mechanism not conducive to her treatment frame." Quinn believed it to be a natural way to live her life and do her job.

She stood in the doorway, watching Jethro gobble down his bacon paycheck, while she adjusted her high ponytail in yet another useless attempt to collect the stray tendrils tickling her cheek.

"One of these days I'm calling the health department about that dog." Wilbur's voice boomed across the room and landed on her. This morning he sounded even more like a cement mixer with a tumbler full of rocks than he normally did.

Silas limped past him. "I'd think you'd call them about Jake's food."

"I'm telling Jake." Quinn came out from the kitchen carrying a full coffeepot. Jethro trailed after her; sad, droopy eyes ever vigilant for more bacon. She opened the front door of the diner and ushered Jethro out, thumping him on his side as he passed her. "Don't do anything I wouldn't do."

As one of the town dogs, Jethro had a cushy life of doing absolutely nothing. He was owned by none, loved—and fed—by all.

Herman cocked a quizzical eye at Quinn, still holding the door. "Jethro is a dog. I doubt there's a Venn diagram overlapping with anything the two of you would do."

"Don't be so literal, Herman," Bob said, smoothing his movie-star hair.

"Yeah, Herman." Larry shuffled, slightly stooped, to his seat, dragging a chair from a neighboring table with him.

"Yeah, Herman," Quinn repeated. "If I had time and didn't have to start catering to every single one of your whims this morning, I'd absolutely draw you a Venn diagram showing just how much Jethro and I have in common." She began pouring coffee for the Retireds already sitting.

A man Quinn didn't know took the chair Larry had dragged over next to him.

"Coffee?" Quinn asked. After he nodded, she said, "I don't believe we've met. I'm Quinn."

The man held out his hand and smiled up at her. "Hugh Pugh."

Quinn stifled a giggle, but none of the other Retireds did.

"Your folks sure had a warped sense of humor," Silas said.

"That they did," Hugh said. "They named my sister Sue, but she learned early on to go by Susan. I got used to it. Could be worse, I guess."

This was all the encouragement the Retireds needed. They each began shouting and laughing, trying to outdo one another. If wordplay could be done, it could certainly be overdone. Quinn took the opportunity to go seat a party of four that had come in, which didn't mean she was out of range of their conversation. Their voices carried throughout the diner like so much volcanic ash, erupting, then wafting down over unsuspecting diners.

"Fondue Pugh."

"Gym Shoe Pugh."

"Kazoo Pugh."

"Voodoo Pugh."

"Kung Fu Pugh."

"Déjà vu Pugh."

"Kangaroo Pugh."

"Timbuktu Pugh."

"Cardinal Richelieu Pugh." Bob's offering stopped them short.

"Who?" Herman asked.

Bob started to answer, but Wilbur clamped a hand over his mouth, only removing it when Bob gave it a good, solid lick.

"Are you going to hang out with these miscreants every day?" Quinn asked Hugh, pulling out her order pad.

"I'm not sure yet. Maybe just on Saturdays like today."

Larry looked up at Quinn. "Hey. What are you doing here on a beautiful summer Saturday? Aren't you normally off?"

"Yeah, but Jake couldn't bear the thought of seeing you all, so he took the morning off. Was he supposed to clear it with you first?" Quinn used to be scared of these old men, but they had taught her to give as good as she got. And boy howdy, did she got.

The truth was Jake still hadn't been able to fill the weekend cook and waitress position after the last pair, a husband-and-wife duo, just up and took off recently with no warning. When Quinn needed them the most, they were halfway to Boise. Chestnut Station, Colorado, was just a dusty blip in their rearview mirror. Quinn appreciated all the extra money she was making picking up weekend shifts, and she really liked feeling in control at the diner, but all work and no play was beginning to turn her into a bore, much to the chagrin of her friends. She was tired all the time, even begging off from going to a movie with Loma in order to watch *The Rockford Files* on the couch with her parents. Although maybe that was the depression talking. Regardless, Loma was getting annoyed by all the cancellations. As was Rico. When he wanted to go for Mexican food the other night—his treat—she opted for cheese and crackers in bed with Netflix on her iPad, and Fang in his bowl on her nightstand for company.

At least she still found the energy to create her beloved crosswords, a task she could accomplish in bed.

She realized Hugh was speaking to her. He hadn't quite mastered the skill of attention-seeking as well as some of the other Retireds. "I just retired from my tailoring business."

"Oh, yeah," Quinn said, remembering. "My mom and dad went to your party. Nice to officially meet you."

"Of course. You're Georgeanne and Dan's daughter. I should have realized. You look just like Dan."

Quinn sighed. Every girl wanted to be told she looked like her dad.

Hugh continued speaking in his soft, calm voice. "It would be fun to hang out every day with these guys, but I want to be there to say goodbye to Creigh—my husband—when he leaves for work. He still has a few years before he can retire."

"Wait. You're Hugh and Creigh?" This time Quinn did laugh.

Hugh rolled his eyes while Bob launched into one of his know-it-all explanations. "Funny you should mention that—"

"Here he goes."

Quinn took the opportunity to pour coffee and take orders from the party of four, but still, Bob's story wafted down over the diner. Nobody seemed to mind, and in fact, the party of four turned to listen to him. Bob was a minor—very minor—celebrity in Chestnut Station, having spent his career on the stage. But he was revered in this tiny town on the Colorado plains for a series of local television commercials he did where he played second fiddle to a llama, a bucket of spicy chicken wings, and a chimpanzee dressed in a tuxedo. Everyone adored those ads. Bob pretended they never happened.

"I learned about 'hue and cry' when I was performing Shakespeare in the Park. I had to do some research for a role—"

"Was Shakespeare there?"

"In the thirteenth century—"

"When you were already an old man…"

Bob continued as if nobody had spoken. "If you witnessed a crime, you had to make a lot of noise and anyone in the vicinity was required to join in the pursuit. If they didn't, they could be held liable for the robbery victim's losses."

Quinn listened to them squabble and poke fun at each other while she returned the coffeepot to the warming tray.

"You know that movie *Grumpy Old Men*?" Quinn asked them when she returned to take their orders.

"Is that the one where they all swim in a pool then get on a spaceship?" Wilbur asked.

"No, it's the one where they're all butt-kicking spies with Helen Mirren," Bob said.

"She's a national treasure," Larry said.

"She's British," Hugh said, "but I don't think I've seen that one. I think Creighton did, though. He sees a lot of movies. I love it when he tells me about them; it's like I'm right there with him. When we got married our wedding was right out of *Roman Holiday.* We must have watched that one a hundred times."

Hugh got a dreamy look in his eyes that immediately endeared him to Quinn.

"Are you ever going to get around to taking our order?" Wilbur rumbled.

"I was waiting for you all to take a breath so I could get a word in edgewise." Quinn flapped her order pad at him. She knew, however, it would take at least ten more minutes for the six of them to order. They studied the menu, then asked a million questions they already knew the answers to, and then ended up ordering the exact meals they ordered every day. Hugh was the wild card, though, so she began with him. Maybe they could all change their routine.

"I'll have the Mexican omelet," Hugh said, without any prefacing questions.

Quinn scribbled it down. "Do you want guacamole with that?"

"Is it extra?"

"A dollar," Quinn said.

"Scandalous practice, charging for guac," Silas said. "Next thing we know, Jake will be charging us for breathing the air around here."

"Good idea," Quinn said. "I'm going to drop that in the employee suggestion box. Another revenue stream might get me a raise." Turning to Hugh, she said, "So…guac or no guac for you?"

"No guac. Gotta watch my pennies now that I'm retired." Hugh handed his menu to Quinn.

As she went around the table, Quinn was disappointed that Hugh's quick and easy ordering hadn't rubbed off on the Retireds. None of them changed their ordering routine. They asked all the same questions, she gave all the same answers, and they ordered their usuals. When she first began at the diner she joked with Jake that she was going to write up their orders, laminate them, and slap them down in front of each of them like she was a soccer referee "red carding" them for fouls.

She still might.

Knowing the Retireds would be at the diner until lunchtime anyway, Quinn got all the other tables' orders started before theirs.

She made sure everyone knew she was working alone and pointed to the drink station so they could get refills whenever they wanted. She left a coffeepot on the Retireds' table.

She'd become more comfortable in the kitchen since she'd had to recently learn short-order cooking by the seat of her pants, but it still could send her into an OCD tailspin. She knew when Jake accidentally broke a yolk when cracking eggs for an order of fried eggs, he'd just scramble them and serve them anyway. He'd flash his grin and nobody would seem to mind. But when Quinn broke a yolk when making fried eggs, she'd have to scrape the grill clean and start over. Cutting corners was not her style, no matter how much she wished it could be.

Today her eggs were fine and she only had to redo a couple of pieces of toast that weren't quite the right shade of brown to her eyes, so she was feeling pretty good. Any breakfast shift where she could keep her *baba ghanoush*es under a dozen was a win in her book. And, yes, of course she had a book. Every evening she recorded her OCD status for the day. An important statistic for her was how many times she muttered *baba ghanoush* as her "safe word" to keep her from a spiral. She knew other people used positive affirmations like, "You can do it!" or "Don't let the monster win!" but she preferred *baba ghanoush*, as it was more fun to say and didn't seem very therapy-y to her. It had the added benefit of sounding more like an unusual expletive if she accidentally said it out loud, which happened more often than she liked.

She also marked in her journal how often she found herself counting things, or organizing, or touching her fingers to her thumbs, or alphabetizing while attempting to feel in control of herself and her world. She recognized that her OCD journal itself bordered on OCD behavior, but she had no safe word for that. It was also why she kept it hidden.

She carried a tray filled with plates to the Retireds' table and began distributing them. As soon as the plates were in front of them, they began plucking things off them.

Herman bit into a piece of bacon before his plate even touched the table. "It's cold. I knew it."

Bob glanced up at Quinn. "Herman was just telling us how desperate he was for bacon."

"There's nothing more dangerous than a desperate man," said Silas. "That reminds me of a joke—"

"Everything reminds you of a joke," Wilbur said.

"How many vegans does it take to eat a piece of bacon?" Without waiting for an answer, he said, "Just one, if nobody's looking."

They'd all heard this joke fourteen thousand times, so nobody laughed but Silas.

Quinn turned to Herman. "This bacon came directly from the oven to your plate, which you just saw me walk out carrying. The only way I could make it hotter would be to build a fire in the middle of your table and cook it here."

Silas laughed. "I think an irritated waitress might give that dangerously desperate man a run for his money."

Quinn pretended to be annoyed by Herman and Herman pretended to be annoyed by Quinn.

She left them to their food, but returned almost immediately with a full coffeepot and extra packets of stevia. As she bent over Herman's cup, she dropped the packets next to his plate and whispered, "I noticed you were out, you old coot."

He whispered back, "Thanks, whippersnapper," and patted her hand.

An hour or so later, the door chimed again and Quinn peeked out the pass-through, the window from the kitchen to the dining room. She had been hoping the breakfast crowd would thin out soon, so she was thrilled to see Loma's bright, wide grin instead of another party of four.

Loma stopped at the Retireds' table to banter with them. Quinn always tensed the slightest bit when Loma wisecracked with the Retireds, because they were not the most "woke" people in the community. Casually sexist and racist things rolled trippingly off their tongues more often than they probably realized. Quinn knew Loma could shut down a disparaging remark with a grin and a quip because she'd seen her do it before. Many times. She hoped it wasn't just her imagination, but it seemed like the incidents were much more infrequent since Loma started coming around more often.

Loma was Jake's ex-wife, so she wasn't a complete stranger around the diner, but now that she and Quinn had become friends, they saw her a lot more often, which seemed to be fine with Jake, despite the way the two of them bantered. Quinn wondered if Jake regretted their divorce. Loma didn't seem to.

Loma made her way to the kitchen where Quinn artfully arranged an orange slice next to a stack of pancakes on a plate. "Hey, where's Jake? Sleeping in?"

"I don't know. I think he said he had some errands in Denver. I don't pay attention to anything he says after he says 'I'll pay you extra.'" Quinn picked up the plate of pancakes and carried it out to the dining room. Loma followed her.

"More coffee, Mrs. Feinstein?" Quinn set down the pancakes and moved the syrup pitcher closer to her plate.

"Please."

"Ooh, let me!" Loma said. "Always wanted the glamorous life of a diner waitress."

"Knock yourself out. You can do it every Saturday and Sunday, if you feel you have a calling."

Loma topped off Mrs. Feinstein's cup, then said loudly to everyone in the diner, "Anyone else?"

Quinn watched, bemused. When Loma finished topping off coffee cups, Quinn asked her, "So...have you found your calling?"

Loma placed the pot back on the warming tray and accidentally brushed the side of her hand on the hot surface. "Nah," she said, rubbing the red mark. "I'll stick to interior design work. Less danger."

"How's it going out at the old Maynard place, anyway?" Quinn asked her.

Wiping her hands on the hem of Quinn's apron, Loma said, "I'm having a ball out there. My rich Texans gave me a blank checkbook and very vague instructions, so I'm pretending it's my house instead of theirs. I'm stretching out the work so they stay in Texas longer before moving in."

Wilbur said, "the old Maynard place? That house must be over a hundred years old."

"Rumor has it there's buried treasure out there," Larry added.

Herman scoffed. "You'll believe anything."

"I'll keep my eye out," Loma said.

"And you'll give us a finder's fee, right?" Silas said.

"Wrong." Loma turned back toward Quinn. "Speaking of the old Maynard place, you want to help me tear down a wall next Saturday?"

"Do old men complain about bacon?"

Rico Lopez stepped into the diner, plucking off his duty cap with the insignia of the Chestnut Station police department on it. He placed it under his arm, then blotted his sweaty forehead with paper napkins extracted from the spring-loaded contraption on the nearest table. "August is not my favorite month."

This comment set off the Retireds, who began arguing the merits of every month.

Rico walked over to Loma and Quinn. "Hello, ladies. Despite the temperature, I need three coffees to go."

Quinn looked at his uniform. "All of you are working on a Saturday? Has the jaywalking task force come into some money?"

Loma elbowed her in the ribs. "Good one."

"Very funny. These are your tax dollars at work. Donnie is coming off shift and Chief is prepping for a luncheon with the governor."

"And what are you doing?"

"Fetching coffee. Duh." Rico mopped his brow again.

"Are you sure you wouldn't rather have iced tea?"

"Positive. This is coming out of the coffee budget. There'd be paperwork if I switched to tea."

Loma laughed but Quinn didn't. "That's hilarious." Loma saw Rico's puzzled expression. "Oh, I forgot."

"Forgot what?" Rico asked.

"Forgot you couldn't tell a lie." She cocked her head at him. "You really couldn't write that you bought a coffee even if it was a glass of tea?"

He wrinkled his sweaty brow. "Why would I get tea but say it was coffee?"

"Because nobody cares which it is?"

"But it was coffee." He glanced over at Quinn, who just shrugged at him. She didn't understand it much better than Loma.

Rico had never been able to fib. Quinn knew this ever since they'd become friends in elementary school. Being friends with him was like being constantly hooked up to a lie detector, which her mother quickly learned to exploit. For her part, Quinn quickly learned what to keep secret from Rico: that she was certain her boobs were different sizes; who she was crushing on; that time she hurt her jaw eating too many Twizzlers too fast; and that she constructed the crossword puzzles for the *Chestnut Station Chronicle* since they were in high school. She was nerdy enough growing up and didn't need to give anyone more ammunition. Only her parents and Vera Greenberg, the editor-publisher-reporter-photographer and chief bottle washer over at the *Chronicle* knew.

Quinn had been on a quest ever since they were kids to teach Rico the beauty of a well-placed fib. He was not catching on, however. In fact, he was being willfully recalcitrant about it. She simply couldn't get him to understand that sometimes a tiny fib meant nothing, certainly wouldn't and couldn't change the trajectory of the world, but would and could ingratiate him to the women he occasionally dated.

Just last week she overheard him tell a woman who was clearly interested in him that the color of her dress was not flattering to her. "Why didn't you just say it was lovely?" Quinn had asked later.

With a frown, he had said, "Because it was not flattering. She looked terrible in yellow."

"But why—"

"Because she asked." No matter how many times Rico and Quinn had some version of this conversation, it always ended the same way—both of them completely perplexed by the other's thought process. But it was another reminder to Quinn to only ask Rico questions if she wanted the truth. The whole truth. Rico's truth.

Quinn returned with three coffees and an iced tea in a square cardboard container. Before Rico could protest she said, "The tea is on me. I don't want to see you melt into a tiny puddle on the sidewalk on your way back to the station."

While Rico recorded the three coffees in the ledger—actually just a small spiral notebook Jake kept under the front counter—Quinn said, "If I throw in a couple of doughnuts for Chief Chestnut, you think he'll like me any better?"

Rico returned the ledger to its place, then picked up the box of beverages. "No. He hates you. Remember?"

Chapter 2

A few days later, on Thursday, Quinn was standing in the middle of the police station waiting for Rico to finish a call. She gazed at the framed news articles decorating the walls, detailing the history of the Chestnut family, who founded Chestnut Station in the mid-1800s. Chief Chestnut descended from a long line of bureaucrats.

When Rico hung up his desk phone, Quinn handed him his cell. "You forgot your phone at the diner."

"Oh, jeez. Thanks! I've been looking everywhere." He paused. "Well, not everywhere or I would have found it, I guess."

Quinn thought about offering him a quick lesson about hyperbole and its perfectly acceptable use in conversation, but she'd told Jake she'd only be gone for a couple of minutes and a lesson like that, especially with Rico, might take well into next week. She had just turned to leave when the front doors were pushed open by Officer Donnie Garfield and Chief Chestnut, each with a hand gripping Hugh Pugh by the biceps. Donnie easily had nine inches on Hugh.

They were followed by Vera Greenberg from the *Chronicle*; Jose Salazar, the studio photographer and master at Photoshop who had taken Quinn's senior high school portrait, miraculously zapping each of her zits into oblivion, a coveted, lucrative skill to have in real life; and Sherwin somebody, who Quinn knew took photos of tractors and such for the "Farm Equipment Sellabration" circular given away all over town. He had an uncanny resemblance to one of Fred Armisen's characters on the TV show *Saturday Night Live*, the one who always looked befuddled and on the verge of tears.

Quinn backed up toward Rico as the bodies filled the room.

Wiry Chief Chestnut released his bony hand from Hugh's arm, but Donnie held tight. Quinn noticed sweat had dampened the underarms of his rumpled uniform, even through the T-shirt he always wore.

Quinn wondered why Donnie had to support Hugh in such a way, but Hugh looked scared and Donnie did not look solicitous or concerned about Hugh's feelings in any way.

She wanted to say something, to ask if Hugh was feeling okay, but before she opened her mouth, Chief Chestnut stepped in front of Hugh and Donnie and addressed his entourage of photographers. "As you know from visiting the scene of the crime, we have arrested Hugh Pugh here for the murder of his husband, Creighton McLellan."

Quinn gasped, earning her a look of disdain from Chief Chestnut. She searched Hugh's face, but he kept his eyes to the floor.

"What? When did all this happen?" Rico stepped forward, blocking Quinn's view.

"A few hours ago. Where were you? I've been trying to call you."

"I was here. But my phone was at the diner."

Chief Chestnut threw more shade Quinn's direction, as if this was her fault. *Didn't he know the phone number to his own police station?* He turned back, addressing Vera and the two photographers again. "As you saw at the crime scene, Mr. McLellan was found in his bathtub, stabbed with Hugh Pugh's eight-inch double-plated chrome-over-nickel gold-handled fabric shears. Thank you all for getting there as quickly as you did to document the speed with which the Chestnut Station police department solved this crime and arrested the perpetrator. We will continue the press conference here. Do any of you have further questions?"

Vera spoke up. "At Hugh and Creigh's house—"

"The crime scene," Chief Chestnut corrected.

"I saw one of the crosswords from the *Chronicle* with a cryptic note scribbled in the margin." Vera checked her reporter's notebook. "It said, *Spokesperson: who to call when your wheel breaks*. Do you have any idea what this means?"

"It doesn't mean anything. Just another annoying pun."

"Annoying? What do you mean?" Vera caught Quinn's eye.

Quinn continued to gape at the scene unfolding around her. Nothing made sense. Creighton murdered? Hugh arrested? Was the crossword puzzle some bizarre clue?

"I did that puzzle," Chief Chestnut said. "Like I do all of them. Even if they're full of puns."

"You don't like puns, Chief?" she asked.

Quinn stared at Vera. *That* was her question? Nothing about the murder? Vera must have asked all the important questions at the crime scene. They must have been there for hours, if they were there before the coroner came to process the body. Why would Chief Chestnut involve the newspaper and these other photographers before he reached Rico to help with the crime scene? She tugged on Rico's hand. When they locked eyes, she saw her same bewilderment reflected back at her. Quinn began to process Chief Chestnut's earlier words. He'd already solved the crime and arrested the perpetrator. And called everyone in town with a camera to document what happened at Hugh and Creighton's house.

"This press conference is over."

Rico hadn't spoken since he'd explained about his phone being at the diner and Quinn couldn't believe what she was seeing and hearing. Another murder in Chestnut Station? This time by Hugh, who spoke so lovingly about his husband less than a week ago? It was impossible.

Chief Chestnut and Donnie gripped Hugh by the arms again and marched him toward the door to the basement lockup. As they reached Quinn, who had plastered herself against the wall, Hugh looked up at her. "Will you pick up Virginia Woof for me?"

"Virginia Woolf?" Quinn fought to recall her high school English lit class, a million years from this moment. "Which book...*Mrs. Dalloway*? *A Room of One's Own*?"

Hugh shook his head violently. "No! Virginia Woof, our dog. From the groomers!"

"And then what?"

"And then take care of her until I get back. Gin's no trouble at all." They reached the threshold and Hugh's eyes filled with tears. "Please?"

Quinn's mind raced. *I can't take care of a dog! I'm barely taking care of Fang.* She looked at Hugh. A cascade of thoughts flooded her mind. *I don't have a choice. It's not that poor dog's fault. I'm sure Hugh has enough to worry about without worrying about their dog. And dogs...they probably have feelings too. Wouldn't Virginia Woof be sad and confused if nobody picked her up after her bath? It would be so pitiful, like being the last kid picked up from day care. I don't need that kind of guilt. Besides, it'll only be for a couple of days. Surely they'll release Hugh on bond since he's not a flight risk. If he couldn't afford guacamole, he certainly doesn't have the means to jet off somewhere without extradition laws.*

"Of course I'll pick her up!" she called after Hugh as they took him away. She hoped her mom and dad would understand.

Quinn turned toward Rico and saw Vera standing next to him. Jose and Sherwin stood near the door.

Rico spoke in clipped words. "If any of you have photos of Creighton in that bathtub, I want you to forward them to me and me alone. And when you get confirmation from me that I've received them, you will destroy your copies. If I see them published anywhere, you will be charged with..." He faltered, searching for words. "I don't know what you'll be charged with, but you won't like it."

"Is the baler out back?" Sherwin asked, confused. "I thought I was supposed to photograph a baler today."

Jose nodded to Rico, then murmured to Sherwin and ushered him out the front door.

"What is going on?" Quinn asked. "That couldn't have just happened. Hugh murdered his husband?" Quinn had to lean on a desk to keep her balance.

"You know as much as I do." Rico stared at the door to the basement lockup.

Vera said, "All I can tell you is that I got a call from Chief Chestnut to grab my camera and get over to Hugh and Creighton's house. When I got there, Jose and Sherwin were already there and we were led through the house." She shook her head and squinched her eyes tight. "It was horrible. Creighton was...in the bathtub...with those fancy gold scissors...sticking out of his...and Hugh was just standing there. Like he was in shock."

Quinn's knees went weak at Vera's description.

"He probably *was* in shock. And you are too, Vera. Do you—"

Vera snapped out of it. "I'm fine. I've got a story to write." She hurried from the police station.

Rico called after her. "No photos in the paper!"

She waved a hand in acknowledgment.

"Rico, what—"

"I don't know, Quinn. Go back to the diner and I'll call you as soon as I can."

* * * *

At the diner, out of earshot of the customers, Quinn whispered to Jake everything she knew, then fretted about it all afternoon. She replayed it over and over again, starting with everything Hugh had said at breakfast on Saturday juxtaposed with what Chief Chestnut and Vera had said at the police station. She felt herself spiraling down into obsession, trying to make the pieces of this jagged puzzle fit.

She tried to calm herself by organizing the condiments on each table. But even after tidying and aligning all the jelly caddies, salt and pepper, hot sauce, napkin holders, and bud vases, her thoughts remained scattered and wild.

Her *baba ghanoush*es weren't working either, so she tried something different—more proactive—and called the groomer. "I hope this is the right place. Do you have a dog there named Virginia Woof?"

"We sure do. She's a beautiful girl, fresh from the bath. Who's this?"

"My name is Quinn Carr. Hugh Pugh has had an…emergency and asked me to pick her up for him."

"Oh, dear, I hope everything is okay."

"Me too. But I don't have any of her stuff. Do I need to bring a leash or anything?"

"No, she came in on a leash. It's a rule."

"Okay, great. I'll pick her up when the diner closes at seven."

"That's a problem. We close at six."

Quinn glanced at Jake's closed office door. "I can probably come on my break, around four, maybe?"

"That would be great. See you then. Give our best to Hugh."

* * * *

Quinn walked the few blocks to the groomers around 3:30 when there were no customers in the diner. Jake had given her permission to do whatever she needed to do for Hugh; he could handle everything there.

When they brought out the dog, Quinn stared. "Is that a…fox?"

The groomer laughed, holding out the leash to Quinn. "No, probably a Pomeranian-husky mix."

"Are you sure? It looks like a fox."

"*She* is not a fox." The groomer wiggled the leash at Quinn, who reluctantly took it from her. "She is probably a Pomeranian-husky mix, like I said." The groomer dropped to one knee but raised her voice. "Aren't you, Ginny-poo? Who's a sweet girl who just got a bath and a yummy treat?" When Ginny-poo didn't respond, the groomer stood and answered for her. "You, that's who!"

Ginny-poo and Quinn exchanged a horrified look.

The groomer waved off payment, explaining Hugh had an account with them and she'd just send the bill and he could pay it whenever.

Quinn and the dog left the groomers for the walk to Quinn's house. She was relieved that the dog seemed to know exactly what to do.

"You walk like you've been doing it your entire life."

The dog looked back at her. Quinn could swear she smiled.

"So…" Quinn never had a dog before, and felt like they should be making small talk. She refused to use that high-pitched, squeaky voice people, like the groomer, used with dogs, though. She didn't talk to big ol' Jethro that way, and she saw no reason to start with this one. "Would you prefer the more formal Virginia, or do we know each other well enough that I can call you Gin?"

The dog glanced back while keeping a dainty rhythm with her toenails on the sidewalk.

"Was that Virginia?" Quinn kept the pause longer. "Or Gin?"

The dog stopped walking and turned back, blue eyes lasering into Quinn's.

"Gin it is. But don't make me holler for you. I don't want the whole town thinking I'm a lush."

Gin bobbed her head.

"And you can call me Quinn."

Gin seemed to know exactly where they were headed, but that was unlikely. Left here, straight for a while, two quick rights.

"Mom? I have somebody for you to meet!" Quinn and Gin clattered through the back door into the kitchen.

Gin walked to the middle of the room and demurely posed herself. She sat erect, fluffy orange tail swept around, encircling her feet, waiting for an introduction.

"Mom? You here?" Quinn dropped the leash and went in search of Georgeanne. When she returned to the kitchen, Gin had one paw raised and was licking it with a tiny pink tongue.

"She's not here," Quinn said. She watched Gin place her front paw back on the linoleum, clearly waiting for more information about their plans for the day.

Quinn wasn't sure what to do. She didn't think Gin was one of those chewers or whiners or barkers, but what did she know? She'd only known her for a hot minute. Quinn got herself a glass of water, then poured one for Gin. She held it down and let her lap to her heart's content before thinking, *Oh, yeah, she's a dog. Probably drinks from a bowl.* "Next time." She placed both glasses in the dishwasher.

Quinn rolled around options in her brain for long enough that Gin slid her front feet forward to lay down.

"Ohmygosh...you don't have a pelvis!" Gin's hind legs were splayed out to either side, her bushy tail centered behind her. Quinn dropped to one knee and ran a hand down Gin's back from neck to tail. Everything seemed perfectly fine and Gin grinned up at her again. Quinn stood and surveyed her sprawled on the linoleum. "Your hind end looks like a spatchcocked turkey."

Gin crossed one front paw over the other, as if to say, "Yes, thank you, I know. I'm absolutely divine."

Quinn stared at this mesmerizing creature a bit longer. She finally swept her eyes around the kitchen and peered out toward the living room, seeing potential hazards everywhere. She made up her mind. "I can't leave you here alone. It would be dangerous and it would scare the bejeebers out of Mom to come home and find a fox in her kitchen."

They left from the kitchen door and pit-pattered their way back to the diner. Well, Gin pit-pattered. Quinn did more of a sneaker slap.

The effect was the same. They ended up in front of the diner, where Jethro the bloodhound lounged across the sidewalk.

He lifted his huge, droopy face, introducing himself to Gin with his eyebrows. Gin walked right up to him, stuck her pointy snout right up under his ear until it covered her entire face, and gave him a lick.

"Virginia Woof, meet Jethro. Jethro, this is Gin."

Gin gave some dainty shakes of her tail in response, then stepped around him to the door of the diner where she waited to be let in. Jethro thumped his tail on the sidewalk, too lazy and comfortable to indulge in any intricate doggie butt-sniffing rituals.

"You have some fine manners, Virginia," Quinn said, rubbing the soft fur around her neck.

Quinn explained the situation to Jake as he knelt in front of Gin, speaking to her in that terrible high-pitched voice. "Who's a beautiful girl—"

"She doesn't like your voice."

"Says who?"

"She does. Look at that face."

Gin's eyes were half-closed, her ears twisted sideways.

"Look at those ears, Jake. She's trying to dial up a different frequency."

Jake snorted. "Fine. I'm sorry if I offended, Gin," he said in his normal voice. "Of course you can hang out in my office as long as you need to."

Quinn unclipped the leash from her collar. Gin gave a curt nod of thanks, then pranced to the office, where she turned around three times in the center of the room and dropped to the floor. This time she curled into a ball and rested her chin on her tail.

"She looks just like a fox," Jake said.

"I know, right? But I have it on good authority she's not."

* * * *

Late that afternoon Rico walked into the diner.

Gin had migrated into a corner of the dining room. She lifted her head to see if it was anyone interesting, then snuggled her nose back into her tail.

Quinn stopped filling saltshakers.

"Is that a health code violation?" Rico pulled off his duty cap and stuck it under his arm.

"No, that's a dog."

"Are you sure? It looks like a fox."

"I just know what I'm told."

"Maybe you should take her to a kennel?"

"Don't be silly. She's no trouble at all." Quinn knew that Rico was concerned about how much stress she could handle. He wouldn't say it, but she knew he wondered how she could take care of a dog when she could barely take care of herself. "Besides, Mom loves dogs. She'll help. Now, tell me what you found out."

"Hugh walked the dog to the groomers before Creighton left for work today. When he got back, Creighton was dead and the place had been tossed."

"Let me understand this. CBI got there, investigated the murder, and they're already gone? And the coroner too?"

Rico nodded. "VanArsdale had to get back. He had a colicky horse to attend to. Didn't want to be gone too long."

"I know it's a thing in Colorado, but I still find it weird that the coroner is also a large-animal vet."

"Regardless, he signed off already. Chief told him he swept the crime scene with Donnie and a couple of state troopers borrowing our office to get some paperwork done. They were already there, so Chief took advantage of the extra bodies. That's why he didn't try too hard to get hold of me. Chief told VanArsdale he made an arrest. Less paperwork for everyone than if the Bureau gets involved."

Quinn could see how hard Rico was trying to control his temper and modulate his voice. One of these days, though, she fully expected him to explode and ruin his career.

"But still," she said. "Shouldn't investigating a murder take more than a few hours?"

Rico shrugged. They both knew it was out of his control. "Yes, of course, but Chief said he found all the evidence he needed."

"Like what?"

"Like Hugh's good scissors sticking out of Creighton's chest."

"But didn't Hugh call it in?"

"Yes."

"And if he took Gin to the groomers, someone saw him there. Was there enough time for him to get back home and stab Creighton?"

"Chief seems to think so."

"But—"

"I know. But you know how Chief is."

"Terrible?"

Rico sighed. "I know how it looks." Quinn rolled her eyes. They'd had this same conversation so many times, in so many ways, about so many cases. "He used to be an excellent cop, a great investigator. I've read his old reports."

"What happened?" Quinn thought back to something her mom had said to her about Chief Chestnut not too long ago. Georgeanne and Chief Chestnut—back when he was just plain ol' Myron—had been kids together and friends, from what she could gather. Whenever Quinn complained about him, Georgeanne flashed her dimple and told Quinn to cut him some slack. There was something her mom wasn't saying, and Quinn was dying to know what it was.

The only redeeming feature about Chief Chestnut that Quinn could think of was how much he loved solving her crossword puzzles. She had it on good authority he did every single one of them. In ink. It allowed Quinn the ability to slip in some subliminal clues and entries to try to force Chief Chestnut to think about a case in a different way. She'd done it before and would surely do it again, under the right set of circumstances. Which may have presented themselves again.

Rico had told Quinn that Chief Chestnut wanted to retire and become mayor of some quiet midsized town, preferably near the ocean or a lake where he could fish. He thought his chances would be much better if he could show that Chestnut Station had low crime stats during his tenure as chief of police. Never mind that those stats were not quite accurate. If there was a crime he could sweep under the rug he would, whether it was a bicycle theft or a murder. And those he couldn't sweep away, he'd get an arrest—any arrest—so fast it would make your head spin.

"Rico, Hugh couldn't possibly have killed Creighton. He has an alibi, regardless of what Chief Chestnut says. Plus, there's no motive. Plus, I like him."

Rico plucked some paper napkins from a nearby table and blotted his forehead.

Quinn knew it was futile to have this conversation again with Rico. They were on the same page, after all, but Rico's hands were tied. He told her before that he didn't mind her thoughts about any of his cases. He liked having someone to bounce ideas with. And Quinn had thoughts—oh boy, did she have thoughts. And a few skills too.

"Since I have to go over to Hugh's anyway because of Gin, can I straighten up the house for him? You said it had been ransacked? I'd hate for him to have to come home to a huge mess of top of dealing with his grief."

"That's awfully nice of you to do for a murderer."

"He's not a murderer." She didn't want to tell Rico she was also curious. Who wouldn't want to snoop around a crime scene? *Besides, if my organization skills can help, I want to and I should. It's my duty, my neighborly duty.* Who was she kidding? Quinn loved a good deep-clean, especially coupled with reorganizing. She couldn't shake the feeling that there was no possible way Hugh was guilty of this murder, either. He had been saying such lovely things about Creighton that day at the diner, and he sure hadn't looked or acted like somebody who was plotting to kill his spouse in the coming week. "You don't really think that sweet old Hugh murdered his husband, do you?"

"No."

"Then—"

"I know," Rico said wearily. "But I can't go to Chief with anything that's not overwhelming proof. And just like with Jake's arrest, he's absolutely convinced he's got the right guy." He arranged his duty cap over his tight curls, suddenly all business. "Let me ask Chief if you can clean it up."

After Rico left, Gin stretched and walked to the door. She stood, looking outside, then glanced at Quinn. Then at the door. Then at Quinn.

"Oh! You need to go out?" Quinn snapped on Gin's leash and followed her to the planting strip in front of the diner. Quinn and Jethro politely averted their eyes while she squatted. Gin gave her puddle a good sniff to make sure all was well, then trotted back across the sidewalk to the diner. As she passed Jethro, she gave him a little boop on his big nose with her dainty one. Jethro's tail thumped the sidewalk before he settled back into his nap.

Gin waited for her leash to be removed, then pranced to the kitchen doorway. When Jake didn't notice her, she gave a gentle huff, a little doggy throat-clearing, to let him know she was there.

"Oh, hey. You need something?"

Quinn came up behind her. "I think she's hungry."

"Why do you think that?"

"Because I am."

"Logical." Jake held out a piece of bacon to Gin.

She accepted it, then dropped it to the floor in front of her, while she collapsed into spatchcock position. She placed one paw over the strip, then nibbled the end with her tiny front teeth.

Jake held out a piece of bacon to Quinn.

She accepted it and crunched it in three bites.

* * * *

After the diner closed at seven, Quinn walked Gin over to Hugh's house, getting more nervous with every step. She fiddled with the key Rico had dropped off after he'd received the okay from Chief that she could clean up the house.

When they got closer, Gin practically levitated on the sidewalk she was so excited. Quinn braced herself for what she'd find after she jabbed the key in the lock. She was pretty sure there wouldn't be any blood to clean off the floors or carpet, since Creighton was killed in the bathtub. But surely the crime scene guys would have cleaned up the blood anyway, despite Rico saying it was a mess. That's what happened at the diner when that poor man had died in the big corner booth. Of course, Rico had been in charge of the crime scene back then.

As soon as the front door opened, Gin took off like a shot, leash trailing behind her as she raced down the hall. Without thinking, Quinn followed her. Before either one of them could prepare, they skidded to a stop in front of the open door of the bathroom.

Gin gave a whimper and retreated.

Quinn realized Creighton hadn't been taking a bath when he was killed, like she'd thought. Blood was still all over the tub, but it wasn't diluted. There'd been no water in the tub. Creighton hadn't been surprised by an intruder. He was put there to die.

With a shudder, Quinn backed out of the bathroom and shut the door.

She found Gin sitting on the couch, which had no cushions on it. Her eyes were downcast. When Quinn sat next to her, Gin raised her eyes, but not her head. Quinn wrapped an arm around Gin and pulled her close. Gin leaned into Quinn's chest, then slowly slid down until her chin was resting on Quinn's thigh. They sat this way until they had collected themselves, at which point Gin sat up and looked at Quinn with her ice blue eyes. Quinn gave her another squeeze and Gin licked her cheek.

"We're in this together," she seemed to tell Quinn. "Let's make it right."

Quinn stepped over the couch cushions and pillows strewn around the living room and picked her way to the kitchen, where cabinets hung open and pots and pans laid scattered across the room.

Piled on one corner of a catchall counter, Quinn identified some items Hugh must have brought home with him from his tailor shop, now that he'd retired. Thick folds of quality material for men's suits in several dark colors formed the base of the pile. On top of that rested several pairs of scissors: one with weird bent handles, small spring-action snippers, pinking shears, and a couple of scratched and battered silver scissors that had clearly been used for years. There were also packets of needles, both for hand-sewing and to fit in a machine, along with straight pins, tailor's chalk, tape measures and rulers, and something that looked to Quinn like a large white plastic apostrophe. She picked it up and saw the words *French curve* engraved in red on the side.

All of these were clearly tools of the tailoring trade that he'd brought home with him when he'd sold his shop. She spied a sewing machine tucked away on the floor next to the catchall. She squatted and ran her hand lightly over the sleek and sturdy industrial machine, much fancier than the plain Singer machine Georgeanne used.

Quinn stood and fingered the navy blue fabric, then the charcoal gray at the bottom of the pile. Tears welled when she realized he'd probably saved it, intending to make new suits, perhaps for himself and Creighton.

Whoever had killed Creighton had easy access to the murder weapon, which had probably been sitting right here with these others.

Quinn shuddered. Who could pick up a pair of scissors and stab it into someone's chest? She shook her head, trying to erase the image and return to the job at hand.

Gin's food and water bowls were untouched in the center of a laminated place mat artfully designed with prints of Virginia Woolf's book covers.

It took some effort, but Quinn was able to ignore the mess, knowing she'd be diving in to clean it all soon. She pulled her cross-body bag over her chest and dropped it on a kitchen chair. She filled the water bowl, then searched for Gin's food. After a bit, Gin gave her polite throat-clearing huff until Quinn looked her way. When she did, Gin gave a nod of her head at the pantry door. Quinn opened it and found a shelf clearly set aside for Gin.

Quinn compared Gin's size to Fang's. He received twenty flakes of fish food every day, fed to him one at a time so there'd be no question as to exactly how much he ate.

Her OCD monster began to stir, bringing up all the questions she'd already begun asking herself. How much will you feed her? How do you know if it's enough? What if you starve her? What if you feed her too much? Dogs die from being overweight. You'll probably give her diabetes or something. Actually, you probably already have with all the bacon and other treats she got at the diner.

"Baba ghanoush!" she shouted.

Gin startled and Quinn dropped to one knee and held her close. "I'm sorry. I didn't mean to yell."

Gin licked her cheek, readily accepting the apology.

Quinn counted out thirty-five pieces of kibble and dropped them into Gin's bowl. "Please quit eating when you get full."

Leaving Gin to munch her kibble, Quinn wandered around the house. The living room and kitchen were in the center of this ranch-style house. The kitchen had a sliding glass door that led to the backyard. To the right of the living room was the hallway leading to the bathroom where Creighton had been found.

Across from the bathroom was a bedroom they'd turned into their library. Floor-to-ceiling bookshelves lined the walls. Two matching bentwood rockers with their seats and backs caned with light-colored rattan sat in the nook where the closet should be. The doors had been removed, leaving a cozy reading spot with a table situated between the two rockers. Matching reading lights hung over the chairs.

All but the books on the highest shelves now resided in a heap in the center of the room.

The jumble of books alarmed Quinn and she hurried back to the living room.

The knowledge that a man had been killed in here early this morning wrapped the rooms in a melancholy and tragic vibe.

Quinn carefully negotiated her way through the chaos on the floor, returning to the front door. She stood with her back to it, trying to put herself in Hugh's shoes when he had returned after leaving Gin at the groomers. He would have been alarmed by the mess, perhaps relieved, like she was, that the large grandfather clock hadn't been toppled. Quinn pictured him rushing around, calling Creighton's name. Her eyes followed this image of Hugh until it disappeared down the hallway to the bathroom.

Then she tried to put herself in the shoes of whoever had done this to Creighton.

Did they ring the doorbell and greet Creighton as he stood right here? Did they silently pull open the door and surprise him? Where was he? In the bathroom where they killed him? The kitchen? The bedroom? Did he struggle? Did he walk with them willingly? Did they know each other? Was his murderer a stranger? When did the murderer see the sewing scissors and decide to use them on Creighton?

Quinn closed her eyes and rolled her neck. Too many questions and not enough answers.

She returned the couch cushions and pillows to the furniture in the living room. She lovingly smoothed a crocheted afghan across the back of a wing chair in the corner. She froze momentarily, unsure if that would be its proper place. Her OCD told her she must put it all back together exactly as Hugh had it, but after uttering a few *baba ghanoush*es, she calmed enough to let her rational brain take over and allow for differences. As long as it was neat. That was the important thing. For now.

Framed wildlife photos hung crookedly on the wall and she straightened them, admiring the artistry. An eagle in flight. A bear peeking out from some bushes. A herd of deer in full alert. A moose drinking from a river. A pika sunning on a rock.

After the last photo, Quinn saw a framed certificate that Creighton had won in the photography category of an art contest. Quinn straightened it too.

A section of the wall just past the wildlife photos held an array of plaques with Creighton's name engraved on them. Quinn stepped closer to read them. All from Buckley Tech Solutions, awards for exemplary work. Creighton excelled at his job, like Hugh had said. It wasn't just a proud spouse talking; his employer thought so too. Quinn trailed a finger lightly around the perimeter of one of the ornate awards.

Gin hopped up on the couch and watched while Quinn made her way around the room, picking up, straightening, rearranging. She added water to some vases of fresh-cut roses. She returned the fireplace tools to the stand, freezing as she felt the heft of the poker. Was this used as a weapon? Quinn held it like a baseball bat and gave it a few swings. Maybe Creighton defended himself before he'd been stabbed. Maybe he walloped the killer with this or some other weapon. She inspected every inch of it, but saw no blood. She made a mental note to ask Rico if he called any area hospitals to see if anyone had been treated for an injury like that.

She placed the poker with the other tools. When she stood, she found herself staring at a greeting card on the mantle. The front was the logo from the Broadway musical, *Les Misérables*. Maybe it was to commemorate a trip they'd taken to the theater together. Quinn's heart broke with the enormity of Hugh's loss. She made her way to the kitchen, away from the greeting card.

On the floor near the table was a newspaper crossword puzzle. Quinn recognized the *Chestnut Station Chronicle*, folded in a way that Quinn knew to be the mark of an avid cruciverbalist. Was Hugh or Creighton the crossword fan? Perhaps they both were. She picked it up.

After all the years she'd been creating the crossword for the local paper, it still gave her a shiver of delight whenever she knew someone enjoyed solving it. Vera had been paying her five dollars for every puzzle she published, ever since high school. The wage was ridiculously low even then, but Quinn would have done it for free.

She loved the symmetry of a crossword. It was a thing of beauty to her. No matter which way you turned it, the design remained. She also loved knowing there was only one correct answer. No ambiguity in a crossword.

Ambiguity was something Quinn did not enjoy, not today and certainly not back in high school. So when she'd overheard Vera telling her parents she'd like to start running puzzles in the paper, but couldn't afford the syndication fees, Quinn asked if she could try creating them. She swore them to secrecy, citing her deficit of cool points with her peers. She was pretty sure a nerdy pastime like designing crosswords wasn't how the cool kids spent their free time.

She'd come to grips over the years with her general lack of cool points, knowing deep down that the cruciverbalists probably thought she was pretty cool, even though they didn't know her. Many times she wished she could go back in time and tell her younger self to quit worrying about what people thought of her. They probably weren't even thinking about her anyway, busy being too focused on their own cool points.

Quinn picked up the folded newspaper. Messy handwriting angled across the page, *Spokesperson: who to call when your wheel breaks?* That's what Vera had been asking Chief Chestnut about at his bogus press conference. She looked closer at the puzzle and confirmed it was hers from the *Chronicle*. The puzzle was inspired by her parents when they toyed with the idea of getting mountain bikes, even though they lived about as far away from mountains as you could and still say you lived in Colorado. She smiled at the puns. Some she was quite proud of, so of course, Chief Chestnut hated them.

She slid the puzzle into the bag she dropped on the kitchen chair. Hugh might want that and she didn't want to lose it if she got overzealous with her cleaning.

Quinn took a quick tour of the rest of the house to see how much of a mess it really was and to think about her plan of attack to clean it all up. Down the hall to the left of the living room there was a bedroom that had been turned into an office. A four-drawer file cabinet stood open, files littering the floor. Across the hall, the master bedroom closet was open, clothes and shoes tossed everywhere. The mattress was off the frame, sitting askew as if someone had lifted it and given it a push before dropping it back down.

The guest room at the end of the hall next to the office seemed to have been spared. The bed was made perfectly, the closet doors closed. Quinn opened them and saw they were practically empty, just some extra blankets and pillows on the shelf. The master bathroom looked like it hadn't been touched either.

With a sigh, Quinn returned to the kitchen. The only logical thing to do was to tackle the most important places first. The living room, which Hugh would see as soon as he walked in; the kitchen, where he'd have to cook and eat and feed Gin; then his bedroom, then the office, and finally the room with all the books. She debated for a long time what to do about the hallway bathroom, finally resorting to texting herself a list of the most compelling arguments and then toggling back and forth between them.

One, save it for last because the door can remain shut and Hugh has another bathroom he can use.

Two, do it first because it's horrifying.

Three, put a DO NOT OPEN note on the door.

Four, notes fall off.

Five, when Hugh gets released tomorrow, I may not have finished. He can pick up books, but I do not want him to have to clean that bathroom.

Numbers two, four, and five burned into her retinas every time she scrolled past them and that gave her the answer.

Start with the bathroom.

She gathered up rubber gloves, cleanser, scrub brushes, a mop, and a bucket and went to work in there. Just as she was ready to begin, though, she stripped off her gloves and texted Rico. *Are u SURE I should clean this bathroom? Worried about evidence.*

Rico texted back immediately. *No more evidence in there. We have scissors and we know that's Creighton's blood.*

Okay.

Are u sure u want to do this?

Already doing it. I'm fine. Don't worry.

When Quinn finished scrubbing and reorganizing the bathroom, she returned to the kitchen. She piled all the pots and pans from the floor into the sink and ran some hot water along with a squirt of dish soap. She was no germophobe, but there was no way she'd pick them off the floor and simply return them to the cabinets. They'd be put away, clean or not at all. And *not at all* wasn't an option.

Now that the kitchen floor was mostly clear, Gin was running back and forth, pausing every so often to jump straight up in the air, like she was on an invisible trampoline.

"What are you doing?"

Jump, jump.

"Why are you acting so weird?"

Gin slid across the tile like she was sliding into home plate.

Quinn stared at her for a bit, then rinsed and dried her hands. "Is this playing? Are you playing?" She slid open the back door for Gin, assuming she wanted to run around. And the best place to run around was outside, presumably.

Gin refused to step over the threshold, however, opting instead to run through the rest of the house. Quinn could hear her paws on the carpet in the different rooms. She followed Gin into the office. In the middle of the floor Gin pounced on a neon-green tennis ball and raced away with it. Quinn found it dropped in the middle of the living room mess, but Gin was grinning across the room, tongue hanging out.

Quinn picked up the ball and tossed it. Gin, still grinning and panting, watched it roll behind the drapes.

"There it is." Quinn pointed. Gin stared at Quinn's finger. "No, it's over *there*." Quinn jabbed her finger in the air. Gin stayed put. Quinn fetched the ball. As she reached for it, she saw something shiny on the carpet hidden behind the drapes. Picking it up, she saw it was a brass Kwikset key stamped *do not duplicate* attached to a fancy silver fob. She turned it over and saw the fob had been engraved. Holding it to the light, she read out loud, "In life you have many keys, but only one opens the lock to your own story."

At this moment Gin decided she wanted the tennis ball and launched herself across the living room like a projectile, startling Quinn, who lost her balance and grabbed wildly for something—anything—to break her fall. The living room drapes did not save her and she landed on the floor clutching fabric in one hand and the key in the other. The curtain rod crashed down half a second later, hitting her on the top of her head and bouncing into a table. The impact popped the plastic end cap from the curtain rod and Quinn suddenly found herself underneath a shower of cash.

Gin let out a single warning bark, even though it was clearly much too late.

Quinn rubbed her head until she was sure there'd be no lasting damage, maybe not even a bump. She surveyed the cash on the floor, then Gin sitting on the couch, as if this kind of thing happened all the time.

"What's all this, you think?"

Gin cocked her head and Quinn began gathering it up. She smoothed the bills, most of which had been wadded up and shoved in the hollow rod, and arranged them all going the same direction, like bills with like bills. When she'd finished, she had a pile of mostly fifties and hundreds. She counted it, looked at Gin, and repeated the number.

Gin hopped down, sniffed at it, then gave a little nod, as if she concurred.

Quinn took a photo of the curtain rod with her phone, then texted herself with the location and amount of money found.

Quinn and her OCD monster roared to action. Why was there money in the curtain rod and why so much? Her OCD prodded her, if there was money hidden here, there was probably more hidden elsewhere. It needed to be found, organized, counted, and understood.

Gin watched from doorways while Quinn systematically moved around the house. She found bills stuffed in the couch cushions, inside a teddy bear high on a shelf, in the lining of two winter coats, under inconspicuous corners of carpet, under the inside sole of some ratty old gardening sneakers in the front closet, even inside a groove chiseled from the top of the office door.

After each cache was located, Quinn took a photo of the hiding place, organized and counted the bills, then texted herself the location and amount, before returning it to its hiding place.

Her skill at detecting these hiding spots came from countless hours of watching crime dramas and true crime shows, she knew, but was proud of it regardless. She went into the library and began opening random books jumbled on the floor. She expected to find a bunch of them hollowed out, the compartments packed with cash, but found none.

She jumped when her phone rang. "Hi, Mom."

"Quinn, where are you? It's late. I fell asleep and you still weren't here."

"I'm sorry. I completely lost track of the time. I had a…weird day." She didn't want to tell Georgeanne about the murder over the phone if she hadn't heard about it yet. Instead she said, "I'm bringing home a friend."

Georgeanne lowered her voice to a whisper Quinn could barely hear. "Are you on a date? Are you bringing a boy home this late? Should I make something?"

"No to all of that. We'll be home in a little while."

After she disconnected, she looked at Gin, sitting primly with her tail wrapped around her feet. "Ready to meet my parents?"

Gin stood and walked toward the front door.

"I've got to gather up your things first." Quinn piled Gin's dishes, food, bags of treats, and a tennis ball in the center of a bed embroidered with *Virginia* in a beautiful calligraphy font on it. Quinn patted her back pocket for her phone, slung her bag over her torso, and clipped on Gin's leash. She picked up the fully loaded dog bed and set it on the porch, turning back to lock the front door behind her. As she pulled the house key from her pocket, the Kwikset key on the engraved fob came out with it. Quinn pushed it back, deep into her pocket.

Gin trotted home next to her with such calm and quiet poise that Quinn almost forgot she was there. Her brain was in overdrive anyway, trying to digest everything that had happened today. It was a good thing Chestnut Station had well-maintained streetlights, so she didn't need to worry about stumbling in the dark. She had more important things to think about.

What was the deal with all that hidden money? She questioned whether she should have put it all back where she'd found it, but was reassured by having the photos on her phone. Hugh either hid that money or it was hidden from him. Either way, she wasn't sure she should get involved with that. Unless...was that what the killer was looking for? Is that why the place had been trashed?

She remained very uneasy about the investigation Chief Chestnut and Donnie did. Or lack thereof. Realistically, though, the only reason she found that cash was because she pulled down the curtain rod accidentally. Chances were good neither Chief Chestnut nor Donnie would have done that. Besides, they weren't looking for hidden money; they were investigating a murder, assuming you could call what little they did an "investigation."

They didn't even find that key on the floor.

Quinn stopped in the middle of the sidewalk and dropped the load she carried. Gin sniffed at her bed, wondering if she was expected to step into it. Humans wanted the weirdest things sometimes.

Quinn felt for the Kwikset key in her pocket. Since when were keys just loose like that, not with other keys, somewhere it could be knocked across the room?

Rico would have found that key. She called him. "Why weren't you at the crime scene with Chief Chestnut and Donnie?"

"Hello to you too. Chief called me, but my phone was at the diner, remember?"

"So he wanted you there but couldn't find you?"

"No, he was calling me to make sure I was going to be at the station, holding the fort."

"Why didn't he call the station?"

"Maybe he did and I didn't hear it. Or I was on the other line."

The way he said it made Quinn think it was just as big a crock as she did.

"Isn't holding the fort usually Donnie's job?"

"Chief wanted Donnie to learn something. His stepfather, the governor, thinks Donnie is being underutilized."

Gin sighed and stepped her front feet into her bed. She pawed at the bag of kibble until she'd moved it to one side, then the bags of treats and toys to another. She stepped her back feet in, turned around three times, and curled up, nose to tail, her butt pushing the bowls away.

"Underutilized in a town where not much happens? Besides, he was involved in Emmett Dubois's murder."

"In his murder investigation, you mean."

"Whatever." Quinn had been trying to put the details of the previous murder in Chestnut Station out of her mind, so she didn't want to dredge it all up again. "I'm on my way home from Hugh's house. I can't believe he killed Creighton. I also can't believe what a crappy investigation they did over there."

Rico paused a long time. "Then you'll just have to...help. Gotta go."

Quinn watched her phone go dark. She'd forgotten to ask if Rico had called hospitals to see if anyone came in with a fireplace poker injury.

Clearly, Rico knew this was another of Chief Chestnut's rush jobs, a cursory investigation simply to get an arrest. He was between a rock and a hard place with Chief Chestnut. Rico was probably given strict instructions about his investigation into Creighton's murder, walking a tightrope at the station. If history was any indication, there were things Chief would let him do, and things he wouldn't, even though Rico might lobby hard for them. There were also things Rico might do anyway, and if Chief Chestnut ever started asking him direct questions he couldn't lie about... well, then, Rico might never become chief of police in Chestnut Station.

And that was one thing Quinn wouldn't allow.

She pocketed her phone. Gin glanced up at her. Quinn asked, "So, what's with all the money? And that key...what's it for? Anything you can tell me?"

Gin didn't answer, just tilted her head in the other direction.

"Really? You live there and can't tell me anything?" Quinn shooed her out of the bed, centered the bag of dog food, then picked up the load. "Guess I'm on my own, then. Fine. I'll figure this out and get another feather for Rico's cap, ideally plucked painfully from Chief Chestnut's. Pretty soon somebody will figure out what Chief Chestnut's game is and Rico will take the job that's rightfully his."

Chapter 3

Rico disconnected Quinn's call and leaned back in his chair. He glanced over at Donnie staring off into space at his desk. Quinn was right. There was about as much chance of Hugh murdering Creighton as Donnie becoming an astronaut.

He stood and stretched. In the break room he grabbed a couple of granola bars and a soda from the mini-fridge.

He went downstairs to the lockup. Hugh rolled over, swinging his legs to the floor. He sat on the edge of the built-in bed.

At Hugh's expectant face, Rico shook his head. "Nothing new. You hungry?" He held the snacks through the bars of the cell.

Hugh shook his head and lay back down.

Rico placed everything on the floor, just inside the cell. "Don't worry, Hugh. We're working on it."

"We who?" Hugh asked, staring at the ceiling.

"Me and a friend who needs to realize she should be a cop."

"Great." Hugh said it without conviction.

Rico wondered if that was an example of fibbing, like Quinn was trying to teach him, or was it simply Hugh's gloom speaking? There was a fine line between sarcasm and lying, and Rico was never sure which was which.

He was sure of one thing, though. If he could straddle the line between doing what Chief wanted and keeping Quinn involved, even if just at the edges, he could perhaps get her back to the police academy. Maybe they'd let her try again, since she had her OCD under control. Problem was, how to keep her involved in an investigation Chief had all but shut down?

* * * *

Quinn struggled to open the back door with her arms full and Gin dancing excitedly around her feet. She tried to keep quiet, but needn't have worried. Her dad slept like a dead man, and her mom waited up.

Georgeanne rushed across the kitchen. "Hang on! I'm coming."

Quinn handed off the leash to Georgeanne, who led Gin to the middle of the room. Quinn dropped the dog bed and everything in it.

"What's this? Who is this sweet little …"

"Girl. Mom, meet Virginia Woof. Gin, this is your new best friend, chief caterer, and maître d'."

"Oh! Is she hungry? Let me find someth—"

"I have absolutely no idea, but I think she'd be better off with her own food, Mom. She's already had more bacon and chicken salad than is probably healthy. And she ate at Hugh's a little while ago. I can't believe she's hungry, but...."

Georgeanne and Quinn watched Gin as she nosed the bag of kibble, then nosed her food dish.

"Is she a fox?" Georgeanne asked.

"Hard to believe, but no. The groomer said she was a Pomeranian-husky mix."

They both watched as Gin used her ears and eyebrows to explain just how famished she truly was.

"You…bought a dog from a groomer?"

Quinn counted out another thirty-five pieces of kibble and dropped them into Gin's bowl.

Gin delicately plucked out a piece of food and dropped it on the floor in front of her, then began eating.

Quinn laughed at her behavior. "I didn't buy her. She's not mine." The smile slid off Quinn's face. "She's Hugh Pugh's dog."

Georgeanne's hand fluttered to her throat. "Oh, Quinn, I heard about Creighton. I didn't know you knew them."

Quinn filled the other bowl with water and set it next to Gin. "I didn't know Creighton, but Hugh was a customer at the diner. I just happened to be at the police station when they brought him in. He asked me to take care of Gin until he got out."

"It's so horrible, all of it. I've been upset all day. We've known Hugh and Creighton for ages. But at least we can take care of Miss Virginia Woof"—

at the sound of her name, Gin wagged her tail—"until Rico gets it all straightened out. There's no way Hugh...killed...Creigh. It's unthinkable."

Quinn loved that she and her mom were on exactly the same wavelength about this.

"Where have you been, anyway? It's so late and you have your appointment with Mary-Louise Lovely early tomorrow."

Ugh. They were not on the same wavelength about Quinn's therapist. Quinn liked Mary-Louise Lovely, really she did. When Quinn had finally fallen so far that she had called her in the middle of the night that time, Mary-Louise Lovely had helped her. She explained some things to Quinn about OCD, anxiety, and depression, and over several therapy sessions had begun to teach Quinn some coping mechanisms, like saying *baba ghanoush*. They all worked some of the time for Quinn, but none of them worked all the time.

It was ambiguity rearing its ugly head again. Quinn wanted Mary-Louise Lovely to fix her, give her black-and-white answers to black-and-white questions. Just like her crossword puzzles.

Mary-Louise Lovely told her it didn't work like that. It was a process that would take a long time, and maybe Quinn would never feel cured. Obsessive-compulsive disorder was something that would be with her forever, but if she managed her expectations and her symptoms, she'd at least be able to live with it.

That sounded ambiguous to Quinn.

"Maybe I should skip my appointment," she said to her mother.

Georgeanne watched her staring at Gin. "Don't be ridiculous. Because of a sweet little dog? Virginia and I will be perfectly good company for one another. I only have a couple of piano students tomorrow so she and I can hang out all day." Georgeanne squatted next to Gin and waited for her to finish her drink of water. When she did, Gin gave the tiniest burp before turning to sniff at Georgeanne's dimple. "Besides, Jake already gave you the morning off, didn't he?"

Quinn could have explained that she was worried she wouldn't get Hugh's house cleaned before he got out of jail, which surely had to be tomorrow. But if she mentioned it, then Georgeanne would offer to go over and help and Quinn didn't want that. She had clues to sift and was looking forward to putting it all back together, which she couldn't very well tell her mother, who worried enough about her OCD as it was.

No, Quinn would keep this secret, as well as the one where she didn't drive to Denver for her appointment with Mary-Louise Lovely in the morning. Helping Hugh was less ambiguous. More black and white.

Chapter 4

Quinn was awakened at dawn by a cold nose on the back of her neck. "Jeez!" She swatted at it before realizing it was Gin. She rolled over and Gin's nose was one inch from hers. "Did you sleep up here? Why'd I lug that bed all the way over here?"

Gin glanced at it across the room in a "that's my napping bed, not a sleeping all night on the floor like a dog bed" kind of way.

Quinn swung her legs over the edge of her sleeping all night bed and performed a couple of side stretches before feeding Fang. She used the tweezers to count out twenty flakes, but stopped when she reached seventeen. Was feeding him once a day really the healthiest way to go, starving him for twenty-three hours and fifty-eight minutes, then letting him gorge for two? What if she forgot one day, or wasn't home at feeding time?

She stared at his meal in her palm. Using her tweezers, she plucked seven flakes and returned them to the jar, leaving ten flakes in her palm.

"New plan, dude. Ten bites when I wake up, ten when I go to bed. Let me know if that works for you, 'kay?" She dropped the flakes in one at a time, waiting for him to gobble each one before it sank to the gravel.

As she watched him bob and weave for each morsel, she mused about how she still wasn't comfortable in her role as caregiver to him, even though all she had to do was feed him. And the instructions were right there on the fish food.

She watched Gin watch Fang.

Gin was a much more complex creature. The enormity of agreeing to care for her was slowly dawning on Quinn. Even if just for a day or two. Lots can go wrong in a day. And what if it was longer? What if Hugh didn't get out of jail right away? Quinn knew what Chief Chestnut could be like when he got his mind set on something, and it sure seemed like he got his mind set on Hugh's guilt.

Fang gobbled up the last flake of food and swam in place, delicate fins gently waving in the water.

"That's it for now. The rest later. You'll get used to it and I'm sure it'll be better for you. Trust me." Quinn brushed off her hands and returned the jar of fish food to its place.

She scooted back into bed, pulling her laptop toward her. Gin snuggled down near the foot of the bed.

Quinn brought up her internet browser and typed, *how to care for dogs.* Pages and pages of advice loaded. She took a deep breath and dove in, reading, scanning, scrolling, rereading, clicking.

Make sure the dog always has fresh water. *What if we're gone all day?*

Prevent obesity? She glanced at Fang. *How? Only give her twenty flakes? What if all three of us feed her accidentally?*

Schedule regular veterinarian visits. *Yearly? Monthly? Weekly? Daily? Probably not daily, she reasoned, but "regular" was much too ambiguous.*

Give the dog plenty of exercise. *Again, ambiguous. How much is too much? How much is too little? How am I supposed to know?* Quinn thought about walking with her to and from Hugh's house. *Was that too much or too little? She seemed perfectly fine, but would she tell me? Her little legs take about five steps to each one of mine. Is that okay? Does walking like that make her sweat? Oh my gosh, can dogs get sunburned?*

What about her feet? Sidewalks get hot! Jethro doesn't seem to have any trouble, but he's not dainty. He's a tough old street dog. He's Tramp to Gin's Lady.

Quinn kept reading, eyes darting faster.

Vaccination record? Does she already have one? What if Hugh never gets out of jail and I can't find Gin's vaccination record? Will she catch everything and die? What does she even need to be vaccinated against? Quinn read the lengthy list of preventable dog diseases. *That's a lot of shots. Does she get them all at once or what? What if they give her one she's already had?*

Brush her teeth? How in the world am I supposed to do that? Gum disease can give her heart problems just like in humans? Do they sell doggy toothbrushes? And toothpaste? Is it bacon-flavored? How would that give her minty-fresh breath? Do dogs care about minty-fresh? Quinn hadn't seen a doggy-looking toothbrush at Hugh's when she was gathering up Gin's stuff. Did he keep it in the bathroom? She hadn't thought to look there.

She scrolled faster.

High-quality food? So ambiguous! What does that MEAN? How am I supposed to know? I don't even know what's high-quality food for me!

Play with her at least three times a day? For how long? How am I supposed to do that anyway if I'm at work all day? Three sessions after work? Before work? Does exercise count as playing? Once in the morning, twice at night? Twice in the morning, once at night? When should I schedule this playtime? Six o'clock in the morning, two in the afternoon, eight at night? Would Jake let me leave at two o'clock or should that be Mom's scheduled time to play with her?

Quinn's breath became ragged. She jumped when Gin licked her foot. Quinn tossed her computer aside and scrambled to the kitchen, where Georgeanne stood at the stove stirring Dan's oatmeal.

"There's no way I can take proper care of Gin. You'll have to."

Georgeanne kept stirring. "Don't be ridiculous. Of course you can. Miss Virginia Woof will get the very best care possible."

Gin joined them in the kitchen, her toenails clip-clip-clipping across the floor.

"Mom, I can't do—I'm not that—I don't—"

Georgeanne turned to face her and saw how worked up she was. "Shush, now. You'll do your best." She embraced her.

That's exactly the problem, Quinn thought, wiping her nose with the back of her hand. *My best won't be good enough.* She glanced down at Gin, waiting patiently by her food bowl.

She broke away from Georgeanne's embrace. "You better feed her."

Quinn went through the motions of her shower even though what she really wanted to do was crawl back into bed and throw the covers over her head. She'd done that too much in the last few months, though, and she knew it freaked out her parents.

She pulled on a pair of jean shorts and a T-shirt that looked clean enough before shoving her feet into flip-flops. She caught a glimpse of herself in the mirror but couldn't muster the energy to do anything with her hair. Makeup was out of the question.

Quinn said goodbye to her parents, stooped to thump Gin on her side. "Oh," she said, twisting to look at Dan. "Have you two met?"

"We have indeed. She's a sweet girl."

Quinn straightened.

Dan said quietly, "You can do this, Quinn."

It hurt Quinn to see how much pain she caused her parents because of her OCD. At least she'd be going to her therapy appointment, even though last night she was ready to bag it to go finish at Hugh's house. Was that progress or simply deflection and avoidance?

"I'm okay, Dad. It'll be okay. I'll go talk to Mary-Louise Lovely and she'll fix me." Quinn knew full well that "fixing" wouldn't be happening, but hoped her parents believed it. "Have fun with Gin today, Mom. Be sure to give her plenty of fresh water and play with her at least three times. Have a good day at work, Dad. I'll see you later." Quinn mustered a smile from somewhere and hoped it looked convincing. "Oh, and Mom? Gin needs her teeth brushed too."

The drive to her therapist's office in Denver was long enough that Quinn traveled all the way through the eight stages of her OCD spiral. Grief only had five stages, but people with OCD were overachievers.

One: Becoming aware of a problem; in this case, learning she didn't know the first thing about taking care of Gin.

Two: Over-researching on the internet.

Three: Obsessing over everything she can't do.

Four: Obsessing over everything she can do.

Five: Realizing it's all too overwhelming.

Six: Hating herself.

Seven: Becoming depressed.

Eight: Making a plan. In this case, after her appointment to have Mary-Louise Lovely try to fix her, going to every veterinarian in town to get specific instructions for taking care of Gin and passing it along to Georgeanne.

That's the beauty of organizational OCD, Quinn thought. *You get stuff done! No wallowing at Step Five because there were three more steps to get through.*

The monster in her brain cracked that whip. By the time Quinn got to her appointment—twenty minutes early—she had convinced herself that it was a waste of a perfectly lovely late-summer morning because she was fine; great, in fact. Yes, she had spiraled about Gin, but in the last couple of weeks, despite working so many hours at the diner, she'd made a color-coded binder for her mom of all her recipes, cross-referenced as to main ingredient and recommended meal—no easy trick with some of Georgeanne's recipes. She may be ignoring her friends and teetering at the edge of letting her monster win, but she was getting stuff *done*. And now she had a plan to handle Gin. She solved her problem and tamed the monster all by herself. Did she really need Mary-Louise Lovely to sit there and reflect the plan back to her? Quinn gathered up her bag. She could leave now and not waste anyone's time.

Quinn had jumped into therapy like she jumped into everything: with both feet and a binder full of research. But Mary-Louise Lovely wanted her to talk about everything when all Quinn wanted was action. Talking wasn't going to slay this monster, but Mary-Louise Lovely believed differently. She refused to see that Quinn needed action items to check off a list, not nebulous emotions and storytelling about her childhood. It didn't matter how or why or when her brain broke, just *that* her brain broke. Why couldn't a smart lady like Mary-Louise Lovely understand that? And why wasn't she filling a binder with ways to fix it?

Quinn took two steps toward the exit.

Before she reached it, Mary-Louise Lovely opened the door and stepped into the lobby, not at all surprised to see Quinn standing there. "Am I ever going to beat you to an appointment?" She laughed as she found the key to her office. She unlocked it and swept Quinn in ahead of her.

"Why can't I have my binder here?" Quinn asked. "It would be so helpful for creating an action plan."

Mary-Louise Lovely put her keys away and pulled some files from her briefcase. "Do you really think you need an action plan to talk to me?"

"I'm pretty sure I need an action plan to do everything. Doesn't everyone?" Quinn was genuinely puzzled.

"No, Quinn. Some people simply live their lives, tackling problems as they come up."

Quinn sat in her regular chair, the one where she could look out the window. "I tackle problems as they come up. Then my action plan tells me what to do about them."

"Does it? Or is it just busywork that makes you think you're taking action?"

Quinn bristled. "It's how I think through a problem and create solutions. You know that."

"If nothing changes, then—"

"Nothing changes. Yes, I know. You've said it a million times." The irony of the phrase being repeated so often was not lost on Quinn.

"Quinn." Mary-Louise Lovely's voice remained calm. "You come to see me for a reason."

"Yes!" Quinn's voice did not remain calm. "Because I want you to fix me. I want to keep using my binders and colored markers and lists, but I need you to keep the monster from taking over. He's got nothing to do with my action plans." Quinn thought about her research earlier about caring for dogs. "In fact, if I didn't have my action plans, the monster would take over completely!"

Mary-Louise Lovely was quiet, waiting for Quinn to regain control. After the red splotches left Quinn's face and neck, Mary-Louise Lovely asked, "Are you taking your meds properly?"

"Of course I am. If I had my binder, I could show you my chart."

Mary-Louise Lovely smiled, then laughed out loud. Finally, Quinn did too.

"I'm not trying to take away your markers, or your binders, or your Quinn-ness. I just want you to learn that your monster will always be in charge unless you start believing that you don't have to organize or have a plan for everything. You've lived for so long with your action plans that you think you're in control of them, but really, I think it might be the other way around."

They talked for a little longer. Quinn left Mary-Louise Lovely's office not sure if she was glad she'd stayed or not.

Chapter 5

Georgeanne and Dan took Gin for a walk around the neighborhood before Dan left for work.

"She's such a smart girl," Georgeanne said as they passed a gum wrapper that Gin completely ignored.

"She looks just like a fox," Dan said.

"That's what I said too!"

Their next door neighbor, Mrs. Olansky, sat on a gardening stool in front of the four-foot-high stone wall that surrounded her property while she deadheaded her daylilies. "Hey you two," she called to them when they got closer. "You get a new dog?"

"No," Georgeanne called back. "Dog-sitting."

As they approached, Gin slowed her trot and then stopped completely. She crouched and the hair all along her back raised.

Dan and Georgeanne stopped and watched. "Will you look at that?" Dan said with astonishment.

"What's going on?" Georgeanne asked, alarm in her voice.

Mrs. Olansky rose from her stool, clippers in hand.

Hair still raised, Gin began a slow-motion walk along the sidewalk, obviously staring at something.

The three humans tried to figure out what caught her attention so completely. They stared in the same direction, squinting. Georgeanne, holding the leash, followed slowly behind.

Suddenly Mrs. Olansky said, "Oh! Snowball's out."

Dan and Georgeanne followed her finger pointing through the gap in the stone wall where the gate had been removed years ago. A white Persian cat peered at them from under a row of peonies with deep fuchsia blooms so large and heavy they created the perfect hideaway.

Gin did her super–slo-mo walk along the sidewalk, eyes lasered on the cat. Neither animal made any noise. Gin did not take her eyes off Snowball, twisting her neck to look behind as they passed the gap. Snowball took off toward the house as soon as Gin was out of sight.

Gin's hackles lowered and she trotted ahead, toenails clicking happily along the sidewalk once again.

Dan, Georgeanne, and Mrs. Olansky burst out laughing.

Gin turned to see what was so funny.

* * * *

Quinn drove home, contemplating what Mary-Louise Lovely had said. She didn't know what to think. She'd always been praised for her organizational skills. Her teachers held up her term papers and science fair projects as examples to the rest of the class. Which might have accounted for her lack of cool points with her peers, now that she thought about it.

But those cool points wouldn't get her anywhere, unlike her organizational skills, which had worked for her all the way through graduation from college.

They'd worked right up until that blip at her police academy interview.

Quinn felt her face flush and she grasped the steering wheel tighter as the images flooded back.

The three men across the table from her.

The unexpected question she hadn't planned for and couldn't answer.

The tongue, jaw, and brain that refused to work.

Finally, the blessed relief as she counted the holes in the ceiling tiles.

Then the EMTs and her father with her at the emergency room as she tried and failed to explain what had happened.

More than a blip. Much more.

But now, almost eighteen months later, Quinn could see her meltdown wasn't her failure. It was a failure of her skills. She hadn't prepared properly, didn't know the questions they'd ask.

She'd have melted down much sooner if she hadn't had such a skill set to rely on all those years.

Mary-Louise Lovely was smart and clearly wanted to help, but she simply didn't understand.

When Quinn got home, Georgeanne was in the kitchen and asked how the appointment went.

"Fine. Same old, same old. I think I've figured something out." Quinn knew Georgeanne was dying to ask for details, but she didn't, just nodded. Quinn didn't want to worry Georgeanne and knew she would if she told her too much.

"Look at these bananas." Georgeanne thrust a banana at her, changing the subject in dramatic fashion.

"Why'd you buy bananas? None of us eat them."

"I'm trying them as a thickener in a new chili recipe I'm making." She shoved the banana into Quinn's hands. "Read it."

"Read it?" Quinn knew her mom had an odd relationship with most food, but this was something entirely different.

Georgeanne turned it over and then sideways in Quinn's palm, pointing at it.

Quinn squinted and held the banana closer to her face. By golly, there were words on this banana. *I'm bananas for you. Hope you never split.* Quinn smiled. "Funny. Why are you writing on bananas now?"

"I didn't write it."

"Then who did?" Quinn studied the banana closer. The letters had been created by poking holes in the skin. As the banana had ripened, the words appeared in a brownish color. The rest of the banana was still yellow.

"I don't know," her mother said breathlessly. "I bought them a few days ago, and then this morning when I went to use it, I saw this. I just got back from talking to Aaron Janikowski about it."

"Who's he?"

"The produce guy at the grocery store."

"What did he say?"

Georgeanne opened her eyes wide and spoke in phrases, for emphasis. "He said...he didn't know...any...thing...about it." She ended triumphantly, like it was a clue she'd unearthed, when in reality, it was the opposite.

Quinn smiled. Clearly Dan was pranking Georgeanne for some reason. With a banana. *Parents are weird.* Quinn handed the banana back to her mother. "A mystery, eh, Mom?"

"And one I will solve. Just as soon as I make this chili."

Quinn had some time before she had to be at the diner, so she opened a search engine on her laptop and typed in *veterinarians Chestnut Station.* She created a list of small- animal vets starting with those in town, and then in an ever-expanding area encompassing the southeastern quadrant of Denver.

Next, she compiled a list of color-coded questions to ask them. Red for diet. Blue for general health. Yellow for bladder and bowel concerns. Green for exercise. Purple for dental questions. Pink for random but persistent queries she couldn't shake, like, "How do I know if she's sad? Will she tell me if she's scared? How much time is too much for her to be alone? Is it better if I just let my mom take care of her? Will my anxieties rub off on her?"

She checked the time again. Still enough to make a few calls. The vet in Chestnut Station didn't have a record of Gin as a patient and was too busy to talk.

Quinn called the groomer and asked if he knew who Gin's vet was.

"Sorry, I don't."

"It's not on any of your forms?"

"What forms?"

"You don't have forms? Aren't you worried? What if something happened to a dog while they were getting groomed?"

"What are you implying?"

"Nothing. I just—"

"We run a perfectly safe establishment here. We've never had anything happen to an animal under our care."

"But what if you did?"

"Then we'd take them to an emergency animal hospital. But that would never happen because—"

Quinn finished the sentence with him. "You've never had anything happen to an animal under your care."

"Exactly."

She started calling the vets. The first three wouldn't talk to her because Gin was not their patient.

The fourth one said, "A few questions? Sure. Shoot."

Quinn rattled off a bunch of questions from her list.

There was a pause. "Is that all?"

"That's all my questions about feeding her. For right now, anyway."

The woman asked, "What does she weigh?"

"I don't know. How much does a fox weigh?"

Quinn heard her sigh.

"Give her about a cup-and-a-half of high-quality food. Split it between two meals if you like. I've got to go. Make an appointment online if you want her checked out."

Quinn stared at the dark phone. *About* a cup-and-a-half? *If I like* …?

Quinn spent the afternoon at work full of *baba ghanoush*es and doubt. Did Gin need to be checked out?

Chapter 6

After her shift ended yesterday evening, Quinn went to finish up at Hugh's but got sidetracked looking for any notes or files about Gin. She didn't even find any *How to Take Care of Your Dog* books in the jumble on the floor.

She had stumbled home with a throbbing head and fell into bed for a fitful sleep with nightmares about Gin alternately wasting away and being too obese to move.

Today, though, was blessedly diner-free and Quinn looked forward to beating back some anxiety on the wall Loma had asked her to help demolish at the old Maynard place. Gin sat in the front seat of Quinn's car with her head out the window, familiarizing herself with the entire world's scent. It seemed to meet her expectations.

Quinn briefly wondered if she should buckle Gin with the seat belt, but she had hopped up so supremely confident, like she'd done it a million times. Besides, Quinn couldn't conjure one memory when she'd seen a dog in a seat belt. Not even on a funny YouTube video. Not even on *The Simpsons*. If it hadn't been mocked in popular culture it must not be a thing.

When they got to the long, curvy road that led to the Maynard house, Quinn was surprised how hilly it was out there, just a handful of miles from town. Everywhere else around Chestnut Station was so flat. She wondered if high school kids traipsed out here for keg parties, something she had never worked up the courage to do when she was young. It would seem to be an ideal place, plenty of seclusion, no streetlights.

"It's about time you got here!" Loma called when she got out of the car.

Gin waited patiently while Quinn came around to open the car door. "Do you think I need to keep her on the leash here in the boondocks?" Quinn asked Loma.

"Only if she's a runner."

"She doesn't seem to be." Turning to Gin, she said, "Are you a runner?"

Gin grinned up at her and twitched her triangle ears.

"Is that a yes or a no?"

Gin raised one dainty paw.

"I have no idea what you're telling me, but I'm going to give you a chance. You seemed to be right about the seat belt." Quinn unclipped the leash from Gin's collar.

Gin jumped lightly to the ground. After landing, she gave herself a whole body shake. She surveyed her surroundings, then strolled up the stairs leading to the wide front porch. She sauntered from one end to the other, reinspected one area, turned herself in three circles, and plopped down, nose to tail.

Loma and Quinn followed her up to the porch.

"Guess she's not a runner," Loma said.

"Guess not."

Quinn's phone rang. She held one finger up to Loma, then answered. "Hey Rico. What's up?" She listened for a bit. "Oh, no! That's terrible... Well, I wasn't finished anyway...Yeah, I guess. Thanks for telling me."

"What's terrible?" Loma asked after she disconnected.

"Hugh's idiotic attorney didn't submit the paperwork in time to get him out of jail, so he's spending the weekend there. Honestly, I think his own attorney believes he murdered Creighton."

"Ugh. That is terrible."

"At least it gives me some more time to get it all organized for him." The realization actually dialed Quinn's general anxiety down a notch.

Loma took Quinn on a quick tour of the old house, pointing out what was staying and what was going to be changed. Loma described it so vividly, Quinn could easily visualize the beautiful new home those lucky Texans were going to be able to move into as soon as Loma finished.

The tour ended in front of an interior wall whose only purpose seemed to be to divide one big room into two smaller ones. Loma promised the Texans they'd have a great room, so this wall had to go.

"You're sure the roof won't fall in or something?"

Loma shrugged, causing Quinn's eyes to widen.

"We can't knock down a—"

"I'm kidding. It's not load bearing. I checked."

"You're sure."

Loma shrugged again. "Pretty sure."

"Loma..."

"Kidding. It's all good."

They stood staring at the wall. Loma was deciding the best way to attack it. Quinn was wondering why there was still a painting hanging on it. She walked over and removed it. It hung on a single nail caught by a wire on the back of the frame. She studied it up close.

"Nice," Quinn finally proclaimed.

"If you like landscapes."

"And I do. Why? What do you like?"

"Velvet paintings of dogs playing poker."

"I should have known." Quinn leaned the painting against a different wall. Returning to the soon-to-be vanquished wall, she stepped closer to where the painting had been hanging. She frowned, then put her weight on her front foot, then her back foot, and did a little back-and-forth dance, shifting her weight. "This floor feels funny. Like it's got a bounce to it."

"Yeah, there's some damage to the subfloor. I'm hoping we won't crash through to the crawl space today."

"That's a possibility?" Quinn asked with alarm.

Loma shrugged.

Quinn wasn't sure if Loma was teasing her again. But, just in case, she tried to weigh less as she took a step backward. "Have you seen this?" She pointed to a poorly patched area of the wall that the painting had covered.

Loma followed Quinn's finger and squinted. "Oh, that makes sense now."

"What does?"

"Why that painting was hung so low and so close to the edge of the wall. Normally, they're supposed to be about eye level and more centered."

Quinn stepped further back, eyeing the wall now that the painting had been removed. "Somebody punched it."

"Looks like." Loma grazed a gentle hand over the rough patch. "And didn't quite know how to fix it."

"Hence the painting."

"Hence." Loma walked over to a toolbox on a table, pulling out two hammers, two foot-long metal shims, two goggles, and two dust masks. She offered a set to Quinn. "You ready?"

"I've been looking forward to this all week."

They adjusted the eye protection and masks.

Quinn held up the long metal tool. "What's this for?"

"I'll show you." Loma proceeded to wedge the end of the shim under the trim and use her hammer to tap it, causing the wooden trim to pop off.

They removed all the trim, then stood in front of the wall.

"Now?" Quinn asked.

"Now."

They dropped the shims back in the toolbox and readjusted their masks and goggles. With their hammers gripped in both hands above their heads, they counted down in unison, "Three…two…one!"

Loma added a "Towanda!" as an homage to the movie *Fried Green Tomatoes*. Quinn yelled, "By the hammer of Thor. I have the *powerrrrr*!"

Over and over, grunting and screeching their battle cries, their hammers crashed through the drywall between the studs. When they couldn't reach any more to disintegrate by force, they began pulling off the chunks by hand. By the time they'd removed all the drywall on one side, they were giddy, and covered from head to toe in sweat and white gypsum dust.

They stopped for a much-needed water break. Now that some of the subfloor was visible, Loma *tsked-tsked* at it.

Quinn peeked over her shoulder. "Bummer."

"Nah. Just means I get to play here longer before the Texans come. But let's be careful. If that floor has rotted through, it'll drop us about three feet to the dirt below."

Quinn stepped back and surveyed the wall, now just showing studs and the back side of the drywall hanging on the other side. "I bet we could just push the drywall off from this side and it would come off in big sheets."

"But where's the fun in that?"

"True."

Loma picked up her tools and moved around to the other side.

"Don't start without me. I've got to get my Hammer of Thor." Quinn hurried to join her and they shrieked and grunted their way through the destruction of the other side of the wall.

Quinn wrenched the final chunk from the end of the wall where the painting had hung. She saw more of the rotten subfloor and pointed at it with her toe. "Can I do something about this?"

Loma had slumped to the floor, catching her breath while leaning against the perpendicular wall, her goggles and mask next to her. "Can you do it without me?"

"Sure."

"Then go nuts."

"I won't ruin anything?"

"Nothing that's not ruined already, by the looks of things."

Quinn dropped to her knees and pulled a chunk of rotten plywood with her hands. It came off easily. She pulled more of the floor running under the wall they were demolishing before finally sitting back on her heels. Bracing herself using two of the studs, she stopped to pull off her goggles and mask and catch her breath. "Ohmygosh, that...was...so much fun!"

Loma grinned. "More fun than pouring coffee in the diner the other day."

So much adrenaline coursed through her, Quinn thought she might actually escape her body. "How do we take down the studs?"

"We don't. That requires people who know what they're doing."

"Which would exclude us from most things." Quinn peered into the dark abyss of the floor. "Do you have a flashlight?"

"Hang on, big girl takes a while to get going. Like the *Titanic*. Big, beautiful, bold *Titanic*. Can't turn on a dime." Loma struggled to her feet. She rooted through the toolbox, then carried a flashlight to Quinn, keeping her distance from the abyss. "What's down there?" she asked nervously. "Nothing dead, I hope."

Quinn knelt and aimed the flashlight beam into the hole. "Smells wet down here."

"I was afraid of that. When the guy inspected the roof, he told me it looked like the gutters were tweaked. Looks like all the runoff was going right here."

Quinn continued to peer into the abyss. "I don't see any standing water, but there's something shiny down there."

"Please, dear God, tell me it's not a collar."

Quinn reached down into the abyss, straining her shoulder. When she brought her hand back up, she screamed and thrust her fist into Loma's face.

Loma screeched and tripped over herself trying to get away.

Quinn started laughing and opened her fist. "Gotcha back about that load-bearing wall business."

"Girl! You 'bout to give me a heart attack!" Loma took some deep breaths and fanned herself with one hand.

"Sorry, not sorry." Quinn walked toward Loma so she could see what was in her palm.

"Coins!" Loma plucked one and inspected it. "Think they're valuable?"

Quinn held up each coin, studied both sides, then dropped them into Loma's hand. "I don't think so. They're all from the 1930s, looks like. I mean, they might be worth something, but it's not like they're ancient or anything." Quinn thought about all the money hidden around Hugh's house. She dropped to her belly and pulled out another handful of coins. "There's lots of stuff down here." She excavated more coins, a black plastic comb, some green army men, and a couple of candy bar wrappers they'd never seen before. There were also wrappers from Hershey bars, but with different designs than they had now.

Loma studied each item as Quinn brought it up.

Finally Quinn brought up some damp, folded pieces of paper, scattering them on the floor next to her. She shined the flashlight into the abyss again. "I think that's everything." She heaved herself up.

Loma carefully unfolded one of the squares of paper.

"What's that?"

"I'm not sure. Looks like a kid wrote it, but it's like a love note."

Quinn unfolded another one. "*What did one boat say to the other boat? Are you interested in a little row-mance.* That's adorable." Quinn read some more. "*I can't believe how hard that geometry test was, but I almost busted a gut when Gary said, Gee...I'm a tree.*"

Loma laughed and read the note in her hand. "*What did the patient with the broken leg say to their doctor? Hey Doc, I have a crutch on you.* This kid had it bad."

Quinn laughed and unfolded another. "*I love you with all my butt. I would say my heart, but it's just not as big.* That's hilarious!"

"*You're like dandruff because I can't get you out of my head no matter what I try.*" Loma hooted.

"*I think you might be suffering from a lack of vitamin me.*" Quinn looked at Loma. "I think I'm in love with whoever this is."

Loma smoothed open another note. "*You're like my asthma. It takes my breath away too.*" She placed a hand over her ample bosom. "Awww!" She turned it over and over. "None of these are signed."

Quinn gasped. "Loma, listen to this. *I walked across the room today to sharpen my pencil just so I could be closer to you. I looked down and saw I was holding a pen. I must have been beet red. Thank God Mrs. Atwater didn't see.*" Quinn held it out to Loma. "This one is signed."

"Looks like they tried to erase it." Loma squinted. "What does it say?"

"Hugh."

"What?"

They both looked at Gin curled up, fast asleep. She must have sensed them staring at her because she opened one eye. No treats were in view, so she settled back into her nap.

"Do you think it's her Hugh?"

Quinn's head swam. *First the hidden money and now hidden love notes?*

"Did your Hugh live here as a kid?" Loma asked.

"Here in this house? I don't know." Quinn pulled out her phone. "Hey, Mom…how long has Hugh Pugh lived in Chestnut Station?…No, just an estimate…Like ten years ahead? …Do you know where he lived? … No, nothing important, I'll tell you when I get home… She's fine." Quinn addressed Loma, "My mom says hi."

"Hi Georgeanne!" Loma called. "Your daughter is a beast with a hammer!"

Quinn listened to her mother for a moment, then nodded. "Yes, you can't even imagine how satisfying it is to tear out a wall. I gotta go, though. Talk to you later."

"Is it him?" Loma asked.

"I'm not sure, but it could be. Hugh is older than Mom. She remembered that the older kids in school sometimes came in to help the younger kids in class. Hugh was her assigned reading big brother. She read with him for half an hour every Tuesday or something and he helped her sound out the words. She doesn't know where he lived, but thought it was in town someplace, not way out here." Quinn mulled over this information, coming very close to telling Loma about the money hidden all over Hugh's house. In the end, she decided not to. At least not until she could figure out who hid it. Besides, it was surely just a coincidence about these hidden coins. Quinn grabbed a handful and trickled them from hand to hand. "Why would these notes be in the wall?"

Loma shrugged. "Why would the coins? And the army men? And the comb?"

Quinn and Loma read through the notes again. When they finished, Quinn leaned back, supported by her hands, legs stretched out in front of her. She flexed her feet. "They're obviously love notes. But written to who?"

"Some guy would be my guess. You said Hugh's gay, right? Married to that man who died? And that's probably why they've been hidden for four thousand years. How old is Hugh?"

"My mom is fifty-eight, so let's say he's around sixty-eight."

"So, he was a teenager in like, late 1960s. If I remember my history, it wasn't cool to be gay back then. The Stonewall riots were in the late sixties, I think."

Quinn nodded. "If Hugh knew he was gay as a teenager, he would definitely have to hide it and lie about who he really was." *But what else was he lying about? Was he really rich? Did he kill Creighton?*

"All that math made me hungry." Loma struggled to her feet. "You brought lunch, right?"

Quinn gave Gin some treats and a fresh bowl of water, then opened up the cooler she brought with her.

Quinn's inner struggle about feeding Gin had been somewhat alleviated this morning, when Georgeanne pointed out that Hugh would only buy high-quality food for Gin and wouldn't have all those treats if they weren't good for her. Quinn had to concede that Gin did, in fact, look and act perfectly healthy.

She announced each item as she pulled them from the cooler. "Chicken sandwiches on whole grain bread, loaded with diabetes-friendly veggies and avocado. Baked sweet potato chips, courtesy of Georgeanne. More healthy and delicious water. Oh, and for dessert—"

"Please, dear Lord, let it be German chocolate cake."

"Berries!"

Loma sighed.

"Don't be an ingrate. I'm trying to help you eat healthier. I did some research—"

"Of course you did. Does this mean I'll never get German chocolate cake again?"

"I can have my mom work on a recipe for you."

Loma grabbed for the container of mixed berries with fake enthusiasm. "Berries are great!"

While they ate, Quinn and Loma made a plan. Quinn would talk to the Retireds and see if any of them knew the Maynards, and Loma would check the real estate records to find all the prior owners of this place. Quinn pretended it was because they should try and find the owners of those coins in case any of them were valuable, but really, all Quinn wanted to know was if those love letters were really written by Hugh Pugh and how they ended up in the crawl space of a house.

After lunch, Quinn collected up everything they found inside the wall and double-checked that there was nothing else. Loma insisted Quinn take it all with her because who knew what would happen to it here with all the workmen trooping in and out. Loma held open the empty bag their sandwiches came in and Quinn dropped it all inside.

They vacuumed, swept, and mopped to get as much of the drywall dust contained as they could.

Finally, Loma pronounced their efforts good enough. "I have other stuff I need to do today."

Quinn protested. "Just let me—"

Loma yanked the mop from her hands. "I know your standards are higher than mine, but if you mop any more, you'll be mopping the dirt in the crawl space. Ain't nobody got time for that."

"Fine." Quinn knew she had more cleaning and organizing waiting for her at Hugh's. *Let Loma think I can walk away from all this like a normal person.*

Quinn loaded Gin and the cooler into the car and said goodbye to Loma. "Hey, thanks for letting me do this. It was fun."

"Girl, you're on my demolition crew from now on. And thanks for lunch. Even the berries."

Before she drove off, Quinn sat with the AC blasting and called Rico. "Hey. Can I visit Hugh in lockup?"

Rico didn't answer right away.

"What?" Quinn asked.

"Chief specifically said you couldn't go down there. Said you used up your visitor quotient with Jake."

"I had to go see Jake all those times! You know that. How else was I supposed to handle the diner while he sat in jail?"

"I don't make the rules."

"Can my mom go? I'm just…worried about him."

"Sure. I don't see why not. Chief likes your mom."

"Right? You'd think a little bit of that would rub off on her daughter." Quinn paused. "Do you—"

"I've told you a million times I don't know why he doesn't like you."

"What makes you think I was going to ask that?"

"Weren't you?"

Quinn had a split second where she thought she'd pretend like she was going to ask him something completely different, but then let it go. Rico would see right through that. "Yes. Whatever. I'll talk to my mom about it."

"For what it's worth, Quinn, I like you enough to make up for how much Chief hates you."

"Yeah, big whoop. You like baseball too, so your taste is dubious." Quinn hung up with a grin on her face and knew Rico did too.

Chapter 7

She pulled into Hugh's driveway at the soothing time of 3:33 and scooped up the copy of the *Chestnut Station Chronicle* that had been thrown earlier. Gin veered toward a rosebush on the side of Hugh's front yard, but Quinn convinced her to come through the house to the back. When Gin gave her the side-eye, Quinn shrugged. "I'm pretty sure there are leash laws here. And the backyard is lovely. It'll be fine."

While Gin scoped a place to piddle, Quinn sat down on the back porch and texted Georgeanne. Hugh is stuck in jail over the weekend. Can you go visit?

The reply came back immediately. Of course! That poor man. Sitting in a cell all by himself. I'll take him some black bean brownies.

Quinn sent a thumbs-up emoji and then a kissy face.

Gin was still on the hunt for the perfect place, so Quinn opened up Hugh's newspaper. She leafed through the pages, skipping articles about a new pizza place opening out by the interstate, the Rotary Club fundraiser that was coming up in a couple of weeks, and one farmer's struggle to get his farm certified organic. She'd read a version of these articles a thousand times.

She scanned some polite but cranky letters to the editor about the park's new playground equipment. Some people didn't see the need to upgrade the wooden teeter-totter that doubled as a permanent tetanus dispenser, or the well-oiled merry-go-round that could sail kids into the stratosphere if they didn't hold on tight, or the asphalt underneath it all. One said, *If it was good enough for us and our kids, it should be good enough for kids today.* Another letter complained about today's bubble-wrapped kids and helicopter parents. And the third just said, *Why does everything for kids have to be in primary colors? Are kids these days too good for brown and gray?*

Quinn was still giggling at the thought of kindergarten classrooms or toy aisles all decked out in earth tones when she turned the page and saw Creighton's obituary. She wondered who had placed it, because certainly Hugh was not in any position to do so.

The article spelled out Creighton's early life and how he'd lived in Cleveland, Ohio, until 1983, *when he decided to embark on his life of indecency and moved to Colorado, leaving his wife Geraldine McLellan and children Victor McLellan and ValJean (McLellan) Tate destitute. The children had to be placed with their beloved maternal aunt when Geraldine drank herself to death. Creighton died on August 15 in Chestnut Station, Colorado. He will not be missed by Victor or ValJean and will now have to face God's judgment without ever having met his grandchildren or having a relationship with his own children.*

"That's brutal," Quinn said to Gin, who had finished her business and sat primly in front of her.

Creighton's kids were named Victor and ValJean? Quinn held open the door for Gin, then followed her to the living room. Gin snuggled into a corner of the couch, while Quinn picked up the greeting card with the *Les Misérables* logo she'd seen on the mantle. She read the inscription this time. *Like Javert did with Jean Valjean, I tracked you across France. It was my lucky day when we met on that tour. I love you.* There was no signature.

Quinn frowned, then pulled the bag with the love notes from her bag. She compared the handwriting on the greeting card with the note that had Hugh's half-erased signature. She was fairly certain it was the same handwriting because there were similarities despite what must have been a fifty-year gap in time. She was almost certain the card was written by Hugh and given to Creighton, because he clearly had a thing for Victor Hugo's *Les Misérables*, since he named his son after the author and his daughter for the main character.

It was sad to think that when those kids were born Creighton and his wife must have had such high hopes as a family. Quinn had never met Creighton, so she didn't have an understanding of the kind of man he was. Was he a loving father, at least until he left? It must have been hard, though, for all of them. The burden of not being his true self would certainly have locked up his heart, if the vitriol from his children was any indication.

With a start, Quinn thought about the Kwikset key on the engraved fob. She dropped the love notes and the greeting card, then raced to the bookcases in the other room. She'd already organized the books—fiction alphabetized by author's last name, nonfiction by the Dewey Decimal system—so she went straight to the shelf of Victor Hugo books. She opened every edition, as well as the two copies of *The Hunchback of Notre Dame*, and rifled every page. The disappointment of not finding a hidden compartment the Kwikset key fit or any notes written in the margins, nor cryptic clues or ciphers anywhere, hit Quinn hard. If this were a TV crime drama, she'd have found something and they'd be well into the midpoint commercials by now.

But nothing.

She pulled out her phone and searched the words engraved on the fob. *In life you have many keys, but only one opens the lock to your own story.* She'd searched that quote several times already, coming up empty each time. But now she tried it paired with the phrase *Victor Hugo*. Maybe it was a quote from one of his books. Again, no hits.

Even if it was a Hugo quote, so what? What would that show her? Nothing, probably.

She straightened the books she'd disturbed, dwelling on those poor kids of Creighton's. Well, they weren't actually kids anymore, were they? Victor and ValJean would be adults by now. Quinn did some mental math. The obituary said Creighton was born in 1954, which made him sixty-five when he died. Assuming he was in his early twenties when his kids were born, that would be around 1974, which would make them both in their forties probably. Not kids at all.

She sat on the couch next to Gin and snooped around online, assuming that at least ValJean had an uncommon enough name to be visible on social media at least.

A surprising number of *ValJean*s popped up on her Facebook search. None with the last name Tate or McLellan, however. She tried *Val Tate*.

Only three.

One lived in Australia. Quinn clicked on her profile, all very public. This woman seemed to enjoy life. She wrote clever posts, shared hilarious memes, and had a lot of friends commenting and interacting with her. Quinn checked out her "About" information and saw she had three brothers and two sisters. Clicking on some of her photos brought up one of six people who all looked very much alike. The caption read, *Six Pack together again!*

Quinn thought it highly unlikely this Val Tate was Creighton's daughter.

The second Val Tate listed her birthday as January 1, 1940. People lied about their ages all the time on social media, but a quick scroll through this woman's profile showed several "Happy 79th Birthday" greetings from January, and nothing since. This couldn't be Creighton's daughter.

The third Val Tate didn't have a public profile for Quinn to peruse. The only thing publicly visible was a photo someone had posted to her wall with a comment, *Val, I found this pic of you and Vic stuck in an old yearbook. Thought you'd get a kick out of it. How are you anyway? It's been ages!*

The photo showed two teens smiling in front of a homecoming float they'd presumably been decorating. The girl wore her hair in the "Rachel," the trend Jennifer Aniston made popular in the early years of *Friends* episodes. The boy had spiked hair, bleached at the tips, also stylish in the 1990s.

It was a definite possibility these were Creighton's kids. Val hadn't responded to her friend who'd posted the photo. At least not publicly.

Quinn clicked the *Add Friend* button, then opened Messenger and typed, *I was sorry to hear about your dad.* Maybe curiosity would get the better of Val, assuming she checked private messages from strangers on Facebook. Not likely.

Quinn searched for Victor but found nothing on Facebook, and nothing for either of them on Twitter or Instagram.

She called Rico to get Hugh's attorney's name and number, after promising she wasn't going to do anything crazy with the information. She figured that was a safe promise because whose definition of *crazy* would they use? Hers, if she had anything to say about it.

When she got the attorney on the phone, she asked him if he had any contact information for Creighton's previous family, his wife or kids.

"Creighton wasn't married before Hugh."

"Yes, he was, there's information in the obituary about them."

"News to me. Hugh never mentioned it."

"I guess that's why it was in the newspaper, eh?" Quinn waited for a laugh that never came. "Will you let me know their information after you contact them, please?"

"Why?"

Quinn's eyes landed on the greeting card on the floor in front of the mantel. She went over to pick it up. "I'm helping with Hugh's house, and there might be something of Creighton's they'd like. Some keepsake or something." She doubted it, based on the obituary, but the attorney didn't need to know that.

"I won't be contacting them."

"Your investigator, then."

"There's nothing to investigate."

"Are you kidding me?" She picked up the obituary and read it to him, then said, "Secret family? Obviously angry? Maybe even angry enough to kill their father?" Quinn had been pacing around and Gin had taken the opportunity to ask to go outside again.

"Listen, I don't know who you are, but I'll thank you to keep your nose out of my case."

Quinn watched the screen go blank. "What a jerk." She looked down at Gin. "Not you." She slid open the patio door and Gin trotted into the backyard.

Quinn leaned against the kitchen sink. She couldn't understand any of this. How could Victor and ValJean be so angry at someone they hadn't had contact with for so many years? Wait—maybe they did have contact with Creighton over the years. And was it possible Hugh really didn't know about Creighton's other family? Could you be married and keep a secret like that from your spouse? And what kind of attorney wouldn't investigate such an obvious lead?

Quinn called Rico and told him about the conversation.

"There's nothing I can do about Hugh's attorney."

"You can tell Hugh he's incompetent."

"I can't."

"Yes, you can."

"No, I can't."

"Can you at least dig into Creighton's kids some more?"

"Chief doesn't want me to."

"But you're a good cop. You need to rule them out, don't you?"

Rico held a long pause. "I'll make some calls."

"What's with the pause, though? You can't possibly think Hugh is guilty, can you? You said you didn't think he was a couple of days ago."

Rico spoke quietly, as if he didn't want anyone to overhear. "His own attorney thinks he's guilty. So do Chief and Donnie."

"But those Three Stooges are all imbeciles, otherwise they'd be investigating this completely. You're the firewall between Hugh and a guilty verdict. You know Hugh called 911 himself. If he really did it, he'd get himself a better alibi or hightail it out of town." Quinn had her doubts about Hugh, after finding the money hidden around the house, but refusing to investigate Victor and ValJean was spectacularly wrong.

"Murderers try to cover their tracks all the time by being helpful."

"But Hugh loved Creighton. It was obvious."

"You've perhaps heard the term *crime of passion*?"

"That's mean, but it's a solid burn. Regardless, Hugh is gentle."

"Until he gets mad, maybe. And you've only known him for, like, eight minutes."

"But I *know* him. I have a good sense about people." Quinn appreciated Rico not pointing out the profusion of times she had misread people. "Besides, why would he incriminate himself by using his own sewing scissors?"

"To throw us off. Cover his tracks. Make people like you question the facts. It's like you haven't spent your life watching crime dramas or something."

"Ugh. You're infuriating."

"That may be, but I'm also a cop. I need facts."

"But you're not looking for any!"

"Quinn, you have no idea what I do all day. Now, I told you I'd make some calls and I will."

"Fine."

"Fine."

Quinn paused a minute, not wanting to end the conversation on a bad note. "Do you still want to bear my children?"

Rico laughed and hung up.

She knew Chief Chestnut tied Rico's hands when he wanted the investigation to go a certain way. She also knew that Rico was correct when he said she didn't know what he did all day. For all she knew, Rico had already talked to Creighton's children. She hadn't asked him directly, after all. Even if Rico hadn't yet learned how to tell even a teensy white lie, at least he had learned not to put himself in situations where someone might ask him a direct question. Quinn knew he investigated on his own, but it frustrated her to be kept at arm's length, especially when he'd promised they could sometimes work together on his cases.

Quinn felt the tightness in her jaw and gave a quick exhalation through her nose. Why did she care so much? She had her chance to be a cop and blew it. Clearly, she should stick to waitressing and making crossword puzzles.

Quinn sat at Hugh's kitchen table, pulled out her iPad, and opened up a blank puzzle grid. She had to get Chief Chestnut and Rico to look hard at Creighton's children. She typed in some potential theme words. *Patricide* and *sociopath* both had nine letters, so those would work fine for symmetry. She couldn't very well use ValJean and Victor's names outright, but what about Lizzie Borden? Everyone knew the rhyme; kids used to jump rope to it on playgrounds.

Lizzie Borden took an ax and gave her mother forty whacks.

When she saw what she had done, she gave her father forty-one.

Gruesome, and not entirely true, but that's what happened when the public imagination fired up. It was no different a hundred and twenty years later. We just used internet memes now.

Quinn was lucky to have options with *Lizzie Borden* as an entry, since both names had the same number of letters. Even though it would be her preference to have this entry smack-dab in the center of the puzzle, she couldn't use a 12-letter entry in a 15x15 grid because of the symmetry of the black square placement. If she put LIZZIEBORDEN flush left, she'd have to have three black squares at the end to fill out the row. But by placing the black squares there, the computer program would automatically cover up LIZ at the beginning. And if she put the entry flush right, with the three black squares at the beginning of the entry, the matching black squares would cover up DEN at the end.

But what she could do was place LIZZIE at the beginning of the center row, then add the three black squares, then place BORDEN to fill out the row. And she could clue it together, so it would be obvious to Chief Chestnut, or any solver, that it was the name of a woman put on trial for killing her father.

She was a bit nervous about those two Zs, but calmed herself by adding an easy "bro" and "sis" to her theme entries.

Quinn began placing the black squares in her grid.

ACROSS

1. American immigration policy for kids
5. Turf found in bogs
9. Taps fingers rhythmically
14. Terrible Russian
15. Black and white whale
16. Proportion
17. Person with extreme lack of conscience
19. Modify a legal document
20. "___ with your best shot"
21. "___ not okay with this"
23. Maggie, to Jake
24. Perished
25. The Joker's nemesis
28. Word with waste and masculinity
29. Who loves My Chemical Romance, Panic! at the Disco, and Jimmy Eat World?
33. Chemical treatment for wood
38. Week-long Jewish mourning period
39. With 40-across, famous axe murder suspect
40. See 39-across
41. Paul, Eckhart, or Sorkin
42. Chasing
44. "___ 9 From Outer Space"
45. A Marx Brother
47. One-percenters
49. Pokemon cards, Tamagotchis, and Rubik's Cubes
53. Form-fitting undergarment
56. Chimpanzee, Bonobo, or Orangutan
57. "Pinky and the ___"
59. Joaquin's brother
61. Killing one's father
65. Getting an A+ on a test
66. Heed
67. Fanning or Macpherson
68. Sudden movement to avoid something
69. ___ of Capri
70. Made the eggs pastel

DOWN

1. What you bring to a potluck
2. Steer clear of
3. Prickly pear and saguaro
4. Japanese art style
5. Soda
6. Constitutional amendment seeking to end legal distinctions between men and women
7. "Sister ___"
8. Largest island in a South Pacific archipelago
9. "No ___ Obama"
10. Colorado State University mascot
11. Native Americans from the western United States
12. Really short skirt
13. Installs turf
18. Definitive record of the Eng lang
22. Theater chain
25. Software app that runs automated tasks
26. "Lizzie Borden took an ___"
27. Style of jacket with a mandarin collar
28. What you might draw a line in the sand with
30. Not so short skirt
31. "Easy-Bake ___"
32. What you did in the shower, maybe
33. Word with trap and board
34. Currency of Iran
35. Poet Pound
36. Protection from the sun's ultraviolet radiation
37. Transgression against divine law
38. Distress signal
40. Jake, to Maggie
42. Earlier than post
43. Package delivery company, for short
45. Very trendy
46. What you did at the luau, maybe
48. Bigger than medium
49. Investigator of organized crime
50. Moved in a curved trajectory
51. "The ___ Show" with Trevor Noah
52. Walk furtively sideways
53. Garrett, Renfro, or Pitt
54. Second in command at Chestnut Station Police Department
55. Enthusiastic
58. According to the Beatles, love is all you ___
60. Country in Eur.
62. Workout target
63. ___ Aviv
64. Kind of bread or whiskey

Chapter 8

Two hours passed in an instant, but Quinn felt she had a solid puzzle.

Stretching every which way began loosening her tight muscles. As she bent at the waist to touch her toes, she expected to see Gin curled up in the corner of the couch. She wasn't there. Quinn started to call for her, then with a start, remembered she'd let her out before she began work on the puzzle.

She hurried to the patio door and yanked it open, calling for her. When Gin didn't come, Quinn searched the backyard and was horrified to see the side gate standing wide open. She raced out front. "Gin! *Virgiiiiinia*! Come here!"

The next-door neighbor was outside dropping mulch around a flower bed. "She's there." The elderly woman pointed to Gin, sprawled on her belly in that spatchcocked pose in the shade of some rosebushes.

"Ohmygosh, I should have made sure that gate was closed!" Quinn's hand fluttered to her throat as she caught her breath.

The woman brushed the mulch from her hands, then fluffed her nest of white curls. "It probably was closed. Gin opens it. That's her favorite place. She'll hang out there for hours if Hugh and Creigh—if they'd let her. She watches the world, smells the flowers." She stood, reaching out a hand to Quinn. "I'm Barbara, by the way."

"Quinn. I'm helping clean up the house." They shook hands.

"And taking care of Virginia."

"That too. Although she seems fairly self-sufficient."

"That she is."

There was a lull in the conversation while they watched Gin stand, stretch, and stick her nose completely in a rose blossom, inhaling deeply before sneezing. Quinn had seen Georgeanne do the exact same thing.

"You're the waitress at the diner, right? When that murder happened a while back?"

Quinn nodded.

"Are you involved in Creighton's murder?"

"What? No! I—"

Barbara gasped. "Oh, I didn't mean it like that! I just wondered, since you were a friend of Hugh's, were you investigating anything or"—here she used air quotes—"looking into anything?"

"Like what?"

Barbara shrugged. "Like would you be interested to know that I've seen Creighton leave the house, walk around that corner, and get into a car with an African-American man for half an hour or so, then get back out and walk home while the car drove away?"

"How often did he do this?"

"Lots of times. Sometimes three or four times a week. I'd be sitting right there on my porch or watering the flowers and I'd see it. The car always pulled up right next to where the Shumachers' wooden fence started. I could see the entire car."

"Do you know the man in the car?"

Barbara shook her head, then got excited. "But I'd know him if I saw him again. He wore those dreadful locks in his hair."

"Dreadlocks? Long braid-like things?"

Barbara nodded hard, bouncing her gray hair.

"What kind of car?" Quinn glanced to the corner Barbara had indicated earlier.

"Brown one. Or gray. Maybe blue. It had bumper stickers." Quinn started to speak, but Barbara held up one finger. She tilted her head back, staring at the treetops. "Don't meddle in the affairs of dragons for you are crunchy and delicious with ketchup."

"Pardon me?"

"That's one of the bumper stickers. I remember it because I've been puzzling over it ever since. I almost went over there and asked about it once."

"Why didn't you?" Quinn asked as she texted the phrase to herself.

"Because they always looked so serious when they're talking in there. Like they were conducting business or something. I didn't think they'd appreciate the interruption. I wish now I had. Maybe that man had something to do with Creighton's...murder."

"Did the car have two doors or four?"

"Probably."

"Did you go to the police with any of this?"

"That Chief Chestnut told me to butt out."

"Butt out?"

"Not in those exact words. He's always very polite, but that was the gist. I didn't realize I'd been given the bum's rush until I got home."

Quinn nodded. She'd seen Chief Chestnut be overly and disingenuously polite to people, so she knew exactly what Barbara was saying. "That is interesting information. Can I share it with Rico and see what he thinks?"

"I'd appreciate that. I'm *sure* it means something. And you tell Rico I'd be happy to talk to him about it. Or anything else he thinks would help. I've known Creighton ever since he moved in here with Hugh. He was a kind, lovely man."

"Barbara," Quinn began slowly. "Is it possible…do you think…could Hugh have anything to do with Creighton's murder?"

"Oh, gads no! They loved each other!"

Quinn thought about the crime of passion theory. "Did they ever fight? Argue loudly?"

Barbara shook her head. "Never." She thought a minute. "Oh. There was that one time they argued over who was going to shovel snow for me. They both wanted to do it even though I told them I was perfectly capable—this was several years back, mind you. They finally came to a compromise. One did the driveway, one did my porch and sidewalk." She shook her head again. "Lovely men. Both of them. I still can't believe this happened. Every morning I expect to see Creighton out early, snipping roses for the house."

Gin sauntered over to Barbara and offered herself for petting, which was obliged. Then Barbara said, "Back to my garden. That mulch won't spread itself." She started to walk away, then turned back to Quinn. "You'll talk to Rico?"

"I will. Right now."

Quinn walked with Gin through the side gate, making sure it was latched properly. She sat on the glider in the shady backyard. Gin hopped up next to her, but when it rocked back and forth, she looked startled and jumped back down, preferring to sprawl in the cool grass.

Quinn called Rico again and told him everything Barbara had said. Again, Rico promised to look into it. She made a mental note to ask him point-blank in a couple of days.

She also told him her theory that Creighton might have hit his attacker with the fireplace poker. "You should call around to hospitals and ask if anyone went to the ER with an injury like that. I don't know how strong Creighton was, but those iron fireplace tools could do some serious damage."

She paused. "It's a shame nobody brought it in for testing or fingerprinted it or anything."

"Quinn," Rico began wearily.

She didn't let him finish. "I'm just saying."

"You're always just saying."

"All part of my charm. You'll look into this too?"

"I'll look into it."

Before she went to work inside the house, Quinn searched for the text of the bumper sticker. Search results came up with a zillion products that had this saying on it, but the origins were muddled. *Probably doesn't matter, just a bumper sticker. It will make the brown or gray or blue car with two or four doors easier to find, though.*

Who was this guy with the dreadlocks? And why would Creighton go sit in his car several times a week without going anywhere? It sounded to Quinn like a drug-deal scenario. But who was dealing and who was selling? If Creighton was dealing, maybe that was the source of all the hidden money. *I'm sure he wouldn't want Hugh to know he was a drug dealer, so it would make sense that he'd hide the money.* It also made sense that this guy with the dreadlocks could have killed Creighton if something went wrong one day. Maybe Creighton cheated him. Maybe he made a promise he didn't keep. Maybe Dreadlock Guy was stoned out of his mind that day and thought Creighton was crunchy, delicious dragon food.

Quinn shook her head. "Let's take a walk," she said to Gin.

They walked through the house and she snapped on the leash. Quinn stood on the front porch and began walking the direction Barbara had pointed. She counted her steps. She only got to sixty-three before Gin skidded to a stop and pulled, nose to ground, toward a light pole. Gin would not be deterred, and Quinn forgot which number she had ended on. They turned around and started over on the front porch. As they neared the light pole, Quinn tightened up the leash and Gin kept pace, although she did look longingly toward all the delicious smells.

Quinn reached the Shumachers' fence, where Barbara had indicated the car always parked. "That can't be," Quinn muttered. "Two hundred fifty steps exactly?"

She pivoted and counted her steps back to the front porch. Two hundred fifty. She completed the round trip eight more times, to make an even ten trips. Exactly the same. Quinn knew it had to mean something. But what? Her stride couldn't be the same as Creighton's, since he was probably taller than she was, could it? And even if it was, so what? There couldn't be any rhyme or reason for the car to park exactly two hundred fifty steps away.

She was losing herself in an OCD spiral but couldn't catch herself. It was getting late and she hadn't done any further work inside the house, but her OCD took over, first with the puzzle and now this. She walked the route ten more times. Each time the number was the same, except for once when she stumbled on a loose pebble.

She stood on the front porch, trying to make sense out of it, but knowing she might never understand. At least she'd learned that much about her OCD. Sometimes the monster just wanted to mess with her and made no sense at all.

"One last time, Gin." She doubted this was the proper amount of exercise for Gin, but she had to finish. This time Quinn made the round trip saying *baba ghanoush* instead of counting, hopeful this would break the cycle for her.

Back on the porch, Gin was panting, so after unclipping the leash they both headed into the kitchen where Quinn poured each of them water. She spied another package of dog treats on the counter next to the fruit bowl so she dug one out for Gin, as a reward for being so patient. But was that the right thing to do? Quinn was worn out trying to know the unknowable about Gin. She held tight to Georgeanne's wise words that Hugh would not have treats for Gin if they weren't good for her.

She dropped to one knee and ran her hands along both sides of Gin's sleek body. Gin smiled up at her. "You're completely healthy, right? You'll stay that way?"

Gin pushed the top of her head into Quinn's thigh, making her laugh. "Are you giving me a hug?"

Gin danced away to curl up on the couch.

Quinn slid the package back into its place next to the fruit bowl. As she did, she noticed something on the bananas. She pulled both bunches out of the bowl, inspecting them, becoming more frantic.

Each of the bananas had a message poked into them, just like the one her mom had showed her that read, *I'm bananas for you. Hope you never split.* That seemed much more sinister to Quinn now. Did Georgeanne get a banana meant for Creighton? Was it a threat made by a jealous man? Don't leave me or else?

She read the messages on these bananas, becoming more and more alarmed.

You're so fruity.

It takes two to mango.

Thanks for the fruitful discussion.

But where do you draw the lime?

Try to see it through a fresh pear of eyes.

I'll go to grape lengths for you.
I've run out of juice.
Be careful, get home in one peach.
I can't even think straight.

That last one Quinn knew was kind of a joke in the gay community, but in this case, here, as a note on a banana, was it a confession? A cry for help?

The more she read them, the more the messages seemed like threats. Discussion about what? Taking two to tango? Drawing the line on an argument? Seeing it with new eyes? Did running out of juice mean patience?

Be careful?

A chill ran down Quinn's spine, despite the August temperature. She made sure Gin had water and told her she'd be back in a while.

Chapter 9

Quinn hurried to the grocery store with one of the bananas. The air-conditioning felt like a polar vortex when the automatic doors whooshed open. Her hand gripped the banana so tightly it was a miracle it kept its shape.

Schlubby thirtysomething Aaron Janikowski was placing cantaloupes in a bin. They kept rolling toward him, threatening to escape. How he got to be produce manager was anyone's guess.

"Hey, Aaron. My mom told me she bought a banana here with a message in it."

Aaron didn't look at her, concentrating on trying to wrangle cantaloupes. "I told her I didn't know anything about that."

"Interesting. Do you know anything about the bananas with messages I just found at Hugh and Creighton's house?"

At this, Aaron stopped what he was doing and stared at the cantaloupe sitting in his palm like a bowling ball.

Quinn narrowed her eyes.

Aaron bobbled the melon.

"Should I ask the store manager why his bananas all have messages poked into them?"

He stared at the cantaloupe in his hand a bit longer. "Fine. I'll tell you." He met Quinn's eyes. "It's just a game Creigh and I play. Used to play. He always did his shopping on Tuesday before work so I'd get a couple bunches ready for him. I wouldn't have wanted them to get into the wrong hands."

Quinn leaned in and spoke quietly. "Because you and Creighton were having an affair?" The two of them having an affair was a less-bewildering scenario than Aaron threatening Creighton.

"No." Both his voice and his hand were steady. "Because it would scare the hairnet off some old lady to see a message in her bananas. Like your mom."

She chose to ignore the dig at Georgeanne's age. "I can't even think straight." Quinn pointed at the words on the banana she brought with her. "Aaron, are you gay?"

His voice was frosty. "Is that any business of yours?"

"Not normally. But today it is."

They had a stare down while Aaron held the cantaloupe in his palm and Quinn pointed a banana at him. It looked like the worst holdup ever.

People were beginning to notice them. Quinn repeated, "I can't even think straight."

Aaron became aware of all the shoppers listening in. He tossed the cantaloupe into the bin, causing a melon avalanche. With a body block and arms wide, he attempted to keep them from tumbling to the floor. Quinn jumped in to help, but it was no use. Cantaloupes rolled from the bin to the floor and under the other displays. Shoppers turned their carts to avoid the area. When the bin was empty of all the melons except for three caught at the raised edge, Aaron stuck his face right into Quinn's. "'I can't even think straight' is what a banana would say. Because they're curved? Get it? It doesn't mean I'm gay."

Quinn stared at Aaron until he finally spoke again, his voice still quiet. "I'm only going to say this one more time, so listen up. I'm not gay, but it's okay with me if other folks are. Creighton likes—liked puns, so I hid some in the green bananas he bought. It was fun. I'm going to miss it and him. I'm sorry your mom got one that scared her. Never intended that." He dropped to the floor and began collecting the wayward cantaloupes, effectively ending his speech and dismissing her.

Quinn took her banana and left the store, not entirely satisfied. Aaron's reaction seemed too calm, perhaps even rehearsed. He seemed more rattled by the cantaloupes than by her questions. Why did he lie to Georgeanne the other day? Was he also lying about having an affair or being gay? Was it *really* okay with Aaron if other people were gay? Maybe if he and Creighton had been playing this weird game of bananagrams for a long time, Creighton got the wrong idea and made an unwelcome pass at Aaron. Could he have retaliated with a hate crime?

Chapter 10

Quinn slept in on Sunday morning. When she shuffled into the kitchen her dad said, "Two days off in a row? Did you win the lottery?"

Rubbing her upper arms, she said, "Knocking down a wall wasn't exactly a day at the spa." She didn't tell him about any of Saturday's other activities.

As she reached for a box of cereal she saw Dan was hunched over a banana pulled from a bunch across the counter. "What's with everyone and bananas these days? Nobody here even likes them."

He stage-whispered and pointed an embroidery needle at her. "But everyone likes a surprise love note! I've gotta hurry before she gets back." He hunched back over the banana and concentrated on poking holes in it.

"Where'd she go?"

"Took some treats to Hugh over at the jail."

A couple of hours later, still in her pajamas, after completing the Sunday *New York Times* crossword, Quinn shuffled back out to the kitchen for a soda. Georgeanne was hunched over a banana with an embroidery needle.

She watched her for a minute. "How was Hugh?"

"I think he's depressed."

"I don't blame him. I would be too. What did you bring him?"

"Black bean brownies."

"I guess if his life can't be regular, at least his bowels can be." Quinn poured a root beer over ice. "Where's Dad?"

"Mowing the lawn."

Quinn peeked out the curtain and saw Gin dozing in the freshly-mown grass, lifting her head warily whenever Dan made a pass too close with the push mower. Quinn turned back and watched her mom work for a bit. "So this is your thing now? You two write love notes in bananas?"

"Who said it was a love note?" Georgeanne saw Quinn's face. "Aha! I knew that's what he was doing."

"Why don't you just look at the bananas?" Quinn reached for the bunch of bananas that had been there earlier. Now there were just three. "Ohmygawd, are you guys hiding them too? This is going to be gross. Remember those Easter eggs I didn't find? The ones you forgot to count? It's going to be spring stink all over again."

Georgeanne laughed and showed her dimple. "I'd forgotten about that! What a mess that was. But I don't think this will be like that. Bananas are noble, not sneaky like hard-boiled eggs. Although ..." Georgeanne got a troubled look on her face. "I was reading this book about the history of bananas. Maybe they're not noble at all. Did you know that scholars think that it was really a banana that Eve ate in the Garden of Eden?"

"There are banana scholars?"

"Yes, actually. Maybe not scholars, exactly, but scientists. And aficionados."

Quinn sipped her root beer and nibbled from a bowl of smoked almonds, letting her mother's voice wash over her.

"... and that's why they're called banana republics ..."

Quinn thought about everything that happened yesterday.

"... there's this banana blight, you see ..."

She watched Georgeanne poke holes in a banana. Was this the same thing Aaron and Creighton had been doing? Sending love notes via fruit? Hugh must have seen the message bananas. How would Creighton explain them? By saying he wrote the messages for Hugh?

"...the bananas we eat today are not the same as the bananas my grandparents ate..."

And what about those love notes Hugh wrote all those years ago? How did they fit in? They were punny too.

"...growing them in test tubes..."

And Dreadlock Guy? Drug user or drug dealer?

"...did you know bananas are technically herbs because..."

Did Rico follow up on Creighton's children yet? Did Victor and ValJean have alibis? Had Chief worked my puzzle yet?

"...Cavendish bananas outsell every variety of apples and oranges combined..."

What about that Kwikset key? What lock did it open? And did the engraved phrase mean anything or was it simply a handy dime-store fob to attach a key to?

"...in most of the world bananas are used as a vegetable crop..."

Quinn finished her root beer. "You know a lot about bananas, Mom."

"Bananas are fascinating."

"Maybe we should start eating them."

"Adding that one to my chili did make it creamy and delicious." Georgeanne started to get up. "Let me heat you up a bowl."

Quinn waved her back to her seat. "Nah, I'm not hungry. I've got to go back and finish at Hugh's. I didn't do as much yesterday as I should have. I dove into making a puzzle. And I've been loafing around here all morning performing that *self-care* Mary-Louise Lovely always preaches."

"That's what Sundays are for. Want some help at Hugh's?"

"No. You stay here and play hide-the-banana with Dad." Quinn blushed at her inadvertent double entendre and took the opportunity to flee before Georgeanne asked why she was blushing.

* * * *

Quinn took a long shower and tried to figure out Creighton's relationship with both Aaron Janikowski and Dreadlock Guy. Her thoughts were so scattered that when she got out, her hair was deodorized and her armpits were soft and manageable.

She clipped the leash on Gin, calling goodbye to whichever parent might be in earshot. "Going to Hugh's. Be back later!"

They reached the front porch of Hugh's, and Quinn looked to where the mystery car had been parking around the corner. Two hundred fifty steps. Her OCD monster took control of her feet and she pounded down the sidewalk. She reached the edge of the fence and stomped her feet in time with her words, "two forty-nine, two fifty." *This is insane*, she thought. She paced further along the sidewalk and then back again, determined not to count her steps.

By the time she was halfway back to Hugh's house, her counting had morphed to: "Liz-zie, Bor-den, Vic-tor, Val-Jean, Les Mis, cross-word, love notes, May-nard, mon-ey, key fob." Ten words, two syllables each, right, left, right, left. Then the eleventh, three syllables…"ba na nas." Three syllables, three steps. Pause. Start it all over again, but this time beginning with the opposite foot. Symmetrical. Another twenty-three steps.

Back and forth from the porch to the edge of the fence.

No matter how hard she tried, she couldn't land her final footfall in the same place with her chant as she did when she simply counted her steps. Eleven sets of twenty-three steps would have allowed her to travel almost the same two hundred fifty steps, but she couldn't bring herself to use the odd eleven sets. Instead she used the even ten sets of twenty-three steps, but tried to lengthen her stride a bit.

She recognized her unhealthy spiral beginning almost as soon as it began, but her *baba ghanoush* coping mechanism felt too puny against all this. The monster was winning. She wrestled with the demon in her brain by telling herself she was simply processing clues. Like Sherlock Holmes, but with her feet. She pushed away the thought that he didn't do it over and over, obsessively. She didn't think so anyway. Sherlock had many problems, but she wasn't aware that OCD was one of them.

Gin trotted beside her on every trip, seemingly unperturbed by the repetition or the exercise. Maybe this counted as her playtime.

After eight of these trips between the porch and the fence, Hugh's neighbor Barbara called out, "Quinn! Don't you know it's a thousand degrees out there? Come inside where it's cool and have some water before you keel over from heat frustration!"

Quinn saw Barbara holding her front door open. It took all of her willpower, but Quinn pivoted halfway through her mumbled chant and led Gin into Barbara's house.

After Barbara had given them both some water, she motioned Quinn to the loveseat. Gin looked at Barbara for permission to join her.

"Sure, go ahead."

Gin hopped up, placed one paw on Quinn's thigh, then curled up in the corner.

"Now, tell me what in the Sam Hill were you doing out there?"

Quinn took a long drink of water while she wondered what to tell her. "I just…I don't know…" Telling Barbara about the counting and the chanting of the mantra seemed impossible, so she decided to tell her the secondary truth. "All of these clues are spinning around in my head and I just don't know what to think. I was trying to organize my thoughts."

"Clues about Creighton's murder?" Barbara leaned forward when Quinn nodded. "Like what? Did you find out who the man in the car was?"

"No, but it seems important, doesn't it? And Creighton has adult children from a previous marriage. Did you know that?"

"He did? Does Hugh know?"

"I don't think so. And apparently, both the kids hated Creighton. Didn't you see the obituary in the paper?"

Barbara jumped up and pulled a newspaper from the top of a pile on the kitchen table. She turned pages until she found it. Quinn was quiet as she read. When she finished, Barbara said, "That's awful. Did you tell Rico about it?"

"He says he'll look into them."

"Well, then he will. He's not anything like that Myron Chestnut," Barbara said with conviction. "What other clues have you found?" She refolded the paper and dropped it on the floor near her feet.

Quinn sighed. "Just some weird stuff. Like a key I found that doesn't seem to fit anything. Some money I don't understand—"

"A lot of money?"

Quinn wished she hadn't mentioned it. She didn't think Barbara was going to break in and steal it or anything, but she shouldn't have mentioned it. She decided to ignore the question. "And my friend Loma and I found some stuff that might be related out at the old Maynard place. She's working on it for the new owners."

"Oh, you found Maynard's hidey-hole."

Quinn's jaw dropped. "You know about that?"

Barbara laughed. "Everyone knows about that. Well, everyone over retirement age, that is. Or at least me, Wilbur, and Larry. We used to run with Maynard, Jr."

"Wait. I thought their last name was Maynard."

"It is."

"Then why was he called Maynard, Jr.? What was his first name?"

Barbara thought hard, for a long time. "Honestly? I don't know. We always just called him Maynard, Jr.—Junior for short. Well, anyway, I was kind of a tomboy back then. Junior had sisters, but they were older and didn't want to hang out with me. Besides, the boys always looked like they were having more fun. This would have been"—Barbara tapped her temple—"Oh, I don't know. Sometime between the Great Depression and the war. Those boys ran wild."

Quinn was interested to hear what some of her Retireds had been like as boys. "Tell me."

"Well, let's see…as I recall, Maynard, Sr. was furious when the bank called his loan early during the Depression. So mad he punched a hole in the wall. Then he had to go find work in Denver. He'd come home on the weekends. Betty, his wife, could barely manage those kids. Let's see… Dorothy was the oldest—she just died earlier this year—then Ruth, then Margaret, then Junior."

"Dorothy. Was that Larry's wife?"

"Yes, the poor dear. Larry may never recover."

Quinn thought about Larry hanging out with the Retireds. He was never as vocal as the rest of them. Quinn hadn't known him when his wife was alive, but he always struck her as sweet and melancholy. Now it made sense.

"Go on."

"Well, Betty was out of her depth; kids she couldn't control, barely enough to get by, husband gone all the time and when he was home he was angry and exhausted. The town came together back then—they still do—to help anyone who needed it. The Maynard family was fed, clothed, taken care of, just like everyone else in Chestnut Station. People barely had anything, but the town scraped up enough money to hold off the bank. But for Betty, it began a lifelong distrust of banks. She started dropping what few coins she could into that hole in the wall. Covered it all up with a painting. Everyone knew about it."

"How was she going to access it if she needed it?"

"She'd send one of the kids under the house if things got dire. But my impression is that she thought of it as a kind of a retirement savings account. Out of sight, out of mind. People who live through hard times want to make sure they have a plan for the next hard time." Barbara tilted her head at Quinn. "Is that what you found there? Bunch of coins?"

Quinn nodded, but kept mum about Hugh's love notes. That was too personal to share with Barbara. But it might have shed some light on the hidden money at Hugh's house. Maybe that was Hugh or Creighton's version of having a plan for the next hard time. "That clears up a lot of stuff for me. Thanks for telling me." Quinn stood. "I should go finish up at Hugh's now, though. Thanks for rescuing me."

She reached for her empty glass, but Barbara waved her away. "I saw you out there in that heat and you were making me hot. Just thought I should share my air-conditioning with you."

Quinn couldn't help herself and hugged Barbara tight. *If she only knew what else she'd rescued me from…*

"Need any help over there?"

"No, I've got it under control. But thanks."

"Before you go—" Barbara stopped herself with a flap of a hand in front of her face. "Never mind."

"What is it?" Quinn assumed she needed a jar opened or a light bulb changed. It was the least she could do for her.

"It's just…I don't want to get anyone in trouble. No. Don't mind me."

Quinn perked up. Another clue? "Tell me." Quinn reached for Barbara's hand, thinking she'd pat it reassuringly, like a normal person would. Instead, it was more like she'd batted it away. Awkward. "Tell me, Barbara. It must be important if it's bothering you."

Barbara paced back and forth across the room a few times, finally stopping near Quinn.

Quinn carefully reached over and caught up Barbara's hand in hers, then covered it with her other one. Success! "Tell me."

"Do you know Dick Darnell?"

Quinn shook her head.

"Ask Rico to find out where he was when Creighton was killed."

"Why?"

"There was some bad blood between them. I don't want to gossip."

"Why don't you call Rico?"

"I don't want to gossip!"

"It's not gossip if it's a crime tip." Quinn didn't point out that bringing up Dreadlock Guy could be construed as gossip too. Maybe Barbara didn't count that because he was a stranger.

"Can't you please tell Rico for me?" Barbara pleaded.

"What's the bad blood?"

"I don't want to gossip! Besides, Rico will know. He probably already talked to Dick Darnell anyway. I'd just feel better if I knew for sure."

"What exactly would you like me to tell him?"

"Tell him to make sure he knows exactly where Dick Darnell was during the murder."

Quinn agreed with a squeeze of Barbara's hand, then motioned to Gin. "C'mon, let's go."

Gin stretched, then lightly jumped from the loveseat and waited patiently for the leash.

"You don't need it just to go next door, do you?"

Gin's eyebrows agreed that she didn't and they left Barbara's house. Quinn didn't want to risk anything or wake her monster by stepping on the front porch, so they went through the gate and in the back door.

She leaned against the kitchen sink and called Rico. He didn't answer, so she left a message about what Barbara said about Dick Darnell.

Quinn walked through the house, making a list of priorities, then tackled them one by one, keeping her obsessive thoughts occupied with order and neatness, all her energy focused on Hugh seeing his house again and having it in perfect condition. Being in control kept her on track and the monster at bay. By the time she was finished, she had found seven million tennis balls and lined them up against a wall.

"I'm starving. Let's go see what Georgeanne made for dinner."

Gin trotted over to her leash draped over the doorknob.

Quinn clipped it on her collar, then reached for the front door. *Better not risk it,* she thought. They headed around back, then through the gate. Gin pulled toward the roses and Quinn followed. They both inhaled the velvet aroma before turning toward home.

She was barely past Barbara's driveway when the words began keeping time with her footsteps.

Except this time, instead of the litany of clues, she found herself chanting, "Baba ghanoush, baba ghanoush, baba ghanoush" with every step.

Her safe word. The one to get her out of her spirals.

The view ahead of her swam in her vision as her eyes welled.

She couldn't control anything.

Chapter 11

All weekend Quinn ignored the call from Mary-Louise Lovely reminding her to make a new appointment after failing to do so the other day.

The last thing she needed was for Mary-Louise Lovely to find out just how screwed up she was, with her chanting and step-counting. She'd get hauled back to the hospital so fast she'd leave cartoon contrails behind her. Her parents would freak out. Jake would fire her. She'd lose any chance at moving out of her childhood bedroom and being normal. If she could just avoid Mary-Louise Lovely, she could also avoid the truth.

But maybe all she needed was a bit more time. *After all, Mary-Louise Lovely had said that I didn't have to quit counting and organizing. It was only a problem if I let it get in the way. I'm still doing what needs to be done and, in fact, doing more, with taking care of Hugh's house, and Gin, and helping Rico investigate Creighton's murder.*

As Monday dawned dark and rainy, Quinn had almost talked herself into being proud of her obsessions and compulsions. It would have to do for now.

It was odd to wake to a rainy day in August in Colorado. Typically, thunderstorms formed over the mountains in the west around midday, then traveled to the eastern plains in the mid- or late afternoon. It was another indication of the upside-down turn her life had taken in the last few months.

Quinn sat on the edge of her bed, listening to the rain on the roof and staring through the window at the gloomy sky. It was such a cliché that the weather matched her mood. She threw on clothes without bothering to shower. She gathered her hair in a messy ponytail, using her hands for a hairbrush. It was not effective, but she didn't have the energy to care.

Her parents were still asleep so she didn't need to lie to them about having already eaten, another thing she didn't have energy to care about.

She drove to the diner, apparently beating Jake because Jethro sat in a small dry spot under the awning, waiting for someone to let him in for his rounds. When Quinn walked up jingling her keys, his wrinkles perked up the slightest bit. He looked behind her, then accusingly into her face.

"I'm sorry, Gin stayed with Georgeanne today." Quinn unlocked the diner door and ushered him in. "Come on in, but please don't shake everywhere."

Jethro stepped inside and began to flap his long ears.

"Uh-uh-uh! I said *don't*."

Jethro stopped his shake, took three steps, then did a full-body shake, spraying droplets everywhere.

Quinn couldn't even be mad at him. She wasn't any better at controlling herself.

Jethro made his rounds, got his bacon reward, then sat outside in the dry spot. Quinn wiped off all the tables and chairs and while she was mopping, saw that Jethro had gone. Hopefully somewhere dry.

After Jake had prepped the kitchen and Quinn had prepped the dining room, the Retireds shuffled in, complaining about how the rain bothered all of their various ailments. Herman dragged an extra chair over.

"Think Hugh's coming?" Larry asked.

"I think he's supposed to get out today," Wilbur said.

"When?" Bob asked.

They discussed at length the ideal time to be released from jail. Finally Herman said, "If he gets released and comes here, he'll have a chair."

Quinn poured their coffee.

The Retireds were all subdued, perhaps because of the weather, perhaps because of their ailments, perhaps because of Hugh, or perhaps because of the vibe they got from Quinn, so they didn't make jokes or fusses about ordering breakfast. No special requests, except the usual ones, of course.

When she delivered their food to them, Quinn saw she had no other diners waiting for breakfast so she sat in Hugh's empty chair. She looked at Larry and Wilbur. "I hear you two hung out at the old Maynard place when you were kids."

"I told you that last week," Wilbur growled.

"Yes," Larry said. "That's where I met my Dorothy. Why do you ask? Is your friend still doing work out there? Has she found the hole in the wall yet?" He smiled.

Quinn nodded, pouring herself a cup of coffee.

"Did you find all that buried treasure?" Silas's eyes twinkled.

"Yeah, we're going to split it and go live in the Caribbean. Or at least use it to buy a slice of pizza."

The men laughed. “Not a lot there, eh?”

Quinn didn’t know if any of the coins were valuable or not, so she let them think there wasn’t much there. Which was probably the truth.

“When did the Maynards live there?”

Everyone deferred to Wilbur, since he was the oldest. “Let’s see…Old Man Maynard was born in that house on January sixth, 1900. I remember my pops telling me that he’d say to anyone who’d listen that it was some kind of prophecy to be born on Epiphany at the turn of the century.”

“What prophecy happened nine months before that?” Silas joked.

Wilbur ignored him. “All the Maynard girls and Maynard, Jr. were born there, ain’t that right, Larry?”

“Yep. All of ’em.”

“That family was top-heavy with girls, but then Junior was born and it seemed nobody never had another girl in that family. Chockful of boys ever after.” Wilbur tapped the rim of his cup. Quinn filled it, then topped off everyone else, including hers. “Had a whole passel of ’em—kids and grandkids—trooping through there all the time.”

“Grandkids would come and spend summers out here, keep them out of trouble, get them out of the city.”

“What city?”

“All of them.” Wilbur slurped from his cup. “One Maynard or another lived in that house until they sold it to the Jorgensons.”

“What do you guys know about Dick Darnell?” Quinn asked.

Wilbur peered at her from over the rim of his mug while he took a long, noisy sip of coffee. “He didn’t kill Creighton, no matter what you heard.”

“Why do you think that’s what I was getting at?”

“You were, weren’t you?”

Quinn didn’t have the energy to argue with Wilbur. She’d let Rico deal with it. She scooted her chair out. Before she stood, Larry covered her hand with his large, liver-spotted one.

Quietly he said, “Dick Darnell was Dorothy’s nephew. She loved that boy.”

Quinn couldn’t read Larry’s tone, but noticed the other men had gone silent. Was this a threat? A warning? Or was it just a sad man spreading gloom on this gloomy day?

Customers began to trickle into the diner, so Quinn got back to work. It got busy despite the rain, and Quinn didn’t even notice the Retireds had gone. She counted their cash and gave a long, low sigh as she pocketed her tip. Exactly 10 percent. She wondered if she could ever wow them with service that would budge them from their lowball tip. She also wondered if there was anything more she could ever do for them since she already catered to their every whim. Luckily, she wowed other diners, so maybe someday before she was ninety she'd be able to have enough money to move out of her parents' house.

When it slowed down, she took the opportunity to slump into the big corner booth and return Loma's call from earlier.

"Hey, did you ask Hugh about those notes? Are they love notes? Who are they for?"

"I haven't seen Hugh yet, and I don't know if I'm going to ask him about the notes or not, but I'm ninety-nine-point-nine percent sure it's his handwriting. I've been asking the Retireds about the Maynards, and if my math is right, Hugh could have been friends with one of Old Man Maynard's grandkids. Wilbur says there were always a bunch of kids staying out there during the summers. And almost all of them boys."

"Do you think they were *special friends*, as my granny would say?"

"I don't know. Maybe. There must have been girls that would spend summers, but maybe not. Larry said they'd come out to keep them out of trouble. Maybe the girls weren't as likely to get into trouble. Times were different then. I remember my mom telling me that her dad wouldn't let her get her driver's license until she was seventeen, even though her brothers got theirs when they turned sixteen."

"And if it was a boy that Hugh was writing to, it makes sense he couldn't let on. Had to keep lots of things in the closet back then."

"Maybe the boy himself didn't even know. Maybe that's why there were no letters to Hugh, only from Hugh."

"Poor Hugh had a case of the unrequiteds." After a bit Loma added, "You should ask him."

"I can't imagine how *that* would come up."

"You'll figure it out."

"Hmph. What did you figure out about the previous owners?" Quinn asked.

"When Maynard, Sr died, it went to Maynard, Jr—"

"Did you find out his first name?"

"Why?"

"Just curious. Everyone calls him Junior or Maynard, Jr. One of Hugh's neighbors hung out with them as kids and she didn't even know it."

"Good reason for that." Loma snorted. "It's Mortimer."

"Ouch."

"Anyway, Mortimer—Maynard, Jr.—kept it until he had to go to assisted living in 2015. A couple named Jorgenson bought it, but only lived there a couple of years. Didn't like living so far from town. Too dark out there for Mrs. Jorgenson, gave her the willies. I called, but they didn't know anything about the hole in the wall. I showed them a picture of the painting on the wall. She said it was there when they moved in. She liked it, so they just left it there the whole time they lived there. Never even moved it. And didn't take it with them because she said it seemed like part of the house. Sold the house in 2017 to my Texans. So the coins have to belong to one of the Maynards."

"Oh! I forgot to tell you!" Quinn related the story about Betty Maynard's distrust of banks. "So, I don't think any of those coins are worth anything. Just her weird little savings account."

"You should check, just to be sure."

Rico opened the diner door and shook the rain off his duty cap before stepping inside.

"Yeah, I will. But I've got to get back to work now."

"Busy?"

"No, but Rico just came in. Maybe he has news."

Jake came out of the kitchen to greet Rico. Quinn made her way across the seat of the big booth, but Jake waved her back down and slid in next to her. Rico remained standing.

With Jake there, Quinn couldn't ask Rico everything she wanted, so she just said, "Rainy, huh?"

Rico narrowed his eyes at her. "Yeah. Rainy. They let Hugh out this morning."

"Finally!" Quinn had a zillion questions that would all have to wait.

"That's great," Jake added. "Want some lunch?"

"Gotta take it to go. Can I get a ham on rye with tomato and onions?"

Jake stood. "Toasted?"

"Nope. And don't heat my sandwich, either."

"Looky, Jake, Rico made a funny!"

"Correction. Rico made an *attempt* at a funny." Jake headed for the kitchen.

"Wait, Jake. Can I take my break and collect Gin and her stuff to take to Hugh? He's probably dying to see her."

Jake flicked his chin at the booth. "Weren't you just taking a break?"

"Can I take my *official* break?"

He tried to look stern, but Quinn knew asking permission was just a polite formality.

"Go. Fine. What do I care?"

After Jake went to the kitchen to make the sandwich, Quinn asked Rico what he'd found out from the hospitals he'd called. "Anyone come in with a whack injury?"

Rico stared at her. "You were serious about that? No murderer is going to go to the hospital after getting hit with a fireplace poker. You said there was no blood on it and no blood was found in the house, other than…you know."

"Well, what about Creighton's kids, then? What did you find out from them? I bet they don't have alibis, do they?"

"Don't know. I haven't talked to them yet."

"They're ducking your calls?"

"I don't know." Rico pronounced his words precisely, as if English wasn't Quinn's first language. "I haven't talked to them yet."

Quinn exaggerated a sigh. "What about Dick Darnell? Barbara said—"

"I don't care what Barbara said. Gossip about Dick Darnell isn't germane to my investigation."

"You're infuriating."

"But he's so adorable," Jake said as he came out of the kitchen and handed a bag to Rico.

"Thanks. Write it in the ledger for me? I'm in a hurry."

"Will do," Jake said.

He and Quinn watched Rico leave.

"Why is he infuriating?"

"I don't know. Born that way?"

"I thought you were taking your break."

"On my way."

* * * *

Quinn drove home through a downpour to tell Georgeanne the good news about Hugh, and the bad news that they'd have to relinquish Gin.

While Quinn gathered up Gin's bed, toys, treats, food, leash, and dishes, Georgeanne had some time to cuddle her and say goodbye.

"Virginia Woof, you have been excellent company and a model houseguest. You are welcome here anytime."

Gin placed a paw on Georgeanne's forearm, then generously allowed Georgeanne and Quinn to snivel and hug her too tightly.

"It's the best thing for Hugh and for Gin." Quinn wasn't sure if she was trying to convince Georgeanne or herself. Both, probably. She shoved her face in the soft fur around Gin's neck. "Hugh needs you right now more than ever. Let's go." Even so, Quinn stayed on one knee a bit longer.

Quinn found an old tarp and wrapped all of the doggy paraphernalia in it as protection from the rain before piling it all into the back seat of her car. She returned to the house for Gin. Quinn had to keep the window up because of the rain. Gin fogged it up and covered it in nose prints before they even backed out of the driveway. Her tail was wagging so hard Quinn thought she might rub the vinyl right off the seat. *What was it about dogs and cars?* she wondered.

At Hugh's, Quinn tapped her horn to let him know they were there. Gin raced to the front door, making excited little huffs. Quinn grabbed everything from the back seat, glad that Hugh would be there to open the door for her. The rain had let up, but not by much.

Gin was wiggling to her happy dance on the porch. But the door remained closed. Quinn reached up with her elbow and rang the doorbell.

Hugh didn't answer.

Quinn dropped her load out of the rain. "He probably went to the grocery store. His cupboard was pretty bare, eh?" Quinn kicked herself for not laying in some supplies; at least staples like eggs, bread, fresh fruit, vegetables, and Fig Newtons. Digging out the house key, she let Gin in, then collected everything and wrangled it all inside. She hoped Hugh would be back before she finished. Jake was flexible, but she didn't want to have to wait with Gin and push her luck with him.

She placed Gin's belongings where she thought they should go. "There. How's that?" She turned, expecting to see Gin next to her, due to the rattling of the treat bags and boxes, but Quinn was alone in the kitchen. "Gin?" She didn't come, so Quinn went to find her.

She heard her softly whimpering in Hugh's bedroom. Gin sat on the bed next to a lump.

"Hugh? Is that you?" Quinn took a few tentative steps closer.

Gin looked at her, then back to the lump.

"Hugh…it's Quinn." She tiptoed around the end of the bed. "Are you okay?"

The lump stirred.

Quinn sidled closer. She could now verify the lump was indeed Hugh. She bent closer. "Hugh, you're scaring me. Are you okay?" She had a terrible thought. "What did they do to you in jail?"

Hugh turned over, facing Gin now. He pulled the covers over with him, practically covering his head.

Gin pawed gently at the bedspread, pulling it down from his face. Hugh pulled it back up without even acknowledging Gin's adorable use of her front paw.

Quinn stared down for a long time, trying to figure out what to do. She was quite familiar with full-blown depression and certainly knew Hugh's darkness right now. But she couldn't decide if leaving Gin here with him would be a good idea or a bad one.

There was a possibility Gin would whimper to go out or because she was hungry and Hugh would rise to the occasion and take care of her. It hadn't been too long ago that Quinn was the lump in bed. Remembering her darkness, she knew there was no possible way she would have been able to rouse herself to care for Gin in that situation.

It didn't look like Hugh would be able to either. It wouldn't be fair to Gin, or even safe, to leave her here with someone who couldn't see to even her most basic needs.

Quinn placed a hand lightly on Hugh's back. "It's okay, Hugh. I'll take care of her."

She loaded everything back in her car, then went to collect Gin, who hadn't left Hugh's side. "C'mon, Gin. We're gonna let Hugh get some sleep, but we'll be back later this evening."

Gin shoved her snout into Hugh's face and licked his cheek. She started across the king-sized bed, but at the edge looked back at him. She offered a little prayerful huff, looked at Quinn, then hopped to the carpet. She led Quinn to the car and waited for her to open the front door.

Back at home, Georgeanne was surprised to see Gin stroll through the kitchen door. Quinn explained everything as she organized Gin's life back into the Carr household.

"That's terrible," Georgeanne said. "Should I go over there?"

"I don't think so. Let's give him the afternoon and see what happens. I'll go by after work. He's been through a lot…first, finding Creighton like that and then sitting in jail for all this time. It's a lot to sort out." Quinn bent to thump Gin on the side. "I think for now, the best thing we can do for him is to take care of this munchkin. After work, I'll swing by the store and pick him up some groceries. Maybe take him some of Jake's meat loaf and mashed potatoes."

Georgeanne placed a palm on Quinn's cheek. "You're a good girl."

"I had a good role model."

Georgeanne stared at her daughter with a tilt of her head that Quinn knew meant she was worried about her. Georgeanne, Dan, and Rico were the ones who got Quinn through her darkness, and it was never far from any of their minds. They were all still feeling their way through the aftermath of Quinn's OCD breakdown right along with her.

She wished she could reassure her mother that everything would be okay. Trite words wouldn't be enough, but they were expected. "Everything's going to be fine, Mom."

Quinn wished she believed it.

Chapter 12

Quinn drove back to the diner, where Jake took one look at her and said, "What happened?"

She told him while she busied herself with loading the dishwasher with lunch dishes. It was only a little after two, but she wanted to make it up to Jake for her longer-than-normal break at an inopportune time. The dinner rush would start before they knew it—assuming people wanted to go out in the rain—and Quinn wanted to be ready.

Jake listened while leaning against the prep table. When she finished, he said, "That's a shame. Well, you did everything you could. I'll keep my fingers crossed for him."

"And your toes."

Jake checked the dining room. "While it's quiet, I need to get some bills paid. Will you start a batch of bacon? And do it in the oven. Your mom was a genius with that trick, by the way."

It pleased Quinn that Georgeanne was able to put her fingerprint on the diner in a small way when she'd been needed the most. "Why do you need so much bacon in the afternoon?"

"This rain must be giving the residents of Chestnut Station a collective case of cabin fever, the only cure for which seems to be a BLT. What is it about rain that makes everyone crave a BLT? I'm betting money tonight will be the same."

Quinn was glad to be kept busy. It might keep her from worrying about Hugh. Creating a hypothetical research study about the effect of weather on diner orders would be an excellent diversion between customers this afternoon.

Rico walked into the diner about twenty minutes later. Quinn marched right up to him and whispered into his face, "What happened to Hugh in jail? Has he been like this the whole time?"

"Like what?"

Quinn grabbed his hand and dragged him into a corner for a little privacy. "Like almost comatose."

Rico rubbed a hand across his face. "I was hoping being at home would snap him out of it. I drove him there myself. I think he's depressed."

"Ya think?"

"Why are you mad at me?"

Quinn released Rico's hand and slumped into the nearest chair. "I'm not. It's just so sad…and stirs up some—never mind."

"I know," Rico said softly. "But this is Hugh's fight to win. Not yours."

"He needs help."

"Of course he does. I'm not saying don't help. I'm saying it's his fight." He looked at his feet. "Just like yours was your fight to win."

"Yeah." The word spoke volumes between them.

After a bit, Rico said, "I need to pick up something for Chief."

"Let me guess…BLT?"

"Weird. How'd you know?"

"I'm psychic."

* * * *

A while later, when they were alone in the diner, Quinn and Jake took a midafternoon break in the big corner booth to eat. Not BLTs, though. Cheeseburgers.

They were almost finished eating when a girl who barely looked old enough to drive opened the diner door, letting in a windy blast of rain. She struggled to close the door behind her. She stood on the mat, dripping. It looked to Quinn like she'd been out in the weather all day. The sopping-wet look didn't diminish her attractiveness, though. Her blond hair, full lips, and doe-like eyes still managed a certain allure. Quinn didn't have that kind of glamour even when she tried.

"Let me get you a towel." Quinn popped the last bite of her burger in her mouth and pointed to her French fries. "I'm not done with those," she said to Jake as she hurried to the back.

Quinn handed a clean towel to the girl, who used it to dry her long hair. She pulled the length over to one side, bending at the waist so it hung away from her body, then rolled the towel around it. She had so much hair and it was so wet, the towel was immediately soaked through.

When she handed the towel back, Quinn noticed the back of one of her hands was covered in an intricate henna tattoo. Each finger had a matching design leading to a large sunburst design covering the back of her hand. The fingernails were polished in glossy black enamel.

Quinn took the towel from her and returned to the back for a few more. As she tossed it with the other dirty linens, she saw it wasn't just wet, it was filthy. That hair was dirty.

When Quinn returned to the dining room, she heard Jake offer to make her something to eat, on the house.

The girl replied quietly, "I can pay. If you'll take a check."

"Sure," he said. "What do you want?"

"I don't really care, as long as it's hot."

Jake thought for a moment, then gave her three choices: a cheap option, a medium option, and an expensive option. "Cup of chili? Tomato soup and grilled cheese? Chicken-fried steak and mashed potatoes?"

She didn't hesitate. "Chicken-fried steak, please."

Maybe she wasn't homeless, Quinn thought as she handed her the other towels. She waited for the girl to dry herself as best she could under the circumstances and then held out her hand for the wet towels. "Sit anywhere you like. Do you want tea or coffee? Something to warm you up?"

"Coffee would be great. Thanks." The girl sat at one of the tables.

Quinn poured her coffee, then went back to the booth to finish her fries. She finished Jake's fries too while she cleared the table. It occurred to her that she did have an appetite, as long as someone else put food in front of her.

She mopped the puddles on the floor, waving away the girl's apology. As she returned the mop to the back, she passed Jake as he carried out a plate with a huge slab of steak covered with crispy seasoned batter, crowding out a generous scoop of mashed potatoes with gravy and a small ear of corn dripping with butter.

The girl actually groaned with delight. "That smells great."

Jake laughed. "Enjoy!"

Jake and Quinn went about their business to finish preparing for dinner, Jake in the kitchen and Quinn in the dining room. Quinn filled, wiped off, and reorganized the condiments on each table.

The plastic holder for individual jellies sat centered, grape packets to the left, strawberry to the right, exactly full. Salt and pepper shakers were centered on the right side of the jelly caddy, hot sauce on the left. A vase of fake flowers centered at the rear of the caddy, dispenser for paper napkins at the front. She still wasn't sure if the flowers and napkins should be switched, but the flowers were taller—she'd measured. She also wasn't sure if the placement made sense for tables not pushed up against a wall. She hoped that no matter where anyone sat in the diner, they'd be pleased with the arrangement of the condiments. She had the tiniest inkling, however, that she might be the only one who cared.

While she worked, she snuck peeks at the girl. She ate like she hadn't had a real meal in a while, but she said she could pay. Maybe she was walking in the rain because she enjoyed it, not because she had to. Or maybe her car broke down. Even though Quinn was curious, she knew it was none of her business. And the girl didn't seem like the talkative sort, having only spoken in answer to their questions, except for that groan when her food came.

When the girl finished, Quinn handed her the ticket and cleared her plate. The girl wiped her mouth one last time, then hefted her bag from the floor and walked over to the cash register. The bag left a puddle on the floor.

Quinn itched to get the mop out again, but forced herself to round the corner of the front counter and punch numbers on the ancient register.

"Do you have a pen I could borrow?"

Quinn handed her one from her apron pocket. With her other hand, Quinn lightly touched the girl's henna tattoo, on the hand holding her checkbook. "I've been admiring this. It's beautiful."

"Thank you." Her pride lit up her face. "I did it myself."

As the girl opened the checkbook, Quinn saw the name printed on the check. A flush of adrenaline made her fingers tingle.

Chapter 13

Quinn grabbed the checkbook from her and moved between the girl and the diner door. "Where'd you get this?" She raised her voice. "Jake! Can you come out here?" Quinn shook the checkbook at her. "I said, Where'd you get this?"

The girl didn't answer, but looked on the verge of tears.

Jake hurried out, wiping his hands on the towel over his shoulder. "Something wrong with the register again?"

"No." She held the checkbook out so Jake could see the name on the check: *C. McLellan*. Quinn addressed the girl. "What's your name?"

Pause. "C-C-Cathy."

"Cathy what?"

The girl cut her eyes toward the checkbook. "Mc—Farland?"

Quinn pulled out her phone. "Rico, can you come to the diner right away? There's a girl here trying to use Creighton's checkbook to pay for her lunch." Quinn stashed the girl's bag under the counter. She didn't know what else might be in it, but she knew enough to keep it from the girl.

Without a word, Jake held the girl's upper arm while he guided her to a booth. She stumbled. He slid in next to her and Quinn blocked her in the other side.

Quinn asked again, sharply, "Where did you get this?"

"By a dumpster at a truck stop out by the highway."

"Why are you here?" Quinn bit off every word.

"I came into town figuring that if someone lost it, they'd be asking about it out there, not in town. It was in a reusable grocery bag with a bunch of papers and files. I didn't mean to steal anything, I looked in that bag, hoping there was food, but I found this instead."

"You live around here?" Jake asked.

At Jake's calmer, quieter voice, the girl visibly relaxed a little. "Hitchhiking."

"You didn't answer—"

"Shush." Jake quieted Quinn.

"But she has—"

Jake peered at Quinn. "I know. Shush." Then he addressed the girl again. "You were hitchhiking?"

The girl looked nervously at Quinn, but then concentrated solely on Jake's face. He had that effect on women.

"I'm on my way to art school. Got a full scholarship."

"Congratulations."

"Didn't matter. My parents didn't want me to go."

Jake smiled at her. "Parents have a weird way of showing their love sometimes, eh?"

The girl allowed a quick smile to play on her lips. Because, truly, Jake had that effect on women. "They wouldn't give me bus money, so I left. I'll get to California on my own."

"But you ran out of money," Jake said softly.

"So you decided to—"

"Quinn."

The girl nodded and lowered her eyes. "Almost before I left Hartford."

Rico pulled open the diner door and Quinn jumped up to meet him. She handed him Creighton's checkbook and whispered, "She had this! Arrest her!"

"Did she write a check?"

"No, I grabbed it before she could."

"Well, then I can't arrest her."

"But—"

"Quinn, you know I can't. She hasn't committed any crime."

"That you know of."

"That I know of," he granted. "Simply having Creighton's checkbook is not a crime. Now, if you hadn't grabbed the checkbook…"

"I was shocked. I reacted."

"That's not a crime either."

Quinn's lips were pinched so tightly together they disappeared. Rico looked at her with alarm.

"You're just going to let her go?" She raised her voice.

Rico stepped closer and lowered his. "No, of course not. She was in possession of a dead man's checkbook. I'll ask her some questions, but I can't force her to answer me." Rico glanced at the girl turning the saltshaker in slow circles in front of her. "She hasn't committed forgery, but she knows what she did—almost did—was wrong. I'll talk to her and get to the bottom of this." He handed his dripping duty cap to Quinn, who gave it a shake and then dried it as best she could with her apron.

Rico walked over to the booth, sliding in next to the girl. Jake began to slide out the other side, but Rico cut his eyes at him and he remained where he was. The girl was trapped between them and Quinn stood near the booth. Nobody was going anywhere until Rico was done.

"I'm Rico Lopez of the Chestnut Station police department. I need to ask you some questions and I hope you'll answer them truthfully and completely."

The girl looked him in the badge and nodded slightly.

"First, do you need anything? Glass of water? Something to eat?"

She shook her head. "I just ate." Her voice was barely audible.

"What did you have? Jake makes the world's best cheeseburgers."

She glanced up at Rico. "Chicken-fried steak."

"Ooh, that's good too. Did you have dessert?"

She shook her head again.

Rico turned to Quinn. "What's for dessert today?"

She frowned at him. "Cherry pie and chocolate cake."

"Bring me a slice of each." Rico cocked his head at the girl and smiled. "We'll arm wrestle for first dibs."

The girl looked bewildered. She glanced at Jake, who smiled at her.

Flustered by Rico's overly friendly demeanor, Quinn turned to the kitchen to plate two desserts. She hoped he knew what he was doing.

Rico pulled out his notepad and pen. "So, while we're waiting, let's start with your name."

"Eliza Yorkie." She slid her driver's license from her back pocket and across the table.

Rico examined it. "Where do you live?"

"Nowhere, I guess." She looked into her lap. When Rico didn't respond, she continued. "I used to live in Hartford, Connecticut, but I left home to go to art school in California." She told Rico the same story she'd told Quinn and Jake, but offered a bit more detail to Rico. It was clear the badge and uniform intimidated her. Or maybe she was disarmed by his overly friendly demeanor.

Quinn set a piece of cherry pie and a slice of chocolate layer cake in front of Rico. A can of whipped topping was shoved in the pocket of her apron.

As Quinn walked up, Eliza said, "The Art Institute. It's in Valencia."

Rico wrote that down in his notebook. "Ah, dessert." Rico held them both out to Eliza. "Choose." When she hesitated he said, "You can't go wrong with either one. There's no wrong answer here."

Jake leaned toward her. "Go for the cake. It's perfect."

Eliza reached a tentative hand for the cake.

"Wow. What's all that?" Rico used the plate holding the pie to gesture at her henna tattoo.

Jake said, "She did that herself. Isn't it amazing?"

"It's awesome." Rico set the pie down and motioned for Eliza to set the cake down. "May I?" He gently took her hand and studied it up close.

"That reminds me of a picture I saw once from the Book of Kells in Dublin," Rico said.

Eliza nodded slightly, then said quietly, "I was inspired both by Celtic and Persian influences. But this is my original design."

"That black nail polish is stunning, really sets it all off," Jake said.

"It really does," Rico agreed.

Who are these men? Quinn wondered. *Is Eliza Yorkie actually a witch? What kind of spell does she have them under?* "When I wore black nail polish, you said it looked like a desperate cry for help," she said to Rico, then turned to Jake. "And you told me it was going to scare the customers. Should we get back to the matter at hand? How this girl had Creighton's checkbook?" Quinn shook the can of fake whipped cream harder than necessary and splooched it all over Rico's pie. "Whipped topping?"

Rico locked eyes on her while he used a paper napkin to wipe a bit that had sprayed on his arm. "Yes. Thank you." He picked up his fork and took a bite, savoring his pie. Eliza did the same with her cake, shielding it from Quinn's can of weaponry.

"Eliza," Rico spoke slowly and quietly. "The reason Quinn here is upset is because that checkbook you had belonged to a friend of hers." He paused. "A friend who was murdered recently."

Eliza's fork clattered to the table. "Mur—mur—murdered?"

Rico nodded. "Where were you on Thursday?"

Eliza responded immediately. "Still home. I didn't leave until Friday."

"Do you have a cell phone?"

She nodded, rattling off the number, which Rico jotted down. "It's never charged, though. It's in my bag."

Quinn retrieved the bag and handed it to Rico.

"Do you mind if I take a look in here?" he asked Eliza. She shook her head, so Rico pawed through her belongings, finally withdrawing a cell phone. He pushed the power button. "Dead as a doornail." He dropped it back in the bag. "What about your parents? Your mom, maybe?"

"I haven't talked to her since I left."

"Then she'll be happy to hear from you."

Eliza looked at Rico with wide eyes. "Can't you just arrest me? Don't you have to give me three hots and a cot? I don't have to be in California for a few more days. I could use a break from…traveling."

Quinn was appalled at Eliza's naivete in practically begging for an arrest record. She'd lose her scholarship for sure, and it would follow her around the rest of her life. All because she didn't want to call her mom? And she was hitchhiking cross-country? Out in the world? By herself? Yikes.

"Let's talk to your mom instead. You don't need a police record." Rico told her to type her mom's name and number into his contacts. She handed his phone back to him.

He pushed the *call* button. "Is this Teresa Yorkie?" Rico identified himself and asked some questions to verify the story Eliza told them. Her answers must have all checked out because then he said, "Yes, she's perfectly fine…Absolutely…Fed and dry…We've had some rain here. Do you want to talk to her?…Of course." Rico handed the phone to Eliza, then slid out of the booth. He walked over toward the cash register with Quinn while Eliza moved to a corner of the diner for a bit of privacy.

"I don't think this girl killed Creighton," he whispered to Quinn.

"Well, she must know who did, then."

Jake walked up. "I don't think she murdered Creighton."

"I just said that."

"You two are nuts. You've both had your heads turned by long blond hair and black fingernail polish."

Rico looked at Jake. "I'm not wrong. That's a cool tattoo, right?"

"It is indeed," Jake agreed.

Quinn released a frustrated growl. "Look. I have a gut feeling…and doesn't the academy teach—"

"Quinn. Gut feelings are perfectly acceptable. Especially when backed up by investigation. Which is what I'm going to do." Rico's voice was calm and controlled. "I have a gut feeling too. I don't think she killed Creighton, but I will check out everything she told us. However, I can't bring her to the station without putting her on an investigative hold, which will derail her plans. She'll never get to art school." Rico looked directly at Quinn. "I know you don't want to be a part of ruining this girl's life. It's good you didn't let her write that check. Then I would have been forced to arrest her. Look at her."

They all turned toward Eliza slumped in a chair. She wiped her cheek with the back of her hand. "I will, Mommy, I promise," they heard her say. Then, "I love you too. Be sure to take Inky in for her shots next month. I put it on the calendar."

Rico whispered, "You don't really think she stabbed Creighton to death on Thursday, stole his checkbook, hung around town, then tried to write a check six blocks from his house, do you?"

Quinn let out a hard breath. "No. I guess not. But I still think it's fishy and weird and she probably knows more than she's letting on about all this. And nobody going off to college calls her mom *Mommy*. And they're sure lovey-dovey again after just having a big enough fight to make her run away from home."

"I'll check everything out." Rico looked out the window. "It's still raining. I need to get to the truck stop and rescue whatever evidence is still out there." He looked at Jake. "I'll pay for her meal, but can she stay here with you two until I get back here?"

"Of course," Jake said.

Rico called Eliza over and held out his hand for his phone. He explained the situation to her and snapped a photo of her with his phone. "I'll be back as soon as I can."

Jake told Eliza to finish her cake and hang out in the big corner booth until Rico got back. Jake freshened her coffee and left the pot on the table for her.

Eliza pulled a sketchbook from her bag and flipped it open to a clean page.

Jake motioned for Quinn to follow him into the kitchen. He took his apron off, smoothed his hair, then faced her with an apologetic look. "I have to get to the bank and the grocery store, so I want you to—"

"You're gonna leave me alone with a potential murderer?"

"You heard Rico. The chances of that are slim."

"But you admit there's a chance?"

"There's always a chance someone would murder somebody. Don't you watch TV?"

"I'm serious, Jake." Quinn looked nervously toward the dining room.

"I am too. I think there's much less chance of that girl out there killing someone, than how close I come every day to killing Wilbur. Besides, I know you can handle yourself just fine. She's not going to give you any trouble. Look at her." They both stuck their heads out of the kitchen door. Head down, focused on her sketchbook, Eliza drew with a pencil, smudging a line here and there with her finger.

Quinn realized whether she liked it or not she was going to be left alone with Eliza. "Can't you at least wait until a customer comes in?"

"Then I'll have to cook."

"I can cook."

"Yes." Jake's voice was tinged with impatience. "You've proved you can cook, and you'll have to if someone comes in before I get back, leaving her alone out here where she might bolt. The sooner I leave, the sooner I get back."

Quinn followed Jake into his office where he unearthed a seldom-used umbrella. He whispered, "I'll go out the back so she doesn't know you're here by yourself, okay?"

"I guess it better be. Hurry back, though. No dinking around, flirting with that teller who's half your age."

Jake laughed. "No dinking. No flirting." He pointed at her. "No freaking."

"Fine."

Quinn busied herself in the dining room where she could keep an eye on Eliza, who hadn't moved from the booth. While Quinn was staring at her instead of filling ketchup squirters, Eliza looked up and caught her eye. They both looked away immediately. And now it seemed they were trying so hard not to look at each other, that they locked eyes more and more often.

Quinn couldn't help but run through everything Eliza had said, poking holes in it all, despite everything Rico had said.

Why would Creighton's checkbook be way out at the truck stop for her to conveniently find? Why would she look in a bag by the dumpster for food? Why wouldn't she go into one of the fast-food places and beg, or at least look in the trash cans there? And if she was really an artist, she would have offered to sketch somebody's portrait in exchange for food. That happened all the time in movies. And she had a cell phone but no charger? *Puh-lease*. Quinn felt her chest begin to tighten. Everybody had a charger—it came with the phone. And you could use it in any car these days. She could hitchhike, but couldn't ask for that? Did she even call her mom on Rico's phone? She probably just called one of her cohorts, one of her partners in crime, to pretend. And really? Art school in Valencia? *That seems bogus. I've never even heard of Valencia.* But it was one thing Quinn could verify.

Quinn typed *Valencia California* into her search bar. *Okay, fine. So it's a real place. But what about that art school? What did she call it? Oh, yeah.* Quinn searched for *The Art Institute Valencia*. What popped up surprised her and affirmed her suspicions. "California Institute of the Arts, CalArts for short," she muttered. Who didn't know the name of the college they were risking everything to attend? But was it truly suspicious, or was it like how everyone in Colorado called the college in Boulder

"CU" instead of its real name, the University of Colorado at Boulder? Technically, if we called it CU, it should be Colorado University, but it wasn't. *Baba ghanoush.*

Quinn squinched her eyes. She was beginning to confuse herself and she knew the monster hovered just beyond. She rolled her neck and shoulders. When was Jake going to be back? Or Rico? Quinn decided being more physical would help get her out of the OCD spiral she felt coming on. She grabbed the broom and thrust it around the dining room like it was her swing dance partner. Eventually she settled into a pattern rather than simply a cardio workout and found herself near the corner booth where Eliza still sat, sketching.

Without raising her head, Quinn tried to see what she'd been drawing.

"It's the diner."

Quinn glanced at the pad. Not only was it the interior of the diner, but it was an intricate, fully representational illustration with the rudimentary lines of Jake leaning on the doorframe of the kitchen, and Quinn herself behind the register. How'd she do all that with just a nubby little pencil?

"That's awesome."

"Thanks," Eliza said shyly.

* * * *

Rico drove his patrol car through the pouring rain out to the truck stop near the highway. He pulled up to the overly-full dumpster, squinting through the windshield to spot the reusable grocery bag that Eliza mentioned. He didn't see it. A slow circle put him parallel to the dumpster. Bags and boxes of all types had been deposited all around the dumpster, since nothing more could be fit inside. He thought he saw something sitting at the bottom of a pile that could be the bag. He rolled down his window to see better.

Bingo.

The top of the grocery bag had been folded over by the plastic trash bag atop it, giving it a modicum of protection from the rain.

He popped his trunk, then leaped from the car. After briefly checking the bag to verify it was indeed full of Creighton's papers, and the surrounding bags and boxes to determine if any of them held similar items, he secured it in the trunk. He was happy to see it was one of the coated reusable bags rather than just plain canvas, or it might have been completely waterlogged by now.

Rico drove to the gas pumps and parked under the awning. He opened the trunk and explored the bag a bit more thoroughly. The papers at the top were the soggiest, but everything in the bag seemed to belong to Creighton. Slamming the trunk, he went into the truck stop.

"Hey, Roscoe."

"Well, don't you look like a drowned rat."

"Feel like one too."

"Need some coffee?"

"Nah. Here on business." Rico pulled out his phone and showed him the photo he snapped of Eliza. "Seen her around today?"

"Yep. She came in with the Sandys." Roscoe glanced at a monitor mounted on the wall. "Truck's still here. They're around somewhere."

An older, jovial couple, Sandy and Sandy Shore, owned a long-haul trucking business and stopped in Chestnut Station whenever they passed through Colorado. If anyone asked about their names, Mrs. Shore said, "It was fate!" while Mr. Shore said, "It was inevitable." Usually in unison.

Rico walked through the aisles of the convenience store area scanning for the Sandys as he made his way to the restaurant in back. He finally found them playing cards at one of the tables in back.

Sandy grinned wide. "Hello, there, Constable. It's been a long time."

Rico shook the man's hand. It was like grabbing on to an Easter ham. "Sure has. How you been?"

Sandy jumped up from her seat and gave him a quick hug. She barely reached his armpit. "Handsome as ever, Rico. You keeping out of trouble?" She settled back into her seat.

"That I am, missus, that I am." Rico pulled out a chair and sat between them. "Roscoe tells me you came in with this girl." He showed them the photo.

Sandy's eyes darkened as she studied the photo. "That's Eliza. Why? What happened? Is she okay?"

"Now, now, Mother, calm yourself. Rico don't look like he's the bearer of bad news." He looked at Rico. "Are you?"

"No, she's fine."

Sandy let out a whoosh of air that blew some of the playing cards around the table. She scooped them into a pile. "Why are you asking about her?"

"Hope it's not illegal in Colorado to have hand tattoos, because then she'd be locked up for sure!" Sandy's deep laugh boomed across the restaurant, startling a waitress, who bobbled a cup of coffee. She accepted the mess in the world-weary way of a well-seasoned truck stop waitress.

Rico smiled at him. "Since marijuana is legal, I'm pretty sure the state legislature wouldn't be too bothered by tattoos."

"Then why?"

"Oh, she had something that didn't belong to her and I'm just checking out her story."

"She stole something?" Sandy jogged the deck of cards by pounding it on the table.

"I don't think so. Was she traveling by herself?"

"We picked her up in St. Louis and brought her all the way with us. Sandy here don't like to see youngsters out hitchhiking, especially by themselves. If she had her way, we'd start a charter service." He boomed his laugh, again startling the waitress. She looked down at the coffee spilled on the well-worn, ratty carpet. Without even glancing around to see if anyone was watching, she dug her sneaker into the coffee spill and ground it into the carpet. She raised her foot, studied the stain, shrugged, and walked away.

"What'd she do when you got here?"

"She and I went to the ladies' room, and when I asked her if she wanted to join us for lunch, she said she'd love to but had other plans." Sandy rubbed a thumb on the deck of cards. "I'm so stupid. I should have told her it was on us. She obviously didn't have any money."

Sandy reached out his meaty paw and gently rubbed his wife's forearm. "You can't do everything." He looked at Rico. "We're headed to Boise, but she said she was going to California, so this is where we parted company."

"Shame too. She was real nice company. Drew us our pictures, even." Sandy pulled a folded paper from her purse and showed Rico quality portraits of themselves, wearing the clothes they still wore.

"She sure captured your essence, Sandy." Rico handed the pencil drawings back to her before turning to her husband. "And you look like you always do." Rico grinned at him.

He grinned back. "I asked around the truckers I knew and had a ride all picked out for her—Cal Gentry was going all the way to San Diego—but when I looked around, she was gone."

"This Cal Gentry still here?"

"Nah. I saw him pull out while we was eatin'. Seriously, Rico. She in trouble? The missus and me won't forgive ourselves if we coulda helped her and didn't."

"Everything's fine. Don't you worry about any of it."

Sandy pulled his wallet from his shirt pocket. Digging around, he pulled out a twenty and three ones. "It's all I can spare, but can you give this to her? Tell her it's payment for the artwork."

Rico waved the cash away and leaned in. "Just between you and me, I'm going to do my darnedest to see that the Chestnut Station police department buys her a bus ticket." He stood and held out his hand. "You two stay safe out there and get to Boise in one piece. Call me next time you're passing through and I'll come out and have a bite and a game of gin rummy with you."

"Gin rummy! This is high-stakes poker here. I'm up three toothpicks."

Before he left the truck stop, Rico made the rounds to ask if anyone else had seen Eliza, but nobody had. He waved to Roscoe and headed back to the diner, wondering how he was going to pry money from Chief Chestnut's petty cash for a transient's bus ticket.

* * * *

The diner door chimed, causing both Quinn and Eliza to practically snap their heads off their necks to see who entered. Jake had returned about ten minutes earlier, and came out of his office tying his apron around his waist. He waved to Rico, then stepped into the kitchen.

Quinn dropped the rag she was using to wipe down already clean tables and raced over to him, dragging him behind the cash register, out of earshot of Eliza. She spoke fast and quietly. "What did you find out? Did you find the bag? Why would she be looking for a bag near the dumpster? Why wouldn't she go to one of the fast-food places or the restaurant? Why out by the dumpster? That makes no sense at all. And that phone charger nonsense. How can you believe she wouldn't ask to charge her phone in somebody's vehicle? You can do that in almost all cars these days, except for really, really old ones. Why wouldn't she ask to—"

Quinn stopped midsentence when she saw Rico's horrified face. She took a deep breath. She hadn't even gotten to the part where she extended her theory that Eliza never actually called her mom. *Baba ghanoush.* "I'm not in a spiral, Rico. I'm just really, really not sure I believe this girl." She bit her tongue to keep herself from saying one more word.

Rico didn't speak, but pulled her in for a bear hug. When he let her go, he looked directly into her eyes. "Quinn Carr," he whispered. "I love your passion, but you can stand down. I talked with the truckers who drove with her from St. Louis. The only reason they parted company was because they were going different directions. They had nothing but nice things to say about her. Everything checked out exactly as she said. I found the grocery bag"—he lofted it in the air—"right where she said it would be and as far as I can tell, she was right. It just has a bunch of papers and files in it. In fact, I'd like you to go through them. Would you do that? If you find anything important, set it aside for me."

Quinn's voice and heartbeat had slowed considerably. "What about fingerprints?"

"It's a soggy mess. There won't be any fingerprints."

"What about chain of custody?"

"It's been sitting outside at a truck stop for who knows how long. No way it would be admissible but I'd still like to know what all is in there." He paused. "Wouldn't you?"

"You ask the dumbest questions sometimes." This was her OCD nirvana, after all. Wrangling a mess into tidiness was what she lived for. Quinn stowed the bag under the front counter.

Rico said, "But now I need to powder my nose."

As he stepped away, Quinn called him back over. "Hey. Can I borrow your phone a minute?"

He raised his eyebrows but handed it over.

When he came out of the restroom, he whispered, "Did you get ahold of Eliza's mom?"

"No, you peed too fast." Quinn handed him the phone.

He held it back out to her. "Here, get the number."

"Already did." She grinned at him.

Rico stuck his head in the kitchen. "What do I owe you for Eliza's lunch and our desserts?"

Jake waved away the question as if it were an annoying gnat. "Everything okay?"

Rico nodded. "Yeah, I think so. I'm going to take her into Denver to the bus station."

"Let me help." Jake pulled out his wallet and handed Rico some cash. "If there's any left over after the ticket, let her keep it."

"Very generous, dude." Rico returned to the dining room and Jake followed. "Okay, Eliza. Thanks for waiting until I got back."

"No problem. It was nice to be out of the rain, someplace I could draw." She tore the page from her sketch pad and scooted out of the booth. "Is everything…okay?"

"Yes," Rico said. "But I'd really like it if, in the future, you didn't find yourself in possession of anyone's checkbook but your own."

Eliza looked at the floor.

"C'mon, now, none of that."

She raised her head. "This is for you. To say thank-you." She handed him the pencil sketch of the diner.

Jake and Rico huddled around it.

"This is exquisite," Jake said.

"Absolutely perfect," Rico said. "Quinn, come look."

"I already saw it."

"Did you see she put you in it?"

Quinn sidled over and peered at her image. It only had a few lines when she'd seen it earlier. Now it looked better than if it had been a snapshot of her. "That's remarkable." It was as if Eliza had known her before she had her OCD meltdown. The drawing of Quinn looked calm and in control, the opposite of how she knew she truly looked. *Maybe this girl really was on her way to art school.*

Rico handed it to Jake. "You should have this."

"I'm going to frame it," Jake said.

"It's just a messy pencil sketch." Eliza blushed. "But I'm glad you like it."

"When you get famous, this'll be worth a ton of money. Hey, wait! You didn't sign it."

Eliza blushed even deeper, then took the sketch and signed the lower corner before handing it back to Jake.

Quinn looked over his shoulder and studied it closely. "Eliza Yorkie." *And maybe that really was her name. It doesn't mean she doesn't have any accomplices, though.*

"There's just one more thing you need to do," Rico told Eliza as she gathered up her things.

Leaving her bag where it was, she turned toward Jake. "I promise you I'll send the money for my lunch just as soon as I get it."

"Your lunch is on me. Don't worry about it."

"Then what?" she asked Rico.

Rico said, "You need to come with me to Denver and let me put you on a bus to California. We"—Rico gestured at Jake and Quinn— "won't be able to sleep at night if we knew you were out there hitchhiking."

They argued about it for a bit before Eliza finally relented. "I appreciate it," she said quietly. "I didn't know how bad this…" She trailed off.

After Rico and Eliza left, Jake went back to finish prepping for dinner. Before Quinn even had a chance to glance through the grocery bag of Creighton's papers, people started coming in for dinner. She wanted to lock the doors and go through the papers right then and there, but knew she couldn't. Even if she could convince Jake and shoo away the customers, there wasn't enough room anyway. Not even in the big corner booth in the back, her command center for the last murder she helped investigate. She also couldn't do it at home. Not only would Gin step all over everything, so would Georgeanne and Dan. Plus, they'd ask questions she might not want to answer.

After she got water for table seven and handed menus to table ten, she remembered the Maynard place, big and wide-open without any furniture. She texted Loma. Can I come over tonight? It's not a movie, but I have a fun activity planned!

Loma texted back immediately. Yes! Bring food!

Quinn stepped into Jake's office to call Georgeanne. "Hey Mom, I have to be out at the Maynard place with Loma after I get off work tonight. Can you take Gin to Hugh's? I'm worried about him. See if you can get him to eat something. But nothing…um, fancy. Just open a can of soup for him. Or applesauce. Or make him a PB and J. Something that's no effort for him to eat. Just like…" She wanted to say, "Just like you did for me for so long," but she didn't want to stir things up for Georgeanne. Besides, who was to say Hugh was depressed? Maybe he was just exhausted.

"I'm on it," Georgeanne said.

For the rest of Quinn's shift, she peeked into the grocery bag whenever she had a free minute. As soon as her shift was over and the diner was ready for the morning, Quinn raced out to meet Loma at the Maynard place.

Chapter 14

Georgeanne rang Hugh's doorbell until he answered. She held up a pot she carried with oven mitts. "Chicken pad Thai stew with Grandma's dumplings. Comfort and protein, that's what you need," she said, pushing past Hugh.

Gin danced around their feet in the foyer. Hugh reached down and stroked her velvety ear.

"Now you come on out here and sit yourself down while I get your food ready. Soup's no good cold, now, is it?"

Hugh didn't answer, but slumped into a chair at the kitchen table. Gin leaped into his lap. She barely fit, but he put a protective arm around her so she wouldn't fall. She gave him a dainty lick on his cheek.

Georgeanne opened cupboards and drawers until she found everything she needed. She ladled soup into a bowl. "Is this bowl microwave safe?"

Hugh barely answered and Georgeanne hoped his grunt meant it was, in fact, safe.

She zapped the soup and placed it and a spoon in front of Hugh. She gently shooed Gin off his lap so he could eat. "Croutons?" When Hugh didn't answer, content with staring into space, Georgeanne shook some Grape-Nuts cereal on top of his soup. "For crunch. Everybody likes a little crunch."

She stepped back, out of his view, and stared at him staring across the room. She followed his gaze, but couldn't ascertain if he was just unfocused or there really was something captivating on the far wall.

Gin looked up at Georgeanne and they shared a moment of concern.

Georgeanne made sure Gin had fresh water, then gave her a treat from the bag Quinn had left on the kitchen counter. She poured Hugh a glass of water.

He began staring at it instead of the far wall.

Georgeanne pulled out a chair and sat close to him. "Listen, Hugh. I get that you're not hungry. Or maybe you just don't like my soup, and that's perfectly fine. But I am not leaving here today until you drink that entire glass of water. Dehydration can do terrible, terrible things to a person. And whether you like it or not, you are still a living, breathing human and I want you to stay that way." When he didn't respond and just kept staring at the water, she picked it up and handed it to him. "I mean it, Hugh." Her voice was soft, but sturdy. She held it closer and closer to him until he finally took it from her.

He took a tentative sip, then a couple of gulps before setting it back down.

"Excellent." Georgeanne held out the spoon. "Now eat some soup."

Hugh closed his eyes and shook his head, ever so slightly.

"Maybe later?"

He opened his eyes and lifted his shoulders in the tiniest of shrugs.

It satisfied Georgeanne. "Finish your water." She sat there eyeballing him until he picked up the glass again and sipped. She nodded and smiled before returning to the pot of soup she'd brought. Even though she was fairly certain he wouldn't answer, she asked, "Do you have any small Tupperware I can put this soup in?" She searched the lower cabinets until she found some plastic containers next to a neat stack of matching lids. "Perfect." She ladled all the soup into the single-serving containers. When she heard movement from Hugh, she glanced over, pleased he'd finished drinking the glass of water. She watched from the corner of her eye as he shuffled toward the living room couch. He settled on his side, facing the room. Gin hopped up and curled into a ball in the nest of his bent legs. They both heaved big sighs.

When she'd finished filling all the individual containers with soup and had washed out her pot, she brought Hugh another glass of water. She set it on the coffee table and squatted near him. "I want you to drink another glass of water. And later, when you get up to pee, I want you to zap and eat one of those containers of soup. You don't even need to put it in a bowl. Just zap and eat. And leave it in the sink and either Quinn or I will be back to wash it."

"I used to make lunch for Creigh to take to work in those containers," Hugh whispered.

Georgeanne's heart broke and she dropped to her knees. "Did I ever tell you about the first time I met Creighton? It was during a godawful snowstorm when I somehow managed to get my car stuck in a drift. I shouldn't even have been out driving, but then again, neither should he, but we both were. He helped dig me out and get me on my way. He completely ruined his suede shoes, but wouldn't let me buy him a new pair."

"Shouldn't wear suede in the snow. Disaster waiting to happen. His own fault." Hugh turned over and faced the back of the couch. As he moved, Gin carefully arranged herself to be out of his way, but stayed with him.

Georgeanne pushed herself to her feet, using one hand on the coffee table. She stared down at him for a bit, then pulled a crocheted afghan in earth tones from the back of a chair. She covered him with it, resting one hand on the side of his head when she finished. "Drink that water," she whispered. "C'mon, Gin. We'll leave Hugh to his nap, but we'll be back. Yes, we will, sweet girl."

* * * *

At the old Maynard place, Quinn and Loma spread the soggy papers from the grocery bag all around the room, making sure to stay far away from the area where the floor had rotted. Quinn tried to get Loma to organize as she went, matching like papers with like papers whenever possible, but Loma was hopeless. She wasn't even lining them up in rows and columns with an inch margin at the top and bottom of each. At best, Loma's margins were haphazard.

Quinn followed behind Loma and batted cleanup after her.

Some of the papers were irredeemably wet, but the thick manila file folders saved most of them. Laying them out like this would dry everything the rest of the way. A little of the ink had run, but it was probably better that Quinn hadn't been able to sort through them at the diner. Letting them dry naturally might have kept her from accidentally ruining them.

Loma finished laying a stack of papers and then stepped back and watched Quinn simultaneously place pages from her stack and rearrange Loma's work. By the time Quinn had finished, most of the loose papers had been returned to their appropriate file folder.

"So. This is your fun activity." Loma crossed her arms, heaving her bosom up.

"Not only is this fun and satisfying in every possible way, it's also helping Rico. Maybe the clue as to who murdered Creighton is on this floor somewhere." Quinn waved a hand across the room.

"You really do love stuff like this, don't you?"

"I do." Quinn never stopped placing, scanning, rearranging papers.

"Because of your OCD?"

"That's pretty much over." Quinn's voice was breezy, but she didn't dare look at Loma.

"But I thought you told me it was something you'd always have to deal with."

"I was wrong. My therapist—"

"You've been going to therapy? That's great, especially since it must have helped."

She didn't bother to correct Loma. Quinn was going to say that her therapist appointments were inconvenient, but she'd been reading articles online so everything was fine now. Instead, she said, "There's nothing wrong with being organized."

"You said it, girl. No way could I juggle all these subcontractors I have coming out here if I wasn't organized." Loma went back to the grocery bag for more papers. "Looks like that's all of them. Shall we have dinner and let them dry some more?"

Quinn was itching to read everything, but allowed that stopping to eat wouldn't hurt anything. "Sure." Quinn opened the bag she'd brought with her from the diner. She held out two Styrofoam containers. "Baked chicken or bison meat loaf? Both with roasted green beans, peppers, and onions."

Loma sighed. "I was hoping for one of Jake's cheeseburgers." She reached for the chicken.

"He made both choices for you when I told him I needed something to go."

Quinn pulled out a smaller container. "And for dessert—"

"Let me guess. Berries?"

Quinn opened the lid. "Ta-da! Strawberries!"

"If you want the truth, I'm sick of strawberries."

"Don't be silly. Nobody gets sick of strawberries."

"I do. I've been jonesin' for that German chocolate cake of his. Or the trifle he made that one time." She sighed deeply. "I'd even settle for a stale doughnut."

Quinn stuck the container of strawberries under Loma's nose. "Seriously? You'd prefer a stale doughnut over one of these babies?" She jangled it in Loma's face, knowing she'd picked the most perfectly shaped and ripened berries from the flat.

Loma plucked one out and bit into it. With her mouth full, she said, "I gueth not."

Quinn bolted her food then crawled over to study her perfect grid of papers. She maneuvered around on hands and knees, reading the first page in the upper-right corner and moving down the column. When they'd come across any file folders, they'd decided to keep the papers inside it, so when she got to a folder, she sat back on her heels and went through the pages one by one to see if they all belonged there.

Pangs of happiness shot through Quinn. "Hey! I found Gin's vet info."

Loma enjoyed her food—despite the fact it was healthy—and watched Quinn make her way down one side of the grid. She wondered which direction Quinn would go when she got to the end of the outside row. After spending so much time with her since they'd become friends, Loma knew there was a right way and a wrong way to do everything. At least to Quinn. Would she go all around the perimeter, or up and down each row? "Up and down," Loma murmured, quietly betting with herself while she took a bite of chicken. She gave a flourish with her fork to acknowledge her correct guess when Quinn turned to go up the row.

"Hey. Look at this." Quinn waggled a file folder. "This is labeled *Gardening Catalogs* but it's actually full of stuff about Creighton's kids."

"Like what kind of stuff?" Loma stabbed a green bean with her plastic fork.

Quinn dug deeper. "Oh my gosh…"

"What?"

Quinn held up some pastel-colored envelopes. "These are all birthday cards for Creighton's kids."

"Sweet."

"No, you don't understand. He never sent them. He bought the cards, signed them all *Be Happy*, and drew a little heart." She held one up for Loma to see.

Loma placed a hand over her heart. "That's the saddest thing I've ever seen. What else is in there?"

"Lots of clippings from a newspaper in Cleveland." Quinn held up each piece of paper from the folder and described it. "Victor's team photo from Little League published in the paper. An article giving rave reviews to ValJean as the Sugar Plum Fairy in a local production of *The Nutcracker*. Listings of their names on the honor roll during high school. A picture and short article about Victor's scout troop's tour of a local print shop."

"I thought you said they had terrible childhoods. This all sounds… very middle-class."

"It does." Quinn glanced through some more pages. "Here are birth announcements from the newspaper from, like, fifteen or twenty years ago. They must be Creighton's grandkids. The ones he never met."

"Did ValJean ever accept your friend request or answer your message?"

"Not yet. I'll be surprised if she does." Quinn jogged the papers to neaten them in the folder and replaced it in the grid. She stood and gave a few little knee bobs to get out the kinks. "It's all a big mystery. These papers have to mean something, but what?" She pointed to different areas of the floor. "Why would someone dump Creighton's electric bill, his AARP membership information, his Marriott Rewards, and all these other things out at the truck stop? And why did he have stuff from his kids in a file labeled *Gardening Catalogs*?"

"Oh, that's easy. He didn't want Hugh to find it."

Quinn chewed on that for a bit. "Maybe. And who dumped it?"

"I know you don't want to think about this, but could it have been Hugh?"

"Only if he dumped it before the murder. Rico said Creighton's skin wasn't even discolored yet when Chief Chestnut and Donnie got there."

"So? What does that mean?"

"It means there was no lividity yet." At Loma's raised eyebrows Quinn explained further. "Creighton's blood hadn't completely pooled in the lowest parts of his body yet, so he couldn't have been dead for long before Hugh called 911."

"Gross." Loma wrinkled her nose. "Could Creighton have dumped the papers himself?"

"Why wouldn't he just throw them in the trash at home?"

"Again, because he didn't want Hugh to find them," Loma said.

"The old electric bills? What's so secret about those? And why would Creighton suddenly dump all those things about his kids he'd kept for so long?"

"Because he had a big, ugly fight with them?"

"He wasn't in touch with them, at least according to his obituary."

"Or was he?" Loma's voice had a *dun-dun-duuun* timbre to it.

"They were hidden in a file marked *Gardening Catalogs*. But nothing else was hidden." Again, Quinn jabbed a finger at various points in the grid. "Electric bills in a file marked *Mountain View Electric Co-op*. Dental info in a dental file. Papers for Gin in the vet folder. AARP folder. Marriott Rewards folder." Quinn stooped to pick up the Gardening Catalogs folder. "Each of these papers matched one of the file folders. Except his kids' stuff in this bogus gardening file." Quinn shook it in the air.

"Loma, you know what I'm thinking, right?"

"Hardly ever."

Quinn stared, waiting for Loma's brain to process the information.

Finally, Loma's eyes widened. "Those kids did it!" Her face immediately clouded, though. "But why dump it at the truck stop? It seems very incriminating to kill their father, then leave a big clue at the truck stop."

"Unless you have the timing backwards. What if they found out he'd been keeping all this stuff but never contacting them or engaging in any way as their father, and *then* became enraged enough to confront him." Quinn added quietly after watching Loma consider it, "They killed their own father. How do you—"

"What's that?" Loma pointed to a pattern of lights dancing on the wall opposite the bare living room windows. She struggled to her feet and peeked out the window. "Do you think kids come out here to hang out? And don't know I'm fixing it up?"

Quinn returned the file folder to its place in the grid and hurried to kill the lights. In the dark, she sidled up next to Loma where they tried to see what was going on outside.

"Better view from upstairs," Loma whispered.

They felt their way to the stairs. She led Quinn to the master bedroom that had large windows on two perpendicular walls.

They each took one window, being careful to stay to one side so as not to be seen from below.

Dim lights bobbed in a random pattern across the Maynard property. Quinn thought she could make out legs here and there, but couldn't be sure. "Are those people?"

"I think it's the reflection of stars in the detention pond."

"But it's cloudy." Quinn glanced upward.

"Oh, right." The rain had stopped but it was still completely overcast. No moonlight at all. "Maybe flashlights? Those headlamp thingies?"

Quinn looked closer, trying to make a definitive assessment. But just as quickly as the lights had come, they disappeared, fading to nothingness. Maybe it had just been a plane flying overhead, its lights reflecting off the clouds and the standing water. She gave a shiver and moved away from the window. "Now I know why that lady who lived here got freaked out. It is hella dark out here."

"Right?" Loma peered harder into the black night. "Think we should go out and investigate?"

"Are you nuts? Absolutely not. Haven't you ever read a mystery and some idiot Nancy Drew wannabe goes to investigate something she shouldn't and gets into terrible trouble because of it? Not gonna be us, my friend."

Loma backed away from the window and felt her way to Quinn. They clasped hands and didn't let go until they were back in the living room. Anyone seeing them for the first time would be forgiven in thinking they were an interracial set of conjoined twins.

Loma scrounged for a flashlight in her toolbox and turned it on. "Let's call it a night." She gathered up the trash from their dinner and dropped it into her makeshift trash can, a large plastic bag tied to a doorknob.

"I should call Rico." Quinn gripped her phone.

"Why?"

"Because this is something he should know."

"What is? That we're scaredy-cats? Pretty sure he already knows that. There's nothing to tell."

"He should know that someone—or something—was out here prowling around," Quinn said.

"Some *thing*? Like little green Martians? Colorado contingent of Mothers Against Teenagers Having Fun? Herd of bears?"

"Bears don't come in herds."

"You wouldn't say that if you'd ever seen one."

"You've seen a herd of bears." Quinn didn't ask it like a question.

"With that attitude, now you'll never know." Loma stuck out her tongue, then spoke earnestly. "Quinn, listen, please don't tell Rico, because then he'll have to make a report and it'll get back to my Texans and they'll lose confidence in me and I need this job. I *really* need this job. It's the biggest thing I've ever done and I want more of this. Herd of scary bears or not." She clutched Quinn's hand again.

Quinn squeezed back. *A reasonable request. She's right too. Rico would definitely get the new owners of the Maynard house involved.* "Fine. I won't tell him. But you have to promise me if you're here at night, you quadruple-lock the doors. Or even during the day. Whenever you're here alone. Quadruple."

"Well, that's not possible." At Quinn's stern expression she quickly added, "Quadruple-locked. You got it. And in the morning, in the full light of day, I'll go out there and check everything out. I'll bet you quadrupled boxes of doughnuts that I'll find enough empty beer cans to…do whatever somebody would do with a bunch of empty beer cans."

"You're not supposed to have doughnuts, remember?"

Loma gave a melodramatic pout. "But big girls love doughnuts."

"Which is how they get diabetes. Remember?"

"How could I forget, with you and Jake reminding me all the time."

"If you'd behave, we wouldn't have to."

"Jeez, you're worse than my mother." Loma held the flashlight under her chin and notched up her voice to mimic her mother's. "Loma Prieta Robinson Szabo! You'll catch the sugar disease, you keep eating those Twinkies! Now you save some for me!" Loma rolled her eyes and changed the subject, pointing at the grid of papers on the floor. "What should we do with these?" The flashlight beam danced across the floor.

Quinn stared at her grid. Many of the papers were still damp, so leaving them would allow them to dry the rest of the way. "Will they be in the way here?"

"No contractors scheduled for a few days. We can leave them."

Quinn nodded in the dark. Besides, where else would she be able to set them out like that?

They clutched their belongings to their chests, making sure they both had their keys in their hands before stepping out the front door. Quinn kept her head on a swivel while Loma locked the dead bolt from the outside.

"Ready," Loma said.

Shoulder to shoulder, they sidled to the edge of the wraparound porch, heads twisting and turning at every sound and shadow. At the edge of the porch, they looked at each other.

"One, two…three!" Loma whispered.

They bolted from the porch to their cars. Heaved in their stuff. Locked the doors behind them. They started their engines and took off down the curving driveway to the road.

Loma was in the lead and suddenly slammed on her brakes, skidding slightly in the gravel, her car angling across the road.

Quinn had been staring into the darkness out the passenger-side window and barely stopped in time. She fumbled for the door handle, then thought better of it and fumbled instead for her phone. As she reached for it, it lit up. Loma. "What happened?"

"Almost hit a skunk."

"*CheeseandRICE!* I almost killed you because of a skunk?" Quinn's hands shook.

Loma chuckled. "Sorry, but I—oh, there it goes, off to the right. See it?"

Quinn squinted into the light thrown from Loma's headlights. A fat little skunk, low and wide, ambled across the short grass. Never even looked back, oblivious to its near-death experience, and Loma's. "Cute, for a little hellion." Quinn dropped her phone in the console and they continued, sticking close, but easing up on their gas pedals.

When they traveled the five miles that led to the intersection with the county road, Quinn turned right toward Chestnut Station, and Loma turned left toward Denver.

Loma tapped a soft toot of her horn as goodbye.

As the lights of Chestnut Station came into view, Quinn began to breathe normally, and her *baba ghanoush*es became less frequent. The adrenaline had mostly cleared her system as she drove down Buckingham Palace Way, the main drag of Chestnut Station. Even though it was barely past eleven o'clock, Quinn didn't see any other cars at the intersection with Trafalgar. That didn't mean the stoplights shirked their duty, though. No, Chestnut Station traffic signals never took time off. She came to a dutiful, but unnecessary stop in front of Immaculate Mary Catholic Church, the location of Creighton's funeral tomorrow.

Her eyes wandered. To the left, the dark Chestnut Station Diner, with its ancient wooden sign with the hand-painted cartoon of a grinning brown blob that may or may not have been a chestnut. When she was a kid, Quinn thought it looked more like a half-chewed Tootsie Roll. Or worse. After she worked there for a while, she'd asked Jake why he kept it, since the name of Chestnut Station had absolutely nothing to do with chestnuts.

He'd said, "Why? Because it's Americana, is why!"

When she pointed out the Chestnut family had come from England, he said, "You want me to put up a Union Jack instead? Or commission a cartoon of Chief Chestnut up there?"

Quinn hadn't said it back then, but the more she learned about Chief Chestnut, the more she could see his resemblance in that brown blob.

Still waiting at the light on this quiet summer night, she saw the residential area of town in the distance ahead of her. She pictured peaceful Chestnut Station residents, tucked in for the night. She hoped to be one of them soon.

Movement near the church parking lot caught her eye. She strained to see through the shadows, but couldn't. She was sure something was there, though. Could be anything. Priest out for a smoke. Cat on the prowl. Skunk. Herd of bears.

She glanced at the interminable red light, which, through the sheer force of her will, finally turned green. Quinn stepped on the gas. At the edge of the parking lot her headlights swept over the back of a nondescript sedan parked at the curb with an oversized bumper sticker. *Don't meddle in the affairs of dragons for you are crunchy and delicious with ketchup.* Quinn slowed and stared at the bumper sticker, rereading it. She'd found Dreadlock Guy's mystery car. The one that parked around the corner from Creighton's house.

Quinn was still rolling slowly past the car, staring at the bumper sticker, when an African-American guy loomed directly in front of her. Her headlights captured hostile eyes boring into her, as well as a full head of long, thick dreadlocks.

She swerved to the other side of the road and passed him. With a glance in the rearview mirror, she saw him open his car door and slip inside. Quinn heard the engine roar to life. His headlights clicked on, blinding her. She gunned her engine, taking corners too fast, zigzagging her route home so Dreadlock Guy couldn't follow her, something she learned from Jim Rockford. Before pulling into her parents' driveway, she circled the block with her lights off to make sure Dreadlock Guy was nowhere near. Also courtesy of Jim Rockford.

For the second time in thirty minutes, she gathered her stuff to her chest, clasped her keys defensively in her hand, and raced for the door.

With another adrenaline spike under her belt, she assumed sleep would elude her yet again, but put on her pajamas anyway and optimistically crawled into bed. She thought about calling Rico, but Loma's words rang in her head: *There's nothing to tell.* Still true. She played out the imaginary conversation with Rico. *Um, Rico? I'm calling to report there was a car with a bumper sticker parked perfectly legally near the church. There was also a man wearing dreadlocks I almost hit standing in the street near it. Then I got scared and drove home. Erratically, I might add. But I lost him, even though I have no indication he was actually following me.* Yeah, that would go over well. The only thing that would make that phone call better was if she called—she checked the time—after midnight.

She shifted her worries from Dreadlock Guy to the papers she left on the floor of the Maynard place. Her OCD monster stirred again, this time fully awake. She went over the layout of the grid over and over in her mind, thinking about each folder and the contents. How did they get to the truck stop? Why were those particular papers chosen? Who brought them there? Why were they left? What did it all mean? Was anything missing? Had anything been removed, aside from Creighton's checkbook?

Truck stop. Papers. Who? Why? Missing. Removed. Creighton. Checkbook.

The words traveled in a Möbius strip through her brain. Over and over. No end.

How had she ever had the hubris to tell Loma she was "done" with her OCD?

She'd never be done.

Never.

It was a disease she'd carry with her until she died.

And that didn't seem like such a bad option some days.

Chapter 15

The next morning Quinn woke with a headache, presumably from fighting the monster all night. A normal person might accept this as the time to have a heart-to-heart with Mary-Louise Lovely, but she had other things on her mind. After her therapist left another voice mail for her to set up an appointment, Quinn texted back, Can't. Going to a funeral today.

The monster was in charge. At least for now.

Quinn thought about last night. She believed even more strongly this morning that Victor and/or ValJean had something to do with Creighton's murder. She wondered what they had thought when they saw that file of clippings and cards Creighton saved all these years. *Be Happy*, he'd hoped for them, but had never actually told them.

Quinn thought about that heartbreaking hand-drawn heart. If he had been her absentee father, would it have enraged her instead of breaking her heart? Or does a broken heart lead to rage? She had no frame of reference for bad parents, because she had the best.

How could she locate either Victor or ValJean to ask them to explain their presumably complicated feelings about Creighton? She came up short of viable ideas. She'd leave it to Rico to check out their alibis, even though everyone knew those could be faked. But you couldn't ask someone about their dad and not get a whiff of what they really thought.

Puzzling over this longer only hurt her head more and nourished her monster, so she switched gears and propped a pillow against her headboard. She leaned back and called Loma. "Go outside yet?"

"Perfect timing. I'm out here right now. There were definitely people out here, that's for sure. Muddy footprints everywhere."

"Up near the house?"

"Didn't see any. Probably just kids out looking for a place to party."

"Find any beer cans?"

Loma was slow to answer and Quinn heard her huffing and puffing due to the exertion of traipsing over the hilly land of the Maynard property. "No."

"Awfully quiet for a bunch of teenagers."

"True." Quinn heard Loma hold the phone away and shout at someone. When she finished shouting she spoke again to Quinn. "Hey, I gotta go hold the hand of a new contractor who has no idea what he's doing."

"I thought you said nobody'd be out there. That's why we left the papers—"

"Don't worry. He's working on the septic. No way is he coming in the house."

"Loma, be careful out there." Quinn paused. "I don't think that was a bunch of teenagers last night. I don't know who it was, but it's awfully coincidental to…everything."

"I'll say it again: Don't worry. We let our imaginations run away with us last night. But it's daytime now. All the boogeymen are back in their closets. Gotta go."

Not all the boogeymen. Creighton's killer was still out there.

* * * *

Even though it was a Tuesday, the diner was closed until after the funeral. Then everyone would walk over for the reception Jake had offered to host. Hugh was in no condition to organize it, and neither Hugh nor Creighton had belonged to any church. Quinn wasn't even convinced Hugh would be able to drag himself to the funeral. The plan was that Georgeanne and Dan would pick him up and take him to the church. Georgeanne had quietly gathered a cadre of church ladies to orchestrate the funeral.

Quinn checked the time, then downed some ibuprofen before her shower. Her parents had already left to help Hugh get ready for, and survive, Creighton's funeral.

The day had dawned bright and sunny. Ironic, for a day that stretched so somberly ahead. Yesterday's rain had pushed east toward Kansas. Or maybe it had broken up completely. Quinn didn't really care.

She stepped into the narthex of the church and was immediately blinded by the dark interior. She kept walking, though, because she knew this church well. They'd come here every Sunday when she was a child, which she happily did until she was a junior in high school. Then, the lure of sleeping in on Sunday became greater than the salvation of her soul. She had created an elaborate PowerPoint deck of slides that she formally presented to her parents, and presumably God, right there in the living room. Her thesis was that in her last two years of high school, it was more important that she get an adequate amount of sleep. Her secondary thesis, put forth for their consideration, posited that weekends of study and focused endeavor were necessary to maintain her exemplary grades. It must have been a compelling and effective presentation, because her parents relented and lightning did not strike her down.

Quinn liked Immaculate Mary, but hadn't returned to the habit of weekly Mass. Truth be told, neither had her parents. They were down to less than twice a month, summers being too hot and lazy, and winters being too cold and snowy. Georgeanne wouldn't dream of missing the potlucks, the baby and wedding showers, the food and clothing drives, and the monthly bunco games with the other church ladies, though. Quinn overheard her tell Dan that God wasn't just there on Sunday mornings. She hadn't been struck by lightning either.

Quinn greeted people she knew as she made her way through the crowd.

The Retireds had staked out a corner near the main entrance and clotted there, unofficial greeters, forcing everyone to shake their hands or maneuver around them. Quinn didn't head into the church, instead keeping an eye out for her parents and Hugh. As she passed the Retireds, she heard Wilbur's gravel voice say, none too quietly, "Surprised to see Dick Darnell here after all that ugliness."

Quinn scanned the room, following Wilbur's gaze to a jowly man with deep wrinkles running from the sides of his nose all the way past his down-turned mouth. She recognized him from the diner as one of her grumpier customers. He didn't come in often, but seeing the back of him out the door always made her happy.

He stood by himself, wedged in a corner, stub of an unlit cigarette dangling from his frown.

Quinn veered toward him. Funeral or not, gossip or not, she had to ask him about this bad blood between him and Creighton. She was halfway to him when she heard Georgeanne call her name.

She pivoted and made her way over to her parents as the official ushers began inviting the mourners to take seats inside. "How's Hugh?"

"He's here," Georgeanne said. "That's about all. He'll wait with the priest until the very last minute."

"I doubt he'll even make it to the reception." Dan pulled a handkerchief from his pocket and cleaned his glasses. When he was finished, he clasped Georgeanne's hand and they entered the church. Quinn followed behind.

Immaculate Mary was large and ornate. The church was split in half by the main aisle, with long, traditional pews in solid maple stretching to smaller aisles on both sides.

Quinn and her parents shuffled in behind the crowd and found seats near the back on the right side. Quinn saw Dick Darnell sitting across the aisle to the left and about ten pews ahead of them.

Quinn leaned to the right across Dan and spoke quietly to both her parents. "Do you guys know what ugliness Dick Darnell was involved in with either Hugh or Creighton?"

Georgeanne let out a tiny puff of breath and shook her head in the way Quinn recognized as exasperation. She'd seen it many times in her youth.

Dan leaned close to Quinn's ear. "Every year Creighton buys—bought—all the hunting licenses he was allowed, and put his name in for all the lottery licenses. And then, instead of actually hunting, he'd take his camera out and"—Dan used air quotes—"shoot the wildlife. He posted something about it on Facebook. Somebody made a meme that went viral. It was a picture of Creighton and his camera. The caption was something like *Nobody had to bleed because of this shot.*"

Quinn smiled. "Clever."

"Not to Dick Darnell. He's the president of the Chestnut Station Hunting and Fishing Club. All those wildlife photographers and people who hate hunting started doing the same thing, snatching up all the licenses. So now, his club has dwindled since Darnell hasn't been able to stem the tide. It used to be that he was able to pull some strings to get every member of his club a license for whatever they wanted to hunt. But now, with Creighton's stunt, he can't and people are leaving the club and they aren't getting new members."

"Humiliated by a wussy, tree-hugging camera jockey, he said to me once," Georgeanne said.

"Doesn't seem like such ugliness to me." Quinn leaned back against the pew.

Dan tilted his head toward hers again. "The ugliness was when Dick Darnell publicly confronted Creighton at one of the summer jazz concerts in the park a couple of years ago. Creighton got two of the hard-to-get licenses in one year, one for moose and one for bear. Dick was furious and he'd had way too much to drink that night. Accused Creighton of rigging the system or bribing someone or something—"

Georgeanne leaned across Dan. "Because bribing people was Dick Darnell's job."

"Everyone heard Darnell threaten Creighton. He said…what did he say, Georgie?"

"He said, and I quote, *If I see you, it won't matter if you're wearing an orange vest or not. Orange vests don't protect from everything.*"

"Good grief. When was this? Does Rico know?" Quinn's eyes widened.

"Probably. He was standing right there near us."

"Could Dick Darnell have killed Creighton?"

"The thought crossed my mind," Dan said.

Georgeanne reluctantly agreed.

A mourner tried to get to a seat in their pew, which turned into a big production of everyone scooting down, and then scooting back the other way because the woman was trying to sit next to her husband on the other side of Georgeanne.

The woman finally sat and she and Georgeanne began talking quietly. Dan reached over and shook the husband's hand.

Quinn made a mental note to ask Rico about Dick Darnell's threat against Creighton.

People continued to trickle into the church, greeting people, exchanging sad glances, murmuring what a tragic occasion this was, but wasn't the church lovely? Georgeanne had decorated the altar with a mix of roses, columbine, purple coneflower, and Rocky Mountain penstemon snipped from her garden as well as from Creighton's.

An inappropriate voice, shrill and louder than the others, caused heads to turn, including Quinn's. Chief Chestnut strode up the main aisle, glad-handing everyone within arm's length. Anyone with an aisle seat received a clap on the back with his bony hands. His thin lips were set in an unflattering grimace he must have mistaken for an appropriately somber smile for this grave occasion.

Chief Chestnut made his way to the first row, where he shook the hand of each person, then made his way down each side aisle, working the event like it was a political fundraiser instead of a funeral.

Quinn looked away. Almost directly in front of her, but several rows ahead, she saw long dreadlocks. She leaned this way and that, trying to determine if it was Dreadlock Guy. He finally turned to Vera from the newspaper sitting to his right and spoke to both her and a very handsome man on the other side of her who Quinn had never seen before.

Quinn leaned across Dan again and tugged Georgeanne's sleeve. "Do you guys know that man sitting next to Vera, the one with the dreadlocks?"

Georgeanne craned her neck to see around the heads in front of her. "I've seen him around the church. Don't think he lives here, though."

"Maybe he works here," Dan said. "Or has a gal he keeps company with."

Quinn barked out a laugh, then slapped a hand over her mouth at the outburst. "Keeps company? Are you channeling Grandpa?" She blushed when she glimpsed Chief Chestnut glaring at her. He'd made his way all around the left square of pews and was coming around the back of the church again. She could hear him whispering condolences behind her to the unfortunates who had to deal with his thin lips and permanent coffee breath jutting between them and their neighbors in the back pew. She wrinkled her nose as she watched him travel the side aisle of their block of pews, still thumping backs and reaching over mourners to shake hands with people.

Suddenly there was a shift in the room as everyone quieted. Two ushers escorted Hugh up the main aisle, each man holding one of his elbows. Quinn flinched at the memory of Chief Chestnut and Donnie escorting him into the police department in the same manner.

Hugh stared straight ahead at the altar, upon which sat an urn. Quinn hadn't noticed it earlier, and realized with sorrow it must hold Creighton's ashes.

Hugh was seated in the first pew on the right side of the church. Out of the corner of her eye, Quinn saw Chief Chestnut make a beeline toward the front. He motioned the person sitting on the aisle in the second pew to shove over. Chief Chestnut took his place, directly behind Hugh.

He leaned forward and spoke into Hugh's ear. Hugh flinched, but continued to stare straight ahead. Then Chief Chestnut glanced at the mourners behind him in the church, first over his left shoulder, then over his right, his face smug and implacable.

It appeared to Quinn that he was making a show of telling the congregation that he had this under control. Even though Hugh had been released from jail, Chief Chestnut seemed to say, "I'm still keeping an eye on Hugh. Don't you worry."

Gross.

Seeing Chief Chestnut there with Hugh and the urn just beyond started Quinn thinking about Creighton's murder instead of his funeral. Her mind looped to all of the suspects Chief Chestnut and Rico weren't investigating.

The Processional began. The melancholy low notes of "Amazing Grace" floated through the air. Two altar servers in long robes tied with rope belts held candles in front of their faces, symbolically lighting the way for the acolyte behind them who held aloft the large cross. The deacon followed, carrying the Gospel resting on its ornate stand. The priest brought up the rear, wearing his floor-length white alb, draped with a purple chasuble embroidered with a gold design that caught the light as he moved.

Quinn knew she had to stop her spiral about the investigation before the funeral began. She whipped out her phone and texted herself a list of all the people and ideas she wanted Chief Chestnut, Rico, and Hugh's attorney to explore: Dick Darnell, Victor and ValJean, Aaron Janikowski, hidden money, the Maynards, hate crime, homophobes, Dreadlock Guy.

Georgeanne reached over and smacked at Quinn and her phone as the priest stepped on to the altar.

Quinn made sure her device was silenced and dropped it into her bag. She followed along with the service, using the printed program the mourners received as they entered the church.

The eulogy was given by a friend and coworker of Creighton's from Buckley Tech Solutions. The program listed his name as Jonathan Wilkes. His words were heartfelt and funny. Gentle, soothing words. Creighton was clearly well-liked by his coworkers, who all seemed to be sitting together, taking up several pews near the front.

Without describing exactly what it was Creighton did, Jonathan mentioned how great he was at his job, always beating the other members of his team out of the big bonuses. "He made it look easy. He got his work done every day, left on time, and spent his lunch hour doing crossword puzzles while eating food packed lovingly by his husband, Hugh. Everyone at Buckley Tech learned a thing or two from Creighton about productivity and meeting goals. Although some of us joked with him, wondering where he hid his staff." His coworkers chuckled.

Jonathan pretended to be baffled, and elicited more chuckles from his coworkers when he added, "His output surprised us, because all his time at work seemed to be taken up by telling us how hard he worked to refurbish an old grandfather clock, even though he could never get it to run right. When Joan"—Jonathan gestured at a woman in the third row—"asked him why he didn't just get rid of it, he said, 'Just because it doesn't run doesn't mean it doesn't serve a purpose. Would you get rid of a car just because of a few knocks and pings or a dog just because it starts to limp? That's when they need you the most.' That's what an old"—Jonathan's voice caught—"Softie he was."

Quinn had an image of Creighton with Gin and had to swipe at her eyes. She saw Georgeanne dig a tissue from her purse and do the same.

Jonathan looked out over the mourners. "None of us can believe this happened to him. We'll miss him every day." He shook his head as he made his way back to his seat.

The priest asked Hugh if he wanted to say anything. He gave a barely perceptible shake of his head in response.

At least he made it to the funeral, Quinn thought.

The funeral finished on a somber note. The procession of priest, deacon, and acolytes reversed their course down the main aisle, the same way they entered. Everyone stayed silent and standing while one of the ushers led Hugh out. The mourners knew instinctively to wait as the ushers allowed everyone to leave down the main aisle, one row at a time, from the front to the back.

The organist played "I Dreamed a Dream," one of the anthems from *Les Misérables*. Quinn opened the program to read the lyrics about dreams shattered and extinguished. The hopelessness of the lyrics, the minor key, the harmonic tension, and the final crescendo triggered her emotions.

Georgeanne offered Quinn a tissue, which she used to blot the tears spilling over. Quinn saw many people holding their own tissues to the corners of their eyes.

By the time Quinn and her parents had shuffled from the church, most everyone had regained control of their emotions and made their way to the reception at the Chestnut Diner. They did the same.

Georgeanne hugged Jake, who was welcoming everyone at the door. She peered into the diner. "Everything looks great, Jake. Thank you again for doing this."

"I didn't see you over there," Quinn said.

"I don't like funerals. But this is how I can honor and pay my respects to Creighton and the people who loved him."

Quinn was swept into the diner by the crowd behind her. She looked to see if anything needed to be tended to, but it seemed Jake had it all under control. There was a full buffet set up along the wall with plates of sandwiches, bowls of chips, salads of all kinds, heaping plates of brownies, lemon bars, and assorted cookies at one end, and several silver chafing dishes of hot food at the other end. Across the room he'd even draped the cash register and front counter with a cloth and set up an open-bar station. Quinn identified Bloody Mary fixings, pitchers of mimosas, tubs of beer on ice, and several bottles of wine.

Quinn lined up the wine bottles, situated all the beer bottles so the labels faced outward, and began skewering garnishes for the Bloody Marys in the correct order. When she was pleased with the bar, she plinked a few fat ice cubes in a tall glass and poured herself a mimosa before stepping away from the crowd. She parked herself in the corner behind the register, but it just took a couple of minutes before she became the de facto bartender. Fine with her, it gave her something to do with her hands.

Jake walked over and pulled a beer from the tub, wiping it with the nearby towel. "You don't have to stand here, you know. It's a buffet. People can serve themselves." He twisted off the cap and it made a satisfying *pfft* sound. "Go make a plate. Sit down. Enjoy yourself." He topped off her mimosa and plopped in two more ice cubes. "Scoot."

Quinn filled a plate with a hodgepodge of food, none of which was healthy. She carried her plate and drink across the crowded room, trying not to spill on anyone or get spilled upon herself. The crowd broke apart a bit and she stood in a small clearing, trying to find a seat. She made a quarter turn and found herself staring at a craggy-looking man with long black hair and a mustache that covered his top lip entirely and drooped down both sides of his mouth. He also sported enormous caterpillar eyebrows, the right one with a two-inch scar splitting it diagonally so no hair grew there. It kind of looked like a "not equal" sign in math. She realized she'd been staring and quickly turned away. She propped herself against the wall, placing her mimosa next to the stacked array of coffee cups at the diner's normal beverage station.

She watched Eyebrow Guy meander through the crowd, stopping in front of the Retireds' table. They chatted a bit, his back to Quinn. He squatted down at the end of the table between Larry and Bob.

Quinn scooped onion dip on to a ruffled potato chip. She thought about stuffing the whole thing in her mouth, but at the last second decided to be polite and bite it. Unfortunately, the chip flipped up and dip smeared her cheek. She hadn't remembered to pick up a napkin, so she bobbled her plate while attempting to wipe it off with the back of her hand. As she did, her plate tipped slightly, causing three green olives to roll over the edge. She overcorrected and both a brownie and a lemon bar slid off the other direction. She balanced her plate on top of the coffee mugs, then retrieved the wayward food. As she stood, she saw all the Retireds and Eyebrow Guy turn to stare at her. She blushed, abandoning her plate and drink. She wasn't hungry anyway.

Vera held a glass of red wine while she chatted with Dan near the buffet.

Quinn walked up to them.

Vera greeted her with a slight raise of her glass. "Nice reception. You and Jake did a good job."

"I didn't do anything. It was all Jake."

"He did it while we were at the funeral," Dan said.

"Now that you mention it, I guess I didn't see him over there."

"Speaking of the funeral," Quinn said. "Who were you sitting with?"

"You noticed him, eh?" Vera widened her eyes. "He was truly the most handsome man I've ever seen up close." She shrugged. "Sorry, Dan."

Dan laughed.

"No, not the gorgeous guy. The guy with the dreadlocks."

"No idea. Never seen him before. Why?"

Quinn couldn't very well talk about what she knew about Dreadlock Guy with her father standing right there. After Emmett Dubois had been killed in the diner, he hadn't been thrilled knowing she'd offered to help Rico with his investigations. She had calmed him down by telling him Rico didn't ask her to do much and, in fact, didn't seem to remember the offer at all most of the time. Dan was content, believing her involvement only included the subliminal crossword puzzles to Chief Chestnut. "Oh, no reason. Just wondered who he was." She glanced around casually. "Is he around here someplace?"

Vera shook her head. "Don't think so. I saw him go the other way when we all started across the street."

"What about your new boyfriend?" Dan teased Vera.

"He's not here either. Believe me, I looked."

"Who was he?" Quinn asked.

"He said he worked for Creighton," Vera said.

"Worked for him? I didn't know Creighton had a supervisory position," Dan said.

"I wonder why he wasn't sitting with Creighton's other coworkers," Quinn said.

Three people joined them and started peppering Vera with questions about newspaper advertising, so Quinn excused herself. She decided the humiliation of her party foul had sufficiently passed and went to retrieve her plate. She passed a table crowded with too many people.

"… at the old Maynard place on Saturday night."

Quinn whirled around. "Were you out there? Were you responsible for those bobbing lights?"

The men and women jammed around the table stopped talking immediately and stared at her. Quinn repeated her question.

Two women sitting across from each other exchanged a quick glance.

An older man with a gray ponytail cleared his throat. "I don't know what you're talking about."

"I heard you mention the old Maynard place just now," Quinn said.

"Old Maynard place? What's that?" He looked around the table. "Anybody know it?"

Everyone murmured, all denying any such knowledge.

"Can't help you, miss." He lifted a bottle of beer to his lips.

Did he just wink at me? Quinn hurried away as the table broke out in laughter. She collected her plate and drink and sought refuge in Jake's office. *What was that all about?* Quinn knew they'd been talking about being at the Maynard place. Why the hush-hush? She'd have to make sure to tell Loma and Rico. Where was Rico, anyway? She hadn't seen him at the funeral or here at the reception. Donnie and Chief Chestnut were there. Maybe Rico drew the short straw and had to stay behind to be the designated crime fighter.

Thinking about Rico reminded her about the notes she texted to herself about the other suspects and clues she thought should be pursued.

She ate more chips and onion dip, not caring if she made a mess in the privacy of Jake's office. She wiped her fingers on the hem of her dress and pulled her iPad from her bag, placing it on the other side of her plate. She munched her food while she scrolled through her text.

She wondered about the earlier crossword puzzle with the subliminal—and overt—clues about patricide. She hadn't seen Chief Chestnut solving the puzzle, nor had Rico told her he was taking a closer look at Victor and ValJean.

It's just as well, she mused. *I have more clues and suspects for him now, anyway.*

Her subterfuge with the puzzles worked on Emmett Dubois's murder and she trusted it would work now too. She just had to be patient.

She finished her food, sipped her mimosa, then fired up her iPad. When it showed her home screen, she opened the crossword program to a blank grid. The iPad had been a welcome gift from her parents after she told them how she'd had to leave the Retireds in charge of the diner that day while she ran home to get her laptop. It was when she'd had the brainstorm of creating puzzles with subliminal clues in them for Chief Chestnut. She'd told her parents she'd only left them in charge for a little bit, but Georgeanne and Dan insisted it should never happen again, for the diner's sake and for Quinn's. She thought their reaction was a bit over-the-top, but then later wondered if they'd wanted to reward her for catching Emmett's killer without making a big deal out of it. She smiled at the memory.

She scrolled back and forth through the text she'd left herself, then doodled some words on the back of an envelope she found in Jake's trash can. She crossed out a lot of words, wrote some back in, drew some arrows between some with matching letter counts. When she'd finished, she had a list for her theme words, the ones she wanted Chief Chestnut to focus on, as well as the letter count for each:

hunting licenses (15)
ValJean (7)
Janikowski (10)
Maynard (7)
dreadlocks (10)

She surveyed her list, happy with the word lengths. She couldn't make a good puzzle without having theme words that were symmetrical in length. HUNTING LICENSES would fill the space in the very center of the puzzle. She typed it in the grid, one letter per square.

JANIKOWSKI she put all the way to the left in the top row.

The other ten-letter word, DREADLOCKS, she typed in the bottom row, all the way to the right.

She typed VALJEAN into the grid in row five on the right, and MAYNARD flush left in row eleven. She couldn't be sure Chief Chestnut had thought enough about the involvement of Creighton's children in his murder, so she wanted to be sure to use ValJean as an entry again in this puzzle.

Normally she clued a puzzle after she'd completely filled in the grid, but these were important, and she wanted to make sure she had good clues for them. She tapped the pen on the envelope.

HUNTING LICENSES was easy. *Legal means to venison.*

So was VALJEAN, the same as the other puzzle. *Protagonist in Hugo's Les Misérables.* She made sure to use the cruciverbalist's trick of using a last name in the clue if the entry was someone's last name.

JANIKOWSKI was easy too, as long as Chief Chestnut was a professional football fan. *Retired Raider kicker.* She was fairly certain he followed the Denver Broncos, like she did with her parents. Quinn was just a casual fan, only watching Bronco games, and even she was aware of Sebastian Janikowski, the great NFL kicker. Even though he played for the Oakland Raiders for most of his career, his record-breaking field goal to beat the Broncos in an important game was still fresh in the minds of many fans, even though it had been many years earlier.

DREADLOCKS was easy too. *Hairstyle typified by ropelike strands.*

But how to clue MAYNARD? Quinn brought up her crossword-creating partner, Google. She typed it in to the search feature. She figured it was probably someone's name, and in a moment, she was certain. Unfortunately, she really didn't think Chief Chestnut would know that Maynard James Keenan was the lead singer and lyricist for the heavy metal rock band Tool.

She scrolled the list of other famous Maynards, reading the description for each one. She stopped when she got to "Maynard G. Krebs" and saw that was the name of a character in the sitcom *The Many Loves of Dobie Gillis* from the early 1960s. It further stated that the character was played by the same guy who played Gilligan in *Gilligan's Island*, a show everyone knew.

Chief Chestnut was about the same age as Quinn's parents. Would they know any of these Maynards? Quinn turned her iPad upside down and left Jake's office, searching for her parents. She saw Georgeanne standing with two of her piano teacher friends.

"Do you guys know who Maynard James Keenan is?"

All three shook their heads.

"How about Maynard G. Krebs?"

"*Dobie Gillis*!" one said.

"I loved that show," another said.

"Your dad and I catch it on those weird channels late at night sometimes," Georgeanne said. "Why?"

"I'm, uh, playing a…trivia game." Quinn should have asked her mother in private. If these other ladies worked the crossword in the *Chronicle*, they might figure out she was the one making them. She started out keeping it a secret from everyone but her parents because she didn't want Rico to blab it all over the school. Now, if she wanted to keep planting subliminal puzzles for Chief Chestnut, she'd better watch what she said and who she said it to.

She glanced around for her dad and saw him with Vera, pouring drinks. Vera, as editor of the newspaper, was the only other person who knew Quinn made the crosswords. "Hey, do you guys know who Maynard G. Krebs is?"

Vera rolled her eyes melodramatically. "Everyone knows who Maynard G. Krebs is."

"Really?"

Dan nodded. "Yes, but don't ask who the prime minister of Finland is because he hasn't been on TV nearly as much."

"She. The prime minister of Finland is a woman," Vera said. "Sanna Marin. She's only, like, thirty-five. Youngest world leader."

"Yeah? Good for her. The world needs more women in power," Dan said.

Quinn made a mental note to use the prime minister of Finland as a clue in a future puzzle. She returned to Jake's office.

"Maynard G. Krebs it is." She filled it in.

Quinn sat in Jake's office and worked on the puzzle, only getting up to get another mimosa and more chips, dip, brownies, and lemon bars. One must have sustenance for this kind of mental endeavor, after all.

She was dismayed she couldn't fix the non-connectivity issue with the "O" in JANIKOWSKI and the second "D" in DREADLOCKS. That was a deal-breaker in the *New York Times* crossword, but not much of a problem in the *Chronicle*. She doubted Vera would get a single complaint, but it made Quinn twitchy that she had to bend the rules to get her theme words to work. If only she had more time.

She finished the puzzle and emailed Vera with a request for it to run in tomorrow's edition instead of the one she'd previously scheduled. Vera wouldn't care; it was easy enough to swap out with all the new digital equipment.

The *Chestnut Station Chronicle* bucked the national trend by becoming a daily, rather than a weekly, when most publications were going the other direction.

Vera had been offered a screaming deal on a digital printing press by a friend of hers who was shutting down his print newspaper altogether and going strictly online. Vera, however, was a newspaper purist and grew up with journalists as parents. She jumped at the chance to move the *Chronicle* to a bigger building and bring the printing process entirely in-house, hiring a few people to oversee the digital process, rather than having to pay a large offset printing outfit to print her newspapers for her.

Vera and her team had built up subscriptions to more than ten times the population of Chestnut Station, because she included news from all over the eastern plains of Colorado, utilizing reporters from many towns to be the eyes and ears of the area.

Vera always said—to anyone who'd listen—that local news was the most important foundation for an informed citizenry. Two framed posters greeted you when you walked into her newsroom. One, a quote from Walter Cronkite: *Journalism is what we need to make democracy work.* The other from Helen Thomas: *We don't go into journalism to be popular. It is our job to seek the truth and put constant pressure on our leaders until we get answers.*

Once, Quinn quipped, "That includes crosswords, right?" and Vera launched into a lecture about both Cronkite and Thomas. Quinn never again joked about the Fourth Estate. The more she learned from Vera, the more she respected both her and the bravery of journalists in small towns like Chestnut Station and around the world.

Quinn liked to think that she helped in a small journalistic way with her contribution of the crossword, but acknowledged the increase in circulation and advertising was more likely because of the last murder in Chestnut Station. Nothing sold newspapers like sensational news, especially in a small town.

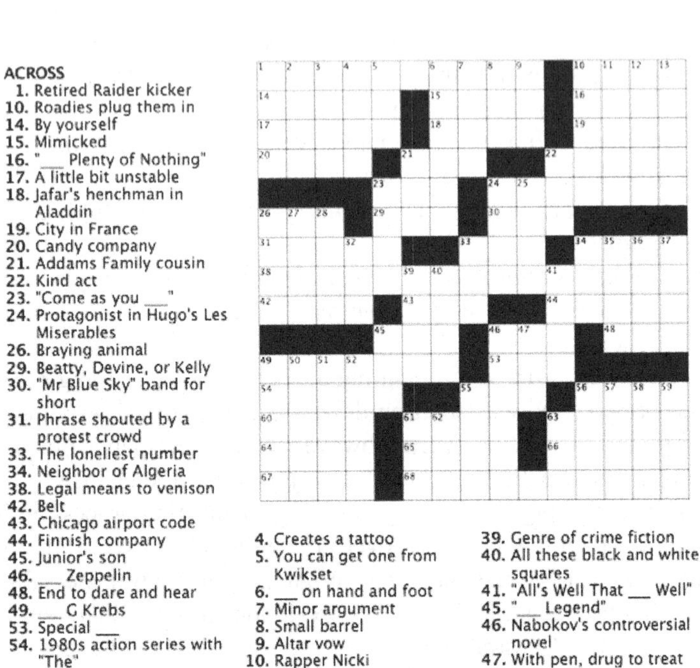

ACROSS

1. Retired Raider kicker
10. Roadies plug them in
14. By yourself
15. Mimicked
16. "___ Plenty of Nothing"
17. A little bit unstable
18. Jafar's henchman in Aladdin
19. City in France
20. Candy company
21. Addams Family cousin
22. Kind act
23. "Come as you ___"
24. Protagonist in Hugo's Les Miserables
26. Braying animal
29. Beatty, Devine, or Kelly
30. "Mr Blue Sky" band for short
31. Phrase shouted by a protest crowd
33. The loneliest number
34. Neighbor of Algeria
38. Legal means to venison
42. Belt
43. Chicago airport code
44. Finnish company
45. Junior's son
46. ___ Zeppelin
48. End to dare and hear
49. ___ G Krebs
53. Special ___
54. 1980s action series with "The"
55. Peyton's brother
56. ___ Linda, CA
60. Chomsky
61. Resident of Bangkok
63. Visit without an invitation
64. In the matter of
65. Hardly the worst
66. Representative
67. The center of concession
68. Hairstyle typified by ropelike strands

DOWN

1. Movie that needed a bigger boat
2. ___ vera
3. "___ of your beeswax!"
4. Creates a tattoo
5. You can get one from Kwikset
6. ___ on hand and foot
7. Minor argument
8. Small barrel
9. Altar vow
10. Rapper Nicki
11. "___ you my word!"
12. Apres ski drink
13. Strict
21. Anger
22. Progressive Insurance spokesperson
23. Against
24. "I came" to Julius Caesar
25. Baldwin or Guinness
26. German interjections
27. Minor biblical figure
28. Without
32. Utmost degree
33. "___ Yeller"
34. Run after JKL
35. Queries
36. Luke's sister
37. "___, old chap!"
39. Genre of crime fiction
40. All these black and white squares
41. "All's Well That ___ Well"
45. "___ Legend"
46. Nabokov's controversial novel
47. With pen, drug to treat severe allergic reactions
49. Frenetically busy
50. When lunch is over, perhaps
51. Many revolutions around the sun
52. Superstars
55. Absence of difficulty
56. Company brand
57. Saudi Arabia, Kuwait, and Venezuela are members
58. Cousin to weasel, otter and ferret
59. Fire and carpenter are common ones
61. Not yet decided
62. Not him
63. Chum

Chapter 16

After she received the confirmation the crossword uploaded properly, Quinn poked her head into the dining room. About half as many people were still enjoying the funeral reception, most of them unfamiliar to her.

The Retireds hadn't moved. Quinn pulled up a chair to their table.

"Hey, who was that creepy-looking guy with the funky eyebrow I saw you guys talking to?"

"Computer guy," Herman said.

"Worked with Creighton," Wilbur said.

"Asking us about VIPs," Bob said.

"VIPs?" Quinn asked.

"No, not VIPs." Silas scratched his chin, thinking. "VCRs?"

Larry shook his head. "No...VHS?" he guessed.

"Was it V-FIB, like on doctor shows?" Bob asked.

"V eight," Wilbur said.

"The juice or the engine?" Quinn asked with a smile.

"He asked us about VPN," Herman said.

The table was quiet for a moment.

"What the tarnation is VPN?" Wilbur growled.

"I think the real question is what in tarnation is V eight juice. That stuff is an abomination," Silas said.

The Retireds all chimed in with their opinion about V8 juice, so Quinn took the opportunity to sneak away before she got drawn into the discussion. *So this is the type of scintillating conversation they spend all day having.*

She searched for her parents, but they weren't around. Probably gone home. Jake was over by the makeshift bar. "Want me to start cleaning up?" she asked him.

He held wine bottles to the light to see if they were empty. "Nah. Let them mourn."

Quinn squinted at the crowd, some of them playing cards, some of them with their shoes off and feet up, all of them drunk. "They don't seem like they're in mourning."

"People mourn in their own way."

"Especially when there's a ton of food and an open bar."

Jake smiled at her. "Best way to mourn."

"I'll be in your office until you need me."

Jake tipped a wine bottle at her.

"Sure. Why not? When in Rome…" She took the plastic cup he poured for her back to the office and settled again into Jake's office chair. Her iPad lying there made her consider starting another crossword, to work ahead, although with the one she just sent, Vera already had two-and-a-half weeks' worth of crosswords and she didn't even place them every day. Depended on how much space she had. If someone wanted to place a last-minute advertisement or there was late-breaking news, the puzzle was the first to get axed to accommodate them.

Quinn sipped her Malbec and scrolled through her texts to see if anything interesting came in while her phone was off. With a start, she saw the hitchhiker's mother's phone number she had pilfered from Rico's phone the other day. She completely forgot about it. Some kind of detective she'd make.

The wine slid warm and welcome down her throat while she considered what to do. There was no way that girl gave Rico her mother's real number, Quinn reasoned. Eliza Yorkie might have charmed Rico and Jake with her good looks and sad story, but Quinn didn't fall for it. It was simply too coincidental that she "found" Creighton's checkbook. Quinn fiddled with her phone. That phone number belonged no more to Eliza's mother than it did to Mother Goose. But who did Rico talk to, then?

Hitchhikers didn't just stumble on important papers tossed into a dumpster at the edge of town. She must have taken them from Creighton's house. If Eliza wasn't involved in the murder itself, she had to know who was.

Could Eliza Yorkie be Creighton's granddaughter? Could Rico have been speaking on the phone to Creighton's daughter, ValJean, who had somehow convinced her daughter Eliza to kill her own grandfather? Someone she'd never even met? Unless, of course, they *had* actually met.

Quinn absentmindedly sipped her wine while she ruminated over all these possibilities. How could she prove or disprove Eliza Yorkie was who she claimed to be? Especially when Rico believed her to be hitchhiking her way across country to go to art school.

She definitely had an artistic bent, Quinn mused, remembering the sketch she'd drawn of the diner. But artistic minds were also imaginative, prone to making things up. Did lies, fabrications, distortions, and other misrepresentations come easier to them? If so, then it was entirely probable she'd made up her mother, "Teresa," who Rico had spoken to.

If it wasn't ValJean herself, maybe Teresa was a friend, some partner in crime. It would be easy to make a pact with someone. *If you get a call from someone asking for somebody named Teresa, you know what to do.*

It was actually pretty smart, though. She and Loma could do the same thing. If either one of them got a call with an agreed-upon fake name, it meant they were in trouble. Whatever the person on the phone asked, play it cool and tell them what they want to hear.

Thinking back to the conversation Rico had with the hitchhiker's mother, even though Quinn only heard one side, she tried to remember the things Rico had asked and how a cohort in crime might answer on behalf of Eliza, if that was even her real name.

Did Rico ask to see her ID? She couldn't remember.

Quinn thought back to the conversation that rainy day but couldn't remember anything Rico had asked Teresa that he hadn't also asked Eliza. Now, looking back, the conversation seemed very generic to Quinn. It confused her, though, that Rico had seemed satisfied, because he was an intuitive and clever cop. But this didn't seem like very good police work.

She picked up her phone and scrolled to Teresa Yorkie's phone number in her contacts. After a couple deep breaths, she dialed it.

When a woman answered, Quinn said, "I'm calling on behalf of Rico Lopez of the Chestnut Station police department." *Not entirely a lie, just mostly.* "I have some follow-up questions about your niece, Elizabeth."

"She's my daughter and her name is Eliza. Is she okay? I thought she was in California?"

Test number one, passed. "She's fine, and yes, in California." *Probably.* Quinn asked all the same questions about hitchhiking and art school as Rico had.

Teresa gave the same answers Eliza had in the diner that day, which didn't prove anything. All of them could have been rehearsed.

But then, Quinn asked the real questions she wanted answered.

"What was Eliza like as a little girl?"

Teresa didn't answer right away. "What does this have to do with—"

She anticipated this response. She'd seen it on cop shows a million times. "Ma'am, we're investigating a murder. We'll decide what questions to ask."

Quinn posed prying questions she could envision Mary-Louise Lovely asking Georgeanne in an attempt to understand their own mother-daughter relationship better. Teresa answered all of them in depth. It became obvious that Teresa missed Eliza deeply.

"Do you have regrets about Eliza going to art school?"

"No." Teresa stretched the word out. "But I do have regrets about everything else. When my husband said we couldn't afford art school for her, I believed him. And when he said she should take that job at the accountant's office and work her way up, I agreed with him about that too. I wanted her to stay close to home, like I did, to keep her safe. Maybe she could marry someone who'd take care of her...like I did. Raise some kids, take up knitting." She paused. "Like I did." After another pause she asked, "Do you have kids, Officer...?"

Quinn didn't supply her name. "No."

"Well, if you do, be prepared for a lifetime of guilt. Everything you failed, everything you did. It's all wrong and it's never enough."

She heard the heaviness in Teresa's voice. This was not some fake partner in crime. This was definitely Eliza's mother.

Quinn had heard the same thing from Georgeanne.

Chapter 17

After Jake finally shooed everyone from the diner and he and Quinn cleaned up the buffet, she went home to collect Gin and walk over to Hugh's house. She'd gathered all the sympathy cards from the funeral and the reception in a large manila envelope. In a bag over her shoulder, she also carried containers of leftover goodies from the reception, in an attempt to bribe Hugh into eating something. If he thought about it, he'd know the food came from Creighton's funeral lunch, but she wouldn't announce it. No discussion necessary.

Quinn knocked, but Hugh didn't come to the door. She hadn't expected him to, but it was awkward to just walk into someone's house when they were there. Gin was having a conniption there on the porch, so Quinn used her key, calling out the entire time. She didn't want to startle Hugh and she certainly didn't want to catch him coming out of the shower or something.

Gin raced in and made the rounds of all the rooms the same way she did every time. Finally making the connection that she was searching for Creighton, Quinn's heart shattered. How could you explain to a dog that her person was never coming back?

Her task incomplete, Gin slowly trotted back to the living room where Hugh sat on the couch.

Quinn held out the envelope. "I brought these cards for you."

Hugh waved a vague hand, which Quinn took to mean, "I'll read them later. Please put them on the table," even though he waved more in the direction of nothingness. Quinn dropped the envelope on the kitchen table.

"Hugh, I wanted to ask you something." Quinn held out the Kwikset key on the fob, which she'd attached to the set of house keys she was using.

"What's this key for? I found it when I was cleaning up, but I can't figure out what it goes to or where I should put it."

It took some effort on his part, but he took it from her hand and focused on it. "Never seen it before." He handed it back, then settled into the couch with his back to the room.

Gin looked at Quinn, then at Hugh. She stood with her front paws on the couch and nudged him with her snout once, twice, three times, each time glancing at Quinn for…something. Help? Encouragement? After the third nudge, Hugh dropped one arm backward. Gin found it and nuzzled his palm.

It was encouraging for Quinn to see that Hugh at least eventually acknowledged Gin's efforts to comfort him, even just a little bit. She always hoped it would be enough to convince her to leave Gin with him, but each time the same worries resurfaced that Hugh still wasn't capable of caring for her yet. She wavered between thinking taking care of Gin would force Hugh back into the world, and being fair to Gin. She settled on the latter. *He'll come around. I hope.*

Quinn was becoming obsessed about what that Kwikset key opened. Why didn't Hugh seem all that curious about it? Because Creighton had lots of keys? Because Creighton had lots of secrets? Because Hugh had too many questions? Because it was really Hugh's key?

Quinn went through the entire house again, despite feeling weird about it while Hugh was curled up there on the couch with Gin. She couldn't shake the feeling it had to be important, though. Maybe important to Hugh's new reality. Like what if Creighton had a secret lockbox filled with Google stock he bought on the cheap? Or jewels handed down from an ancestor. Or the secret recipe to Kentucky Fried Chicken.

Or maybe it was an important clue to Creighton's murder. Maybe the murderer dropped it. Maybe the murderer was searching for it. Maybe… maybe, maybe, maybe.

Quinn sighed. She wanted answers, not maybes.

Again, she found nothing, despite dragging a stool and flashlight around with her so she could search yet again in the tops and dark corners of closets and cabinets.

She slumped into a kitchen chair, debating whether or not to give the key to Rico. If she did, he'd just spend his time doing this exact thing, beating his head against this same intractable wall. She remembered what one of the recruiters for the police academy told her so long ago: Don't bring problems, bring solutions.

She shoved the problem back in her pocket.

She heard soft noises coming from the living room and went to check on Hugh. He had turned over, still lying on the couch, but now he faced the room. His arm dangled over Gin's back, who now sat on the floor, leaning against the couch. Quinn took it as a hopeful sign.

She glanced at the grandfather clock, but the time was obviously wrong. She picked up the TV remote. "Let's see what's on. Maybe it's time for *The Rockford Files*. My dad loves that show." By the time she turned back to him with an episode of *Monk* playing, Hugh was shuffling down the hall to his bedroom. He closed the door softly behind him.

Quinn watched Gin stare after him. "People who say dogs can't grieve should see you right now," she said softly to Gin. Not only had Gin lost Creighton, she was losing Hugh as well.

Quinn muted the TV and sat on the floor, her back against the couch next to Gin. Quinn draped an arm around her. Gin leaned in and returned the hug as best she could. They sat this way for a long time, each wondering, in their own way, how to help Hugh. Quinn stroked Gin's silky fur.

After a while, Gin pushed away and padded out to the kitchen for a drink of water. Quinn stared straight ahead, eyes unfocused on the grandfather clock. The melancholy words from the eulogy returned to her and she pressed a knuckle to her mouth, picturing Creighton excitedly talking to his coworkers about building this clock.

She cocked her head as she examined it from the couch. Why was he so obsessed with it? It wasn't all that attractive, not particularly stunning or ornate in any way. Certainly not a showy piece of furniture that showed off his skilled craftsmanship. And he couldn't even get it to keep time. The rest of their house was practical and had beautiful, personalized touches. The bookcases filled with volumes they clearly loved. The framed wildlife photos hanging on the walls. Those were showy. So, why this boring clock that didn't even work? She stood and moved over to it, running a hand down the side.

The clock stood over six feet tall, made with two compartments. The top compartment took up about one-third of the entire piece of furniture, and the larger compartment below, the remaining two-thirds. Both had thin, decorative keys stuck in the keyholes. They reminded Quinn of the keys that turned her music box and that locked her diary, both tinny, practically useless things. The first time she tried to figure out the Kwikset key, she'd even taken them out to see if it would fit in the lock, as if the others were simply decoys. It didn't come close to fitting.

The top compartment had a glass window to allow the face of the clock to be seen. The key opened the window to allow someone to adjust the hands and set the time. When was the last time Creighton performed that task? Had he ever? Why didn't the clock work? More importantly, why keep a huge clock that didn't work?

The bottom compartment was solid wood, but cheap, like fiberboard. It hid the workings of the clock, the balance weights, and the pendulum.

Quinn opened both compartments and reinspected them for the fourth, maybe fifth time. Still nothing. She closed them both and took a step back, hands on her hips. She'd been so sure there was a Secret of the Old Clock.

She glanced again at the bottom compartment from the outside. She dropped to one knee and opened it again. Closed it. Studied it. Opened it. Studied it. Maybe she was imagining things, wishing there was a secret.

When she opened the compartment, the workings of the clock didn't go the entire length of the outside of the compartment. She'd never made—or ever actually seen—a grandfather clock before, but it didn't make sense to her. It almost seemed as if the clock itself could be six or eight inches shorter.

Her eyes widened and she scrambled to the kitchen where she'd left the flashlight. She held it in her left hand while she felt blindly into the bottom of the clock with her right. It was awkward, though, so she dropped to her belly, shoved the flashlight into her mouth, and pushed her way so she was almost inside the bottom of the clock. She methodically inspected and probed every inch of the bottom of the clock. She began to feel foolish. It was just a crappy grandfather clock kit that Creighton built in a crappy manner.

Then her hand brushed something.

Chapter 18

Cool metal low on the far wall of the clock met her hand. She dropped her head down as far as her neck allowed. A glint caught in the flashlight's glare. Smooth. Solid. She touched every inch of it.

A lock.

Quinn dropped the flashlight and struggled to her feet. She banged her head on the cabinet, hard, and stopped to rub it. Fished the Kwikset from her pocket. Dropped to the floor and into position again inside the clock. Flashlight in her mouth. Ear pressed flat to the wooden bottom.

She reached an arm in and maneuvered the key into the lock, one smooth movement in and to the right. A *click* and the wooden bottom jumped against the side of her head.

She slithered out, repositioned herself on her knees and reached into the darkness, lifting the square of wood out of the clock. Set it aside on the carpet. Feeling in the dark with both hands, she finally wrapped her fingers around what was hidden in the false bottom of the grandfather clock.

A laptop.

Quinn stared at it with a goofy smile fixed on her face. A laptop! Creighton's hidden laptop. The one whoever murdered him must have been looking for.

She frowned, glancing down the hall toward Hugh's bedroom. Or was it Hugh's computer? Did he lie about never having seen that key?

She sat back on her heels, both hands on the laptop. She knew she should call Rico. She glanced down the hallway again. But what if it incriminated Hugh? Maybe he just used it for porn or something. She stared at it, willing it to spill the beans about what secrets it held, as if by osmosis she could suddenly know.

She knew she'd have to rummage through the computer files. Just as she screwed up the courage to peek, she heard Hugh's door open. She hurried to slide the laptop under the couch and sat on the floor in front of it.

"Maybe I will watch some TV," he said quietly.

It was still on the throwback channel from earlier. Quinn turned it up and they watched an episode of *Friends*. At the commercial she said, "I'll make us some tea."

In the kitchen, Quinn also buttered a piece of toast for him, carrying it all out on a tray, which she set on the coffee table. She almost cheered when she saw Hugh had remained sitting up while she'd made the tea and toast. Returning the tray to the kitchen, she scooped up her bag to have near her in the living room, where she settled on the floor once again, her back against the couch in front of the hidden laptop.

They sipped their tea and Hugh nibbled his toast while they watched Phoebe sing "Smelly Cat." She heard Hugh chuckle. Quinn hoped that now with Creighton's funeral behind him, maybe he could turn a corner. That part of his nightmare was over and now he could concentrate on getting stronger to defend himself. He remained, after all, Chief Chestnut's primary—and only—suspect.

Quinn paid no attention to the show. Her thoughts were under the couch with the laptop.

Hugh returned his empty plate to the table in front of him. He smiled his thanks.

If he did indeed turn a corner, Quinn thought, *what will happen when he learns I found this computer? Would he plunge back into his depression? Maybe even deeper?*

She chewed her thumbnail, lost in thought. It had to be Creighton's laptop. If it was Hugh's, when Quinn asked about the key, he would have looked nervous or said it was to an old desk or something bogus.

Yes. It had to be Creighton's.

"That's enough TV for me tonight." Hugh heaved himself from the couch and Gin dropped lightly to the floor.

Quinn jumped at the sound of his voice. "I'm glad you enjoyed it, Hugh. Shall I leave—" She almost asked if she should leave Gin with him tonight, but didn't want to put too much pressure on his fragile recovery. "Shall I leave some more toast for you?"

Hugh shook his head and shuffled to his bedroom. When he got to the hallway he turned. "Thanks for everything you're doing, Quinn. Your mom too." He waved a hand.

Gin trotted down the hall after him, but returned a few moments later, as if she knew she wasn't staying and simply went to tuck him in.

Quinn cleared the tea things from the table and straightened the kitchen. She loaded up the coffee maker and left a note for Hugh. *Just push the button and coffee will appear like magic. Eat more toast. See you tomorrow. Q*

Before she left, she slid the laptop into her bag, along with the Kwikset key. She made a decision. She'd take the computer home. If it only held porn or something innocuous, she'd bring it back tomorrow and return it to its hiding place. If it held something more serious, she'd give it to Rico.

* * * *

After giving her parents the lowdown on Hugh's forward—but perhaps still tenuous—progress, but not Creighton's hidden laptop, Quinn leaned against her headboard and screwed up the courage to open it. Gin hopped on the bed and curled up at her feet.

"Here goes nothing."

Gin glanced at her, realized she was not being offered a treat, and settled into sleep.

Quinn stared at the screen. Password protected. Of course it was.

She was afraid to randomly guess, in case it locked her out permanently. She took a chance and pushed the space bar, in case it was just a blank password like her parents used on too many sites. Nope. Definitely needed a password.

Quinn considered everything she knew about Creighton. Award-winning wildlife photographer. Software developer. Liked puns. Fan of *Les Misérables*. She thought about those addressed, but unsent birthday cards to his kids, one every year for them both. After a long debate with herself, she tried their names as passwords. She decided it made sense to go in age order. Wasn't that how parents would think of their kids? She also went with conventional capitalization, mainly because she thought Creighton, a fellow lover of word games, would be simpatico with her about that. She hoped so, anyway.

VictorValJean.

Nope.

She rubbed her hands, ice-cold even though the heat of the August day lingered long after the sun had set.

ValJeanVictor.

Nope.

She pressed the heels of her palms to her forehead and sat that way for a long time.

One last try. She typed *Be Happy*, hen added the less-than sign and the number 3. The old-fashioned way to make a heart emoji.

She held her breath. Crossed her fingers. Looked skyward. Pressed *enter*.

Chapter 19

Momentarily thrilled she'd guessed Creighton's password, Quinn felt overwhelmingly icky poking around in someone else's computer. She found herself squinting, as if that could keep her from accidentally seeing something terrible. Nothing terrible jumped out at her, and in fact she didn't see much of anything. Lots of dull business correspondence she didn't understand, much of it between Creighton and someone named JM, but nothing terrible or even incriminating. She read through the emails twice, trying to see if they were written in some kind of code. And maybe they were, if "tedious geek" was the code. Everything seemed fairly innocuous. Other than being under lock and key in a hidden compartment of a grandfather clock, this could be anyone's boring old computer.

Despite the relief she felt, she also felt some pangs of frustration. "All this for a handful of work files?" she muttered. She clicked around more confidently and more haphazardly. *All the searching and angst over that stupid key and this is what I find?* "It's no different from Dad's laptop." She clicked into one more desktop folder. "There's nothing on here to take to Rico."

Gin looked up at her with sleepy eyes as if to say, "If you're not talking to me, I'd appreciate it if you'd pipe down."

Quinn closed the lid and set it aside before snuggling down into her covers. It would go back into its hiding place tomorrow.

Her eyes closed, but her thoughts were still on the laptop. She felt horrible for snooping, but relieved she hadn't found anything incriminating. Why was Creighton hiding it, though? Maybe it *was* for porn, but he hadn't loaded any yet. Why were there any files at all on it? Maybe it was an old work computer of Creighton's and he just hadn't wiped the hard drive yet. Maybe he was going to upgrade it as a gift for Hugh and the grandfather clock was his hiding place. Maybe Hugh was a notorious snooper. Georgeanne and Dan had hiding places for Christmas and birthday gifts too, because they thought Quinn had been a bit of a snooper. In reality, though, she stumbled on everything when she was cleaning and organizing. Her parents did not believe it to be accidental.

Quinn fell asleep, annoyed this had all been for nothing.

Chapter 20

The next day at the diner Quinn got a call from Loma.

"Will you help me pick out carpet, drape, and upholstery samples tomorrow night?"

"Thursday? Sure."

Loma let out so much breath, the phone filled with static, causing Quinn to hold it away from her ear.

"Why do you need a lowly waitress to help? You're the design professional."

"I'm the design professional who is drowning in excellent taste. Everything I pick out I fall in love with. You gotta help me break up with some of these."

"Ooh, so much power. I'm at Hugh's every evening until nine or so, making sure he eats at least once a day. And I don't want to go back out to the Maynard place—I still have the creeps—so you'll have to bring everything to my house."

"A-OK. Bringing all my boyfriend swatches so you can explain it's them and not me."

Quinn made the rounds of the diner, refilling drinks and cleaning up after lunch. She poured more water for Chief Chestnut, who was working her newest crossword. She stared at his answers instead of watching her pitcher and water sloshed out, earning her a sour look from him.

She blotted the spill with a napkin and scurried away to busy herself with any mundane chore she could find, as long as it was far away from him.

Jake walked across the diner to the cash register.

Chief Chestnut barked out a staccato laugh. "Maynard G. Krebs! I haven't thought about *Dobie Gillis* in ages!"

"Who?" Jake asked.

Quinn lowered her head so nobody would see her smile. She couldn't imagine the day she would be blasé about someone doing her puzzles, especially when those puzzles fed clues to Chief Chestnut.

"Maynard G. Krebs...Dobie Gillis." Chief Chestnut peered over his glasses in disbelief. "From the old TV show?"

"Never heard of him."

"Too bad you don't have as much smarts as whoever creates this puzzle." Chief Chestnut frowned, tapping his pen on the newspaper.

Jake veered off course to take a look at the puzzle. "You having a problem with it? Puzzle creator smarter than you?" Jake laughed.

"Just trying to figure out the theme of this puzzle."

Quinn felt her heart clutch. The only theme of this puzzle was Get Chief Chestnut to Investigate Creighton's Murder.

Chief Chestnut pointed at one of the entries. "Isn't the produce manager at the grocery store named Janikowski?"

Jake nodded. "Yeah. Like the football player. I don't think they're related, though." He went back to the register and started running the credit card deposit.

Chief Chestnut picked up his phone. "Hey, Donnie. Rico around? ... Oh, well, guess you'll do. What was Creighton McLellan's daughter's name? ...That's what I thought...Yeah, but with a capital J. ...Nothing. Just thinking...When I'm good and ready, that's when."

Quinn couldn't help herself and sauntered over to exchange the condiments on Chief Chestnut's table. "Ya know, sometimes crosswords have no specific theme."

"Only crappy crosswords by crappy creators have no theme."

Ouch.

Chief Chestnut collected up his things and left.

It irritated Quinn that she allowed Chief Chestnut to hurt her feelings. Especially when he had just praised both her and her crossword. Inadvertently, of course. She didn't have long to pout because there was a commotion at table six, men she recognized from Creighton's funeral reception.

Three men were laughing uproariously at a fourth who said good-naturedly, "I said I'd pay, didn't I?" He stood and dug his wallet out of his back packet. "But not for you two losers." He handed Quinn some cash. "This is for our lunch." He pointed at himself and one of the other men.

"Tell her why, Dewey."

"I lost a bet."

Quinn took the money. "What was the bet?"

"Who could catch the most night crawlers in an hour."

Quinn suddenly realized who the men were. “You were out at the old Maynard place last Saturday night.”

“Along with a bunch from the Chestnut Station Hunting and Fishing Club,” Dewey said.

“After that rain it was perfect conditions,” one of the others said.

“Perfect conditions for what?”

“Hunting night crawlers, of course.”

“Why didn’t you just tell me that at the reception instead of teasing me?” Quinn wanted to take the high road and let them have their fun, but she was irked.

Dewey shrugged. “Not supposed to be on private property.”

“Then why were you—You know what? Never mind.” She was relieved to know the truth and didn’t really want to dig too deeply into the innermost secrets of worm hunters. “So how many did you get?” she asked the winner while she rung up the ticket.

“Thirty-four,” he boasted. “Tell her how many you got, Dewey.”

Dewey sighed heavily but Quinn saw the smile in his eyes. “Twenty-seven.”

None of those numbers sounded particularly impressive to Quinn, but she was, admittedly, not a worm expert.

“Well, congratulations to you both.”

Over the course of the afternoon Quinn wondered how many night crawlers she could collect in an hour. What if you pulled one out of the ground and it broke in half? Did that count as two? How much rain was the optimal amount of rain to get worms to the surface for capture? Did people catch worms for anything other than fishing? Questions raced through her mind as she prepped for the dinner rush. If thirty-four was the winning number in Chestnut Station, what was it elsewhere? Were there state and regional competitions? Nationals? International competitors? What country boasted the highest number of native night crawlers?

When she took a break she started searching online for her obsessive questions. Unfortunately, she couldn’t find statistics on capturing worms, but found the world record for eating worms, much higher at sixty-two in thirty seconds.

* * * *

After the diner closed, Quinn went home to collect Gin to take her to Hugh’s, hopeful she’d find him sitting on the couch, watching TV with an empty plate of food in front of him.

She hadn't even realized she was chanting her "clue step" cadence as she walked—*Liz-zie, Bor-den, Vic-tor, Val-Jean, Les Mis, cross-word, love notes, May-nard, mon-ey, key fob, ba na nas*—until a woman she passed said, "Excuse me?"

She reddened, mumbled, "Nothing" and hurried onward. *Don't chant, don't chant, don't chant*, she chanted silently.

As she neared Hugh's, she skidded to a stop, sneakers kicking up gravel.

Dreadlock Guy's mystery car with the bumper sticker was parked around the corner.

She fumbled for her phone and texted Rico.

Quinn tightened Gin's leash and held her close. She stared at the car. No movement inside. They tiptoed toward the car but Quinn didn't see anyone.

If there was nobody in the car, where could he— "Oh no!" She dropped Gin's leash and dashed toward Hugh's house, Gin overtaking her. When she got to the front porch she saw the door was open. She burst in, letting the dog in first. "Get him, Gin!"

Gin streaked through the living room and into the kitchen.

By the time Quinn got there she saw Gin attacking a man, but not with her teeth, with her tongue. Gin's tail wagged so hard Dreadlock Guy had to hold her in place with his hands on either side of her.

Quinn processed the scene slowly. Hugh smiling, actually smiling, for the first time since that morning in the diner, which seemed so long ago, when he officially became a member of the Retireds. Gin in danger of breaking her tail, it smacked so hard against Dreadlock Guy's leg. And Dreadlock Guy, sitting there at Hugh's kitchen table, not even close to killing Hugh.

They both had plates in front of them, along with a big pot of macaroni and cheese on a hot pad in the center of the table. A long-handled spoon jutted from it. Dreadlock Guy's plate was scraped clean, but Hugh's was pushed away, even though three-quarters of his serving remained.

"You're alive."

Hugh smiled at her. "I do seem to be among the living again."

Quinn meant that Dreadlock Guy hadn't killed him, but she decided against clarifying.

"Quinn Carr, meet Malcolm Johnson, a good friend of Creighton's. Malcolm, this is Quinn. She's been taking care of me and Virginia Woof since…for a while."

Malcolm extricated himself from Gin's quivery love, standing and offering his hand. "Good to meet you, Quinn."

She took it, squeezing harder than was necessary, as a show of courage and strength. She didn't trust him. "How did you know Creighton? Why did you park around the corner?"

Hugh and Malcolm exchanged glances. Finally, Malcolm returned to his seat and placed one hand on Gin's head. She began to calm, her tornado tail down to EF3 level.

"I'm an alcoholic. We met at AA. Creighton was my sponsor."

Quinn stared hard into his eyes. He returned her gaze, unperturbed. To Hugh she said, "Why didn't you tell your neighbor? Barbara was ready to call out the National Guard."

"Um…anonymous. Remember? It's right there in the name," Hugh said.

She narrowed her eyes at Malcolm. "Why weren't you at Creighton's reception if you were so close?" Before he could answer, Quinn's face turned burgundy. "Oh, open bar."

Malcolm smiled. "Lead me not into temptation."

"I'm an idiot," she said. "And now I have to make a call."

She stepped through the kitchen into the backyard and called Rico. When he picked up, she said, "False alarm. Never mind. But why aren't you here yet?"

"Because the text I got from you said 'Dreadlocks. Hugh.' While I was curious about Hugh's new hairstyle, I didn't really have the time to race over there to see it. Chief is running me ragged, making me follow up on a bunch of stuff."

"Like what?" she asked innocently.

"All of a sudden he wants me to go out to the Maynard property, talk to Janikowski at the grocery store, talk to Creighton's kids—"

"Which I asked you to do days ago! You never talked to them?"

"Of course I did. They didn't kill Creighton."

"How do you know?"

"Solid alibis, both of them."

While that was good news to Quinn, and good that Chief Chestnut was acting on her crossword clues, it worried her that Janikowski was still a suspect. Was this a hate crime? She wanted to ask Rico more about the produce manager, but before she could he said, "Gotta go." Finding out about those bananas would have to wait.

Quinn returned to the kitchen where Hugh got her a plate and plopped some mac and cheese on it. "It's good. Malcolm brought it."

"I'll eat this if you finish yours." Quinn pushed Hugh's plate back in front of him. She'd already eaten, but if she could nudge Hugh to eat more, she'd step in front of that cheesy bullet.

Hugh picked up his fork and waved it toward Malcolm. "I told you she was taking care of me."

Malcolm rested a hand lightly on Quinn's forearm. "Thank you. I'm glad he had you to help."

Hugh said to Malcolm, "And I'm glad Creighton had you. He always spoke very highly of you."

They ate and the two of them reminisced about Creighton. Happy that Hugh seemed better, Quinn's feelings were nonetheless bruised that he got out of bed to see Malcolm, but not her. Maybe she should have brought him mac and cheese. When she finished eating, Quinn cleared the table, washed the dishes, and placed the leftovers in a Tupperware.

By then it was clear that Hugh was tired. Malcolm put on a dark red leather motorcycle jacket much too hot for August. "Can I drop you anywhere?" he asked Quinn.

"No, thanks, Gin and I like the walk." For a split-second she wondered if she should leave Gin with Hugh, but all of her food and toys were at the other house. Maybe tomorrow. After Malcolm left, Quinn said her goodbyes.

When they were almost home, Gin stopped suddenly, then moved forward in slow motion. Puzzled, Quinn watched as Gin's hackles rose all along her back. Quinn peered into the darkness ahead of them. Someone sat on Mrs. Olansky's front garden wall. Quinn saw movement and caught a glimpse of red. Malcolm? She couldn't tell.

She let out more leash for Gin in the hope that whoever it was might be scared of this clearly formidable fox.

Quinn peered to her right to see if Mrs. Olansky was home. Lights were on, so probably. She glanced beyond the figure sitting on the wall to see who might be home at her house. Lights were on there too. And across the street at both the Fanuccis and Velasquezes. If she screamed, people would come running.

Gin had reached the end of her leash and stopped her slo-mo walk. Her hackles were still raised. Quinn jerked the leash to the left to direct Gin across the street. Once there, they could either run up to the Fanuccis' front door, or use the shadows past the streetlight to cross again back to her house.

"Are you Quinn?" A man's voice.

He jumped from the wall, landing right in front of Gin. He reached a hand down but Gin didn't greet him. Her hackles were still raised.

"She must smell my cat."

Without responding, Quinn pulled the leash backward. Gin didn't budge or make a sound.

The man stepped closer and Quinn saw it was not the red of Malcolm's jacket she had seen, but a red polo shirt worn by the creepy-looking guy with the funky eyebrow scar from the funeral.

Quinn stepped backward, trying to remember all the defensive and offensive moves she and Rico practiced that summer before the police academy. "Who are you?" she said loudly.

"I hear you've been helping Hugh Pugh. Have you found a computer?"

Creighton's laptop? Was this the murderer who ransacked the house? "No. Why?" Quinn continued to sidle into the street, pulling Gin with her.

Very slowly, nervously watching Gin, whose hackles signified she remained on high alert, the man held out what looked like a business card to Quinn. She didn't take it.

"I'm working for Creighton McLellan's employer and they've asked me to see if I can locate any company equipment he might have had at home." When it became clear Quinn wasn't going to come near enough to take the card from him, he dropped it on the wall next to him.

"Why don't you ask Hugh?"

"I'm asking you."

"I haven't found anything like that." There was no way she was turning over Creighton's computer to this guy. She raised her voice a notch louder. "Maybe talk to my friend Chief Chestnut"—she punched the words—"who processed the crime scene."

"Maybe I'll do that." The man stared at her for a bit. "You're sure you haven't found a computer?"

"I think I'd know if I did." Quinn was certain if the man aimed to hurt her he would have done so already, but regretted her choice of words. Perhaps "No, sir" would have been a better choice. Too late now.

"Well, if you do, I'd appreciate a call." He indicated the business card he left on the wall and sauntered away, giving both her and Gin a wide berth.

Quinn watched until he traveled two houses down and crossed to the opposite side of the street before getting into a car and driving away.

She snatched up the business card and raced home, bursting into the kitchen and startling Georgeanne, who was putting the finishing touches on closing down the kitchen for the night.

"Holy moly, Quinn! Can't you ever just walk into this kitchen?"

"Sorry, Mom." She considered telling her what happened but didn't want to scare her. "Had to pee." She dropped Gin's leash and rushed into the powder room.

Through the door, she heard Georgeanne cooing over Gin and giving her a treat. Quinn sat on the lid of the toilet and studied the business card. It was plain white paper with black type. Hardly any information on it. Just *Pignus* centered at the top, *H. Smith* and a phone number centered at the bottom.

She pulled out her phone and searched *Pignus*, which must be the guy's company name. Terrible company name, to be sure. A cybersecurity website popped right up. Quinn followed the links to the "About" page, where it explained that *Pignus* was Latin for "security" and what better way to keep a language from going dead than to use it in the tech sector. The company might be legitimate, Quinn sniffed, but she doubted "H. Smith" was an actual name. She searched for an employee directory, but there was nothing like that on the website.

She took the business card and her phone to her room, scooping up the bag she'd dropped near the door on her way. She heard the quiet, soothing voices of her mom and dad talking in their bedroom. Gin was curled up in her doggie bed on the living room floor.

Leaning against the headboard and pulling Creighton's computer to her lap, she tentatively opened it again. She slammed it shut and jumped from the bed, making the rounds of the house to verify everything was locked up tight. When she was satisfied, she snuggled back into bed with the laptop.

She took a deep breath and opened it, typing in the password. Instead of opening to the desktop, a tab filled the screen, something she must not have closed when she was in before. Because of the visit by "H. Smith" and the fact she wasn't petrified of finding old man porn anywhere, she searched the computer more methodically. She let her OCD monster guide her this time, clicking on each document in each file and actually reading them, instead of just skimming. She didn't understand any of it, except maybe some of the invoices and emails between Creighton and this JM.

Regardless of how carefully and methodically she searched, she found no connection to anything obviously dangerous or illegal or incriminating.

But why did H. Smith want that computer so badly? And how far would he go to get it from her?

Chapter 21

First thing in the morning, before she was due to help Jake open the diner, she took the computer to Rico. She explained how she came into possession of it.

"Why didn't you bring this to me immediately?" His nostrils flared and Quinn could see every cord in his neck.

"Because I thought it was only going to have porn on it and I didn't want to embarrass anyone." When she heard the words out loud she realized how stupid she'd been. She handed him the business card. "I suppose I should give you this too."

"Pignus? What's that?"

"Latin for 'security,' according to Google."

"Why do I care?" Rico's face and neck began to show signs of returning to normal, but that might have been wishful thinking on Quinn's part.

"Because there's something important on this computer. I don't know what it is, but this H. Smith somehow knew I had it and I don't trust him."

"You met him?"

She explained about him leaning on Mrs. Olansky's wall last night and that she recognized him from the funeral when he was talking to the Retireds.

At that, Rico's face blanched. It worried Quinn much more to see him scared rather than angry. He set the computer on his desk and opened it. They both bent over it. Quinn told him the password, then pointed at the files she'd seen.

"There's nothing there, though. I looked through it all."

He poked around, clicking and reading silently. Finally he shooed her away. "Let me look into this. I'll call you later." Halfway across the lobby, he called to her, "Quinn…be careful."

* * * *

All morning at the diner Quinn's OCD spun her up. She could barely function, catastrophizing and spiraling. Every time the door chimed she expected H. Smith to lurch through it and gun her down, or whisk her away to some secret lair, or clear the diner so he could torture her until she gave him what he wanted.

A million thoughts all slammed into the same wall in her brain: *I've ruined the chance to catch Creighton's killer and Rico will never take his rightful place as chief of police.* She kicked herself repeatedly for getting so obsessed with the Kwikset key finally opening a lock that she forgot to think. *I should have taken it straight to Rico. I ruined all the evidence. I know better. I'm so stupid.*

Quinn barely went through the motions of work, and didn't even notice Rico had come in for lunch until he swatted her arm with the laminated menu. "Is this a self-serve place now? Customers get their own menus?"

"Rico! What did you find out?" She led him to a table away from everyone and sat down next to him.

"First, that cybersecurity guy, H. Smith, is on the level. I've been talking to him and the CEO at Creighton's company. They don't exactly know what's going on, but have been seeing some unauthorized access into the company's servers from a VPN, a virtual private network."

"VPN! Not VCR or V eight juice!" Quinn slapped her forehead, then erupted in crazed, hysterical giggles when she realized two things simultaneously: She probably wasn't going to get murdered by H. Smith, and she'd suddenly become a parody of the commercial for V8 juice by slapping her forehead. *Yeah, I could've had a V8, but I also could've been killed.*

Her outburst alarmed Rico and he stared at her with wide eyes.

She wiped her eyes. "He must have asked the Retireds about that VP-whatever, maybe to find out if Hugh had mentioned it. They didn't know what it was either, and couldn't really remember, so they were trying all kinds of things like VCR and...V eight...and well, I guess you had to be there." She saw the look on Rico's face. *Tighten it up, Quinn.* "So what is this virtual ...?" she asked, more in control of herself.

"A virtual private network, or VPN, essentially hides the location of your computer."

"You mean like in the false bottom of a grandfather clock?"

"No. Like you can be on your computer in Chestnut Station, but make it look like you're on it in Moscow, or Paris...or Denver. It seems like

Creighton had a VPN that used his company's server. And someone else was on there too."

"Is that how the security guy found me? Something I clicked on?"

"I think so. It's all very confusing to me. They're not sure if Creighton was hacked or being blackmailed or was willingly allowing somebody inside. They came and cloned Creighton's computer. They're still looking through everything, but haven't found any corporate damage done."

"That's good, I guess." She picked a nonexistent piece of string from her shirt. "Does that mean you're not mad at me anymore?"

"I'm never mad at you." Rico's nose twitched like a bunny smelling ammonia.

"Liar."

"But I do have a plan I need your help with."

"Anything to redeem myself."

Rico called out to Jake, who stuck his head out the pass-through between the kitchen and dining room. "Yeah?"

"Can Quinn have some time off tomorrow to help me with something?"

"Official police business?" he joked.

"Yes."

"Really?" Quinn asked.

"Really?" Jake asked. "Cool."

"Thanks," Rico said to Jake, then to Quinn, "I'll give you the details later."

"Cool."

Rico looked from her to Jake. "You guys spend too much time together."

* * * *

Late in the afternoon Quinn answered the phone in Jake's office since he was at the bank. A female voice asked for Jake.

"He's not here. Can I take a message?"

"Um...yeah...this is Eliza Yorkie and I—"

"Eliza Yorkie the hitchhiker?"

"Yes." She stretched the word out, unsure of the implications of the answer.

"Where are you?"

"California. I just wanted to tell Jake I got here okay and I'm all set up at school. Tell him I'll start sending him reimbursement for the bus fare starting next month. My mom changed her mind about me being here and decided to pay for school after all. It should all be straightened out by then." Eliza paused, her voice getting soft. "Thank you for talking to my mom. Whatever you said did the trick."

"I don't know what you're talking about," Quinn lied.

"She said some woman from Rico's office called. But I happen to know there are no women who work at the Chestnut Station police department." Her voice got even softer. "And he told me how much you help him."

"He did?" Quinn didn't have the heart to tell her why she had really called her mom. They chatted about California and the school.

Eliza was quiet for a moment. "Quinn, do you believe in fate?"

"I dunno. Why?"

"Something mysterious brought me to Chestnut Station and your diner. And I'm glad."

"I accused you of murder."

"Yeah, but then you called Rico, who believed me, and I got safely to California. For absolutely no reason other than fate."

Quinn chewed on that for a couple of seconds. "Maybe. I guess."

"Anyway, I just wanted to call and say thanks to Jake and tell him that I didn't forget about the bus ticket or the extra money."

After a bit, Quinn said, "You know what Jake would like better than you paying him back? Commissioned art for this place. Can you do that instead?"

"Yes! Absolutely."

Quinn asked for her email address. After they hung up, Quinn stood in the center of the diner and shot pictures from all four directions. She emailed them to Eliza. *Do whatever would look good on these walls.*

When Jake returned from the bank Quinn told him about the phone call.

"Now are you convinced that she didn't have anything to do with Creighton's death?" he asked.

"I suppose. But she *was* conveniently hitchhiking through Colorado, conveniently found Creighton's checkbook, then conveniently convinced both you and Rico to let her go on her merry way. It was definitely convenient she was pretty."

"Sometimes stuff just happens. You of all people should know that."

* * * *

Later that evening, walking with Gin to Hugh's, reusable grocery bag slung over her shoulder, Quinn was more than halfway to Hugh's when she stopped, mid-step on the sidewalk. "Dang it. I forgot to bring your stuff. Mom distracted me with all this food for Hugh." She debated walking back home to get it and then drive it all over, but decided to keep going. She'd deliver Gin, then go home and get everything. That was a lot of walking for Gin's short legs, even after the reassurance she'd finally received from Gin's veterinarian.

Quinn's phone rang. Rico. She and Gin continued on to Hugh's while Rico talked.

"Okay, about tomorrow..."

Quinn listened for a while, then said, "Well, if Creighton's employer and the H. Smith cybersecurity guy are involved, then you don't need me for anything."

"You're the most important part. They just hired a new female executive at Buckley Tech Solutions. Since this 'JM' is presumably getting information about Buckley, then he's heard they're doing some restructuring and she's in charge of it. So it won't be weird for him to get an email from her. I know you'll keep your cool long enough for me to arrest him when he shows up to the meeting. She's kind of a hot mess with all this. Very nervous lady. I think she'd give it away. But I can trust you."

"And you want to do it at the Crazy Mule?"

"Yeah. You've spent enough time over there recently so I think you're pretty comfortable there. Besides, I want him to be in public and away from the company."

"Him? You know it's a him?"

"Eighty-five percent sure."

Quinn was quiet for a moment. "I thought the whole point of that VPN was to hide where you really are. If this JM guy was in Colorado, and Creighton was in Colorado, and the company was in Colorado, why hide anything?"

"That's what we're trying to figure out."

"How do you even know this JM is here if he's masking his location?"

"We've been sending him some strategic emails."

"Strategic? And you think he won't be *strategic* in return? I thought all hackers were in Russia, anyway."

"You're right. He may be lying. But he says he'll be at the Crazy Mule. We'll just have to go and find out. And we need your help."

"You're sure."

"I am. And the cybersecurity guy will be there too. You'll only be alone with this psycho for thirty seconds. I went over there and found the perfect spot. We'll see you come in. I already arranged with the hostess where to seat you. It'll be quick and surgical."

"This guy really replied to your email?"

"Yep. Used our same language and said he was looking forward to discussing 'a more conventional arrangement' in a new position with the company. He said he appreciated them acknowledging what a stellar job he'd been doing."

Quinn took a deep breath. "Okay, then. He thinks he's getting a new job within the company. And I'm going to be giving it to him. I think I can do that."

"I know you can do it. See you tomorrow. Dress like an executive. Call me if you have any questions beforehand. I'll be up late tonight, but you should get some sleep."

"Pretty sure I'm not sleeping tonight, but I'll try."

Rico affected Yoda's voice. "There is no try. There is only do or do not."

"Well, then I guess I have a fifty-fifty chance, right?" Another deep breath. "May the Force be with me."

Quinn and Gin were just coming up to Barbara's house, next door to Hugh's. Suddenly Gin dropped into her slow-motion stance, one foot barely moving through the air. Her hackles raised, just like last night.

Quinn's hackles raised too, and she scanned the area for the cybersecurity guy with the eyebrow scar, convinced that he'd hoodwinked Rico and was not on the level like he'd reported. The streetlights were better in Hugh's neighborhood than her own and she didn't see anything unusual. Gin began pulling toward Barbara's yard and Quinn squinted to see what she was tracking.

"It's just a cat, you goofball." At the sound of Quinn's voice, the cat streaked across the lawn and disappeared. All of Gin's hairs returned to their rightful place. Quinn wondered if H. Smith really did own a cat or if Gin hated two things: cats and cybersecurity guys.

Hugh's front door was locked. Quinn knocked but there was no answer, so she used her key to get inside. "Maybe he went out to get you some more treats, eh, Miss Never Turns Down a Treat?" She unclipped the leash and Gin tore down the hallway. Worried, Quinn followed.

She was dismayed to find Hugh in bed again. He had not turned a corner as she had hoped after the visit with Malcolm. Maybe it wasn't the depression that sent him back to bed. Maybe it was just the visit that had worn him out. "Hugh?" she said quietly. "I was going to leave Gin here tonight, but I forgot to bring her stuff. It'll just take me a little while to go get it."

Hugh didn't move. "She deserves better than me. You keep her."

Gin stood on his hip with her two front feet, as if making a literal stand for what she wanted.

Hugh turned further away from them, stretching Gin's legs enough that she was forced to hop off him. Gin looked at Quinn, as if Quinn could magically make this all better. Quinn's heart broke for Gin, and for Hugh.

"Oh, Hugh. Are you sure?"

He didn't answer.

Quinn turned to leave but Gin streaked past her. She returned with a tennis ball in her mouth. She stood on Hugh's side of the bed and must have dropped it in front of Hugh. Quinn heard it as it bounced to the carpet. Gin slowly walked around the end of the bed and to the living room. She sat in front of the door, waiting while Quinn quickly stored Georgeanne's food in Hugh's refrigerator.

Walking slowly back home with a less-perky Gin, Quinn started down a spiral of worry about them both. Was it possible Hugh got a visit from that JM character that she and Rico were meeting with tomorrow? Or did H. Smith, the cybersecurity guy, stop by and talk to Hugh? Did Hugh slump back into his depression because he learned about Creighton's secret computer? Did one of those men threaten Hugh in some way? Tell him things he wasn't ready to hear?

In her growing fury, she thought she conjured up H. Smith because there he was, leaning up against Mrs. Olansky's stone wall again. Gin's hackles weren't raised and she didn't drop into super–slo-mo. Probably because she knew him now. Quinn marched closer, prepared to pepper him with questions about visiting Hugh.

As she neared, a funny feeling tingled in her gut. She stopped and drew Gin closer. The person lurking in the shadows wasn't H. Smith.

A man's voice said quietly, "I hear you've been helping Creighton's husband. Did you find a computer?"

"Why?" Quinn took a step backward.

"There's private correspondence on it." He took a step forward, emerging from the shadows.

Quinn recognized the handsome man from the funeral. "You're JM!" she blurted. She had no idea what was really going on, but knew enough to get away, especially after hearing Rico call him a psycho. She started to run across the street.

He grabbed Gin's leash, yanking it from her hand.

Quinn stopped in the middle of the street. She couldn't leave Gin with a psycho. Something one of the Retireds said popped into her head: *There's nothing more dangerous than a desperate man.* She'd just have to play it cool like Rico expected of her tomorrow. Now it was just a day earlier. And a completely different plan.

She looked past him toward her house. Lights were on. Her dad's car wasn't in the driveway, but she was fairly certain her mother was home.

"I'll trade you the computer for the dog. I'll go get it." She hoped he didn't know that Rico actually had it. She'd call him as soon as she was out of this guy's view.

"I'll go with you."

"My mom is in there. What do I tell her?"

"Tell her we're on a date."

Ugh, but brilliant. This guy knew mothers. "Fine. But the minute you get the computer, you hand over the dog and make some excuse to leave. Tell her you forgot you were married."

He followed her to the kitchen door. When they got there, Quinn had second thoughts about her plan. "You just wait here by the door while I go get it and then you leave immediately, right?" she whispered.

He spoke gently. "You get me that computer and I'll be gone."

They went inside, Quinn first, then Gin, then her bogus date.

"You're home early. I thought you'd—" Georgeanne's eyes widened as she saw the gorgeous man standing in her kitchen holding Gin's leash.

He stepped forward with a hundred-watt smile and an outstretched hand. Georgeanne took it. "I'm Joe. Happy to meet you, ma'am."

He was very polite. For a murderer.

"You're not a dog!" Georgeanne blurted as she shook his hand. "The last time Quinn brought a friend home, it was Gin." She gestured at the dog sniffing for crumbs on the kitchen floor. "Oh, I'm Georgeanne, by the way."

Georgeanne buzzed around the kitchen, apologizing for the messy state of the kitchen, which was spotless. As she straightened things that didn't need straightening, Quinn kept trying to speak.

"Mom, I need to—"

"Where'd you two meet?"

"Mom, don't—"

"How long have you known each other?"

"Mom—"

"Georgeanne," Joe said in his melodic tenor. "Your house is lovely, but you mustn't make a fuss."

"Are you dating? Quinn, why didn't you tell me you were dating someone?"

"We're not dating," Quinn said.

"We haven't known each other very long," Joe said.

"I'll put together some sandwiches for you." Georgeanne looked in the refrigerator. "Roast beef and beets, or tuna and apple on rye?"

Joe grimaced.

Quinn thought it would serve him right to have to eat a beef and beet sandwich, probably served with jelly and mustard, but instead she said, "Thanks, Mom, but we already ate."

Georgeanne poured two glasses of iced tea. "I'll just pop some comfort squares in the oven in case you change your mind." She rummaged through the freezer, then pulled a cookie sheet from a low cabinet.

"I'll be right back." Quinn made her way around Joe but he grabbed her upper arm, not enough to hurt, but enough to make his point.

"Before you go...honey...can I borrow your phone for a minute? Mine's dead." He looked at Quinn in a pointed manner and she knew he'd figured out her flimsy plan.

Georgeanne had her back turned, busying herself with the comfort squares.

Joe looked at Quinn, tipped his head toward Georgeanne and then toward Gin, who had splayed herself on the cool linoleum floor.

Quinn didn't need any words from Joe. The message was clear. Harm would come to both Georgeanne and Gin if she didn't comply. She nodded at Joe, handing over her phone. Her mouth was dry and she took a drink from one of the glasses of tea. Her hands shook as she raised it to her mouth, giving her another idea. She sloshed the tea from the glass down the front of her shirt and shorts. "Oh, what a klutz I am."

Georgeanne turned around. "Better get those in some cold water to soak. Otherwise that tea will stain."

"Good idea, Mom." Quinn calmly walked out of the kitchen, but just beyond the doorway, scrambled like a cartoon cat into her parents' room to find Georgeanne's phone. Not on the dresser. Not in the phone holster of her purse, although why would she expect that since it was the logical place for a phone? Why buy a purse with a phone holster if you weren't going to use it? Quinn stood in the center of the bedroom and turned in a slow circle, searching.

Not anywhere in plain sight.

"What's taking so long, honey?" Joe called out.

Quinn poked her head back in the kitchen. "I'm looking for some... uh...bleach to soak these in so the stain doesn't set."

"Not bleach, Quinn! Just cold water."

"I'm sure I heard somewhere you need to use bleach on tea stains. It'll just take a sec."

Georgeanne began to speak but Quinn cut her off. "Hey, Mom, why don't you tell Joe about bananas. Everything you told me the other day was so interesting!" That would buy some time. Quinn raced back to

Georgeanne's room, listening to the beginning of Georgeanne's long, involved facts about bananas.

"Did you know that the bananas we eat today are not the same as the bananas my grandparents ate?"

Again, Quinn frantically passed her eyes over every surface but still didn't see Georgeanne's phone. She dumped the contents of her purse on the bed. Pawed through it all. No phone.

Was it possible she had it on her right now? If so, Quinn was sunk. She tried to think like Georgeanne. *I own my phone. It's not for me to be at everyone else's beck and call.* She didn't use it at home, preferring the landline in the kitchen. But she took it when she left the house in case she got a flat tire or had to tell a friend about the great deal on ground beef at the grocery store. Quinn tried to remember if Georgeanne said anything about leaving the house today and immediately felt guilty because she didn't always listen to her chatter. She vowed to do better. Assuming neither of them got murdered tonight.

If the phone was anywhere in this room, and it wasn't in her purse or on a dresser, then it had to be in the closet. Quinn opened the door and saw the light pink cardigan Georgeanne wore everywhere on chilly summer evenings. She shoved her hands in the pockets. Success!

She had to search Georgeanne's contacts to find Rico's number. That was the problem with relying on cell phones. You never knew anyone's number in an emergency. She finally found it under *Chestnut Police #2. Jeez, Mom.* "Pickuppickuppickup," she murmured.

"Rico Lopez."

"Rico." Quinn covered her mouth and whispered directly into the phone, trying to be quiet enough that Joe won't hear her. "That guy, JM is here at the house. I think it's him anyway. He wants the computer. Hostage situation. Get over here."

"Hello? Anyone there?"

She moved to the far corner of the room and whispered a bit louder. "Rico! Get over here! And bring that computer!"

"Hello? Hello?" Rico laughed and said to someone else, "I think I just got butt-dialed." Then he hung up.

The phone went dark and she realized he didn't have Georgeanne's cell programmed in his phone. He always called the landline like he'd been doing since he was eight years old. She'd have to text him. Before she got his contact back up, Joe walked in the bedroom.

* * * *

The calm, polite look on his face had disappeared. Quinn stared into a stony scowl and backed further into the corner.

He saw the phone in her hand. "Who did you call?"

"Nobody."

He pushed into the corner with her. Quinn could smell his aftershave.

"Who...did...you...call?" He spoke quietly and over-enunciated each word.

When Quinn didn't respond he grabbed for the phone. "Who?"

She knew *Chestnut Police #2* would come right up as soon as he looked. "A friend of mine. Rico. I was scared...that these stains wouldn't come out and he'd know what to do. I didn't get through anyway." She held her breath, hoping he'd believe her.

He grabbed her arm and dragged her out. This time she felt his anger.

Joe led her back to the kitchen, pocketing Georgeanne's phone on the way. He shoved her toward a chair next to her mother.

Quinn gasped when she saw Georgeanne tied up with her own apron. The bib one that said *There are two kinds of people I hate: people who make lists, people who can't count, and hypocrites* that Quinn had given her for Christmas a few years back. A casing ran on either side of the apron through which a drawstring formed the neck. Georgeanne said she liked it because she could adjust how high the bib went. Right now that was not a feature she wanted.

Georgeanne's eyes were about to bug right out of her sockets, trying to figure out why her daughter's new boyfriend had dropped her favorite apron over her head, backwards, and tied her to the chair with it.

Quinn saw the drawstring pulling across her throat as it held her tight against the chair.

Joe saw her staring at her mother. "I didn't want to, but you left me no choice. You should have just brought me that computer instead of playing games with the phone." Joe's voice had an apologetic tone to it, but Quinn didn't let that lower her guard.

"Sit down."

Quinn sat in the chair he'd indicated, behind the table. Georgeanne was at the end of the table, but Quinn was behind it in a chair against the wall. She saw Gin's leash attached to her collar. The leash had been lashed through the handles of a low cabinet.

Joe placed a bowl of water near Gin and rubbed her head. Gin's tail thumped against the floor. He held out a treat, which she gobbled up.

Then he turned toward Quinn and Georgeanne. "That's not too tight, is it, Georgeanne?" He slipped a finger between her throat and the drawstring.

Georgeanne shook her head. "It's fine."

He put his hands on his hips and focused on Quinn. "I don't have to tie you up, right?"

"Right." Quinn's voice squeaked.

"Um…I don't know what's going on with you two, but my comfort squares are burning." Georgeanne's hands were also tied behind her, so she used her head to indicate Joe should look at the oven.

"Oh, gosh!" He hurried over, found the oven mitts, and pulled the cookie sheet from the oven.

"Go ahead and turn the oven off. I don't think I'll be cooking anything else tonight." Georgeanne paused. "Will I?"

"No, probably not." Joe removed the oven mitts from his hands. He leaned over and took a sniff of the comfort squares.

"Go ahead and have one. They'll help you calm down," Georgeanne said.

"Mom!"

Joe shrugged and placed one on a small plate he found in the cupboard.

Quinn wondered if she should tell him what was in them. Better to let him find out on his own. Besides, he wouldn't believe her anyway.

"You should let it cool," Georgeanne said.

"Good idea." He turned to Quinn. "Go get me that computer now."

She didn't know what he'd do when he found out she didn't even have the computer, so she started asking questions to buy some time to think of another plan. "Before I give you that computer, I need to know some things. I need to know how Hugh is involved in this." She didn't let on that she had no idea what "this" was.

Joe carried the small plate to the table and set it in front of him, though he remained standing, staring at Quinn across the table. "Why don't you tell me what you already know so we can cut to the chase." He picked up a comfort square and blew on it. Still too hot, apparently, as he set it back on the plate.

Quinn spoke slowly. "I know about the invoices."

"What about them?"

She wanted to shout, *I don't know! I don't know about any of this!* but she was pretty sure that wouldn't help anything. Instead, she chewed her bottom lip and tried to decide what she should say.

Joe didn't seem to be in a hurry, which Quinn also didn't understand, but she appreciated nonetheless.

He picked up the comfort square, gave it another sniff, and took a big bite.

By the look of his face, it seemed he got one of the peanut butter and dill pickle ones. It was a shame too, because the mashed-potato-and-cheese was really quite delicious. Peanut butter and pickle might cause backlash. Quinn braced herself.

After he choked down the bite, eyes watering a bit, Quinn was dumbfounded to hear him say, "These are delicious, Georgeanne."

Completely baffled, Quinn hit a mental roadblock. How could a guy tie up Georgeanne, then be so polite as to compliment her on food he didn't particularly like, just to spare her feelings? How could a murderer be so polite?

"I'm glad you liked it, Joe." Georgeanne's dimples appeared, as if she hadn't been tied to her kitchen chair with her own apron. "Have another. There are all different flavors. I think there are some peanut butter and bacon in this batch. Those are my favorite."

"Maybe in a bit. I'm still waiting on Quinn to do as I asked."

"I have more questions." An understatement. "I know you and Creighton worked together—"

"That's a good one. We worked *together*." Joe started to laugh, alarming Quinn when it began to sound a bit unhinged. "There was no *together*. I did all of Creighton's work."

Quinn frowned. "Creighton was blackmailing you?"

"No. He outsourced his job to me."

Georgeanne said, "Like subletting an apartment?"

"Kinda. Except we both lived there."

"I'm confused," Quinn said. Another understatement. "What's on the computer if you two were coworkers?"

Joe dragged a chair over by Gin and sat in it. She rubbed her head against his leg and he reached down to caress her side. "We weren't coworkers in the traditional sense. We had an agreement. I did his work, he paid me half his salary." Gin nuzzled his hand and he complied by rubbing her under the chin.

"Why didn't you just get a job there and do your own work?" Quinn asked.

Joe let out a breath. "I'm unemployable in most industries."

Quinn immediately thought about her OCD. "Mental illness?" Stricken, she added, "That came out wrong. I meant—"

He waved off her concern. "I have debilitating back pain from a car accident. The only thing that works for me to control it is marijuana. I can't pass a drug test."

"Isn't that legal now?" Georgeanne asked.

Quinn nodded, slowly figuring it out. "But not with the federal government or many other states. And software design can be a sensitive area."

"Then just get a different job," Georgeanne said. "I hear Denver RTD needs bus and train drivers. You're a nice, polite man. You'd probably get snapped up."

A nice, polite man who ties people up in their own homes. Quinn bit her tongue. "Mom, everywhere does drug testing these days."

She glanced at Quinn. "Did Jake test you before he hired you at the diner?"

"No, because I was the only one who wanted to work there. Beggars can't be choosers." She turned back to Joe. "But what does this have to do with—"

The doorbell rang and they all froze. It rang again and Quinn heard Loma's voice. "I know you're here. I see your car."

The upholstery samples. "Ohmygosh, I forgot she was coming over tonight." Quinn looked at Joe. "She won't go away. Let me go tell her I'm sick or something."

Joe shook his head. The doorbell rang again, three times in a row. He realized that Quinn had been correct. Loma wasn't going away. Joe untied Georgeanne. "No funny business. Just tell her Quinn isn't here. She got tied up somewhere."

Quinn didn't point out the irony.

Georgeanne opened the door but didn't say anything.

C'mon, Mom. Don't blow this.

Joe hurried to the front door and hid behind it. Quinn slipped to the doorway. Maybe she could signal Loma without Joe seeing.

"Um…hi, Georgeanne. Quinn around? She's supposed to help me decide on swatches tonight."

Georgeanne shook her head, but still didn't say anything.

Not weird at all, Mom.

Joe loomed up over Georgeanne's shoulder. "Georgeanne, Quinn can't find her silk scarf. She wanted to wear it when we—oh, excuse me. I didn't realize you had company."

Loma's grin split her face. "Quinn's getting ready for a date? With you, Captain America? Well, no wonder she forgot to call me. Girl's brain only goes one way with the likes of you, eh?" Loma redistributed all the swatches and samples into her left arm so she could reach forward and poke Joe in the ribs with her right index finger.

Quinn tried to signal her from where she peeked out of the kitchen, but Joe was blocking the view. She thought about running toward Loma screaming, but saw how Joe clutched Georgeanne's upper arm. Instead, Quinn jumped up and down a few times from across the room. Loma never looked her way.

"Well, never mind," Loma said. "I'll catch up with her tomorrow. Have fun, you two!"

Joe locked the front door and ushered Georgeanne back into the chair, tying her up with the apron again. "Not too tight?"

"No. It's fine." Georgeanne gave him a wan smile. She still rewarded Joe with her dimples, though.

Joe looked at Quinn. "I suggest…in the firmest possible way…that you bring me that computer right now."

Despite the fact she hadn't come up with a new plan, Quinn lowered herself heavily into the chair. "I don't have it."

Joe slumped into a chair. "Who does?"

"The police." Quinn dropped her chin to her chest. Loose hair fell in her face.

He rubbed the back of his neck, shoulders still hunched. "That complicates things."

"You're telling me." Quinn thought for a minute. Anyone else would be storming around, ransacking the place, angry at this turn of events. But not Joe. Quinn raised her head. Brushed the hair from her face. He's not acting like a murderer. He's acting like a man who got himself in a jam, involved in something over his head. Quietly, she said, "Joe, why'd you kill Creighton?"

Georgeanne gasped, but Joe looked relieved that someone actually knew and he didn't need to carry the secret alone.

He picked up another comfort square from the cookie sheet, thought better of it, and dropped it on the plate. He spoke softly. "Creighton told me he was going to surprise his husband and tell him he was going to retire too. Up until then, though, he'd been planning to work several more years, which was perfect, as far as I was concerned. He was paying me well enough and I was living really frugally and socking away money as fast as I could until that day came. If I was really, really, careful, I thought I could retire then too." He nodded at Georgeanne. "Or maybe then I could look for a job that doesn't drug test. But like this…everything would… nothing would…" His voice trailed off.

"So you went to his house?" Quinn asked quietly.

* * * *

Loma returned all her fabric swatches to the back seat of her car and left Quinn's house. She pulled a U-turn in the street and grinned as she glanced back at the house. "'Bout time, girl. And Captain America to boot." Loma cackled.

She wasn't nervous about being out at the Maynard property since she found out her trespassers were just out there looking for nasty old worms. But she couldn't do this job alone. She needed her friends, rocky road and chocolate fudge swirl.

She strode into the grocery store, straight back to the freezer section. When confronted with the excellent selection, she wasn't sure she wanted to commit to rocky road and chocolate fudge swirl after all. She prowled up and down the aisle, choosing and rejecting many fine choices. She finally settled on two half-gallons, salted butter pecan and chocolate cherry.

Loma took the long way to the register, deciding to make a pass by the cheese case to see if anything jumped into her arms. She was poking through the fancy cheddars when she heard Rico's voice.

"Hey, Loma."

"Whachoo got there, Officer? Don't tell me it's a bag of doughnuts. Such a boring stereotype."

"While I do love a good glazed, this is actually a sandwich. I thought you had plans with Quinn tonight."

"She stood me up. Got a better offer, it seems."

"A better offer?"

"Yeah, I went to her house, but Georgeanne said she wasn't there. Then this hot snack pokes his head out and says Quinn couldn't find her scarf. I bet it was that lavender one with the butterflies. She loves that scarf."

"Wait. Quinn wasn't there but her date was?"

Loma frowned, thinking. "I asked if she was there, Georgeanne shook her head, hottie says she can't find her scarf."

"Has she told you she's dating someone? She hasn't said a word to me about it."

"No, but she was probably just worried I'd steal him right from under her nose. Big ladies got charms over skinny white girls."

"Have you ever seen him before? What did he look like?" Rico spoke fast, his voice pitched higher than normal.

"Rico, you're scaring me." Loma scooped up her ice cream from where it was resting on cheese wedges.

* * * *

"I went to Creighton's house just to talk to him. Tried to get him to reconsider. I thought if he actually saw me, that I was a real person, not just some internet guy..."

"But then?"

Joe's eyes hardened. "But then I saw all those awards and things he got for *my* work. I knew they came with bonus money. But he never mentioned it. He should have given the bonuses to me. All of it. I earned it."

"Yes, you did," Georgeanne said quietly. "That was a terrible thing for Creighton to do."

But not terrible enough to get killed for, Quinn thought.

Joe began pacing the kitchen, clenching and unclenching his fists.

Quinn tried to change direction by making another guess at all this. "Why'd you take those files and dump them at the truck stop?"

Joe stopped pacing and sat by Gin again. It seemed to calm him to pet her. "I wanted to find proof of what he was doing, find passwords or more information about the VPN or something. But I went a little crazy, trashed the place looking for a computer I knew he had to have there. I needed to let the company know what he was doing. To them and to me. But he started laughing at me."

Georgeanne gave a couple of *tsk-tsk*s in sympathy.

Joe mimicked a singsong voice that Quinn assumed was supposed to be Creighton's. "They're not going to care. They paid my salary for a job to get done. I gave half my salary to you. We both got paid, and they got the work. I'm going to quit anyway. You've got nothing on me."

"So you snapped." Quinn said it like a statement rather than a question, since it was fairly obvious by now.

"Wouldn't you?" His voice was his own again, but calm, resigned. "I was furious. He stole my life. Pulled the rug right out from under me with no warning." Joe let out an anguished sob.

"Oh, Joe," Georgeanne murmured.

He looked away, swiping at his eyes with his arm. "I wasn't worried about me. I could get some crap job to support myself. But I need real money to support my daughter." He raised his eyes, meeting Georgeanne's. "My daughter is blind. How am I going to keep her at that school now?"

Quinn glanced at her mother, who looked like she might start crying too. *Was she buying this sob story? Had she forgotten about Creighton?* "How did Creighton end up with Hugh's scissors in his chest?"

"It wasn't premeditated. You gotta believe me."

Georgeanne said, "We—"

Quinn cut her off. "It doesn't matter what we believe. The fact Creighton was found in the bathtub—"

"When I started trashing the place he came at me with a pair of scissors that were sitting on a pile of fabric, but I got them away from him. He ran to the bathroom and tried to lock the door, but I got there before he could. I was trying to pull him back out to the living room, but he slipped, then I lost my balance. The next thing I knew, I was on top of him in the tub, and he…" Joe shuddered.

Quinn narrowed her eyes at him. "So it was a complete accident but the scissors just happened to be wiped clean of fingerprints. And no fingerprints anywhere in the house—"

Joe shrugged. It seemed all the wind had gone out of his sails. He suddenly looked ten years older.

"After…ward…I still couldn't find the information I needed, but I knew I had to get out of there, so I just grabbed as many files as I could and ran. I was on my way back to Denver, but realized if I was caught with these papers it would look bad, so I parked at the truck stop and looked through them. I didn't find anything about Buckley Tech I could use, so I just dumped it there."

Joe quit talking. Quinn had run out of questions. She had tried to imagine what had happened at Hugh's house when she saw the mess there. Now she knew.

The scene with Joe and Georgeanne in the kitchen seemed so innocuous, in comparison, like any one of their neighbors could have come over to talk over a problem and get some advice from Georgeanne. Nobody else would have tied her to a chair, though.

Quinn had no reason to believe Joe's story. But she had no reason to doubt it either. To her mind it was too elaborate to have been fabricated, and it matched what she'd seen at Hugh's house. She watched him rub his hands across his anguished face. Plus, he just looked like he was telling the truth. He was polite, but not in a creepy, ingratiating way. He seemed to Quinn like a desperate man who was pushed too far—by his pain, by his finances, by the system, by his worry about his daughter, and finally, tragically, by Creighton's mocking.

Creighton didn't deserve to die because of any of it, though.

Quinn was torn. So many bad guys were really bad, but Joe was…what? A good bad guy? A good guy who did a bad thing? A reluctant villain?

She watched him pick up the empty plate from the table and get more comfort squares from the cookie sheet. He set the plate back down and returned to his seat. "These any good cold?" He waved one at Quinn.

"They're as good cold as they are hot," Quinn said diplomatically.

"Thank you, dear," Georgeanne said.

"Either of you want one?" Joe held the plate out.

Georgeanne's hands were tied, but she didn't say anything sarcastic to that effect. Quinn almost did, but thought better of it. Joe hadn't done anything particularly violent here tonight, but it would certainly be better not to press the matter. "No, thanks."

Joe took a bite of a comfort square. "Hey! This one's good. Is that chocolate pudding with mashed potatoes?" He held it out to Georgeanne.

She nodded. "With cheddar cheese. That's one of Quinn's favorites."

"You know what would be good in these? Apple pie filling and cheddar cheese."

"Ooh, I hadn't thought of that, but you're right."

Incredulous, Quinn stared at them having their kaffeeklatsch, a murderer and his tied-up captive. She listened to them while they discussed recipes and argued about the best spices. Georgeanne liked smoked paprika, but Joe lobbied hard for jerk seasoning. Figured.

Quinn wondered briefly if Georgeanne was formulating some plan to get them out of this mess, but the look on her face disabused Quinn of this notion. Georgeanne was simply enjoying a conversation about food and cooking.

After listening to them a bit longer, finally Quinn said, "You know you have to turn yourself in."

Joe heaved a heavy sigh. "I know." He got up and untied Georgeanne. When he was done, she gave him a motherly pat on the shoulder.

"Why'd you come here tonight, anyway?" Quinn asked.

"I got an email from a lady at Buckley Tech, telling me she wanted to offer me a real job." He fiddled with the plate.

Quinn didn't know if he was aware she was supposed to magically turn into that lady tomorrow. "Well, that sounds nice."

"But it was weird too, ya know?" He turned his attention to Quinn. "So I did a bit of digging and found some emails from a guy named Smith. Seems he's been here to talk to you. And that newspaper lady at the funeral told me you were cleaning up Creighton's house while his husband was in jail. I put two and two together and figured you must have found the computer."

Quinn pictured Vera sitting in the pew next to him, absolutely smitten. *She probably would have given up my credit card info, my Facebook password, and my bra size if she knew them. Thanks a lot, Vera.*

"I thought if I could just get my hands on the computer, then I could destroy whatever evidence was on there that might lead them to me. I didn't know you'd already given it to the police." He narrowed his eyes at her, then abruptly softened his gaze. His entire being sagged. "I guess none of that matters now, though."

"Can I have my phone? I'll call Rico. He's a police officer and my best friend. He'll listen to you. Mom and I will help you explain."

Joe nodded and handed over Quinn's phone.

"I'll put some coffee on." Georgeanne began filling the pot with water from the tap.

"Mom, where's Dad? I don't want him bursting in and getting… everyone…nervous."

"Oh, he'll be out late. He's at a party in Denver at one of his agent's houses. He'll end up having to drive someone home."

Joe looked alarmed. "Agent? FBI?"

"Worse. Insurance." Quinn dialed Rico's number. They heard a ringtone outside the kitchen door.

Joe panicked and in one deft movement, grabbed Georgeanne and a knife from the knife block.

Rico burst through the door with his gun drawn, Loma right behind him. "Drop that knife and let the nice lady go."

Quinn stepped between Rico and Joe. She held an arm straight at each of them, palms up. A human demilitarized zone. Loma grabbed the back of a chair and took in the scene, eyes wide.

"It's okay," Quinn said to Rico, her voice steady and calm. "I have it all under control. Put your gun down."

Rico didn't.

Joe walked forward, using Georgeanne as a shield.

"Joe, don't make this worse for yourself. You were all set to turn yourself in. Nothing has changed. Rico is the one I called. You heard his phone ring. You don't want to hurt my mom, do you?"

"No." But he didn't let her go. Nor did he drop the knife.

"Of course you don't, Joe," Georgeanne said.

"So put the knife down and let her go." Quinn's arms were still raised. She caught a peek at Rico from the corner of her eye. He hadn't moved a muscle. Gun still pointed directly at Joe. She turned her attention back to Joe, the unknown part of this equation. "C'mon, Joe. Don't make it worse. Put the knife down and let Mom go over there by my friend Loma." Quinn smiled at Loma, who could only muster a sick grimace.

Joe looked at Georgeanne, then Rico, then Loma, then Quinn. He nodded. He took a slight step forward to place the knife on the table, while still holding Georgeanne, but as he did so, the front door opened with some loud thumps. Dan laughed loudly along with another man.

Rico pivoted with his gun pointed at the living room.

Joe grabbed Georgeanne tighter and raised the knife again.

As soon as he determined it was just Dan and a friend in the living room, Rico swung his gun back and pointed it again at Joe.

Joe continued to use Georgeanne as a shield, this time against whatever was happening in the living room. "Quinn," he said quietly without looking at her. "I'm gonna need you to go sit in that chair behind the table." When she didn't move he growled, "Now."

Quinn sat.

Dan staggered into the kitchen from the living room.

Without taking his eyes off Dan, Joe said, "What's going on here, Quinn?"

"Clearly my dad is drunk."

"And shouldn't have been driving," Georgeanne added with a disapproving frown.

"We Lyfted it," Dan said.

"No, we Lubered it," his friend said.

Neither of them had processed the scene in the kitchen, through their drunken haze.

Dan greeted Joe as he passed by, heading for the sink. "I'm Dave and this is Dan," Dan said.

Dave laughed. "No, *you're* Dave and *I'm* Dan."

As they passed Joe, he turned with them, Georgeanne still held in front of him. By the time everyone had stopped shuffling around the kitchen, Joe had his back to the table, and Rico had moved slightly to the left so he was closer to the living room archway. His gun was still pointed at Joe. Georgeanne was still the shield between them.

"Is there any coffee, Georgie? I'm afraid he's a little drunk." Dan elbowed Dave. "We had fun, though. Sheldon was there. Remember Sheldon? He had that cat with three legs. 'Member? That time I said I'd feed it while he was gone and—" Dan and Dave found themselves across the kitchen. Dan saw the water in the coffeepot that Georgeanne had filled earlier. "Oh, yeah, I was making coffee," he said. He pulled out a coffee filter and wedged it in the machine. Then he and Dave had a short minuet while he tried to get past him to get the coffee from the cupboard. After several tries with the scoop, Dan succeeded in getting a miniscule amount of coffee into the cockeyed filter. He poured the water and pushed the button on and then off again. "Now where was I?"

Dave said, "The cat is feeding you while Sheldon was gone."

"Oh, yeah, Sheldon never told me that cat was a social eater and I'd have to shtay near the food bowl if I didn't want it to starve to death so I—"

While everyone watched Dan and listened to his ridiculous cat story, Quinn slowly rose from where she sat behind the table. Stealthy, she plucked up the discarded apron Joe had used to tie up Georgeanne. She crept directly behind Joe, inch by agonizing inch. She caught Rico's eye and he nodded ever so slightly. She raised the apron strap over Joe's head and yanked him to the floor.

The knife clattered away.

Georgeanne scurried behind Quinn.

Rico dropped his knee to the center of Joe's back and handcuffed him.

It all happened in a split second. Nobody spoke.

Dan and Dave watched everything, uncomprehending. Finally Dave looked at Dan. "But what happened to the cat?"

Chapter 22

Quinn didn't go into the diner the next morning, since she'd already arranged to have the time off for her aborted plan with Rico. She mulled over that plan, lolling in bed, wondering if it would have worked. Joe might have recognized her from the funeral and bolted. Or worse, done something erratic. It was kind of his MO, wasn't it? All things happened for a reason. Quinn thought about Eliza's question on the phone the other day. *Did* she believe in fate? Quinn decided it didn't really matter what she believed. Everything turned out fine.

Almost everything. Quinn rubbed mopey Gin's scruff. Hugh needed Gin and Gin needed Hugh. She threw off the covers and got dressed. She tiptoed around the house, gathering up Gin's supplies and keeping it quiet for her parents, both of whom needed to sleep in after last night. She was pretty sure Dan and his friend both needed aspirin today too. Rico got Donnie to drive Dave home last night, which was a godsend. Georgeanne didn't need to play nursemaid to anyone else today.

Quinn set a bottle of aspirin on the counter and added some coffee to what Dan had measured so poorly into the machine last night. She pushed the button and started it to brewing.

She wrote a note. *Coffee's made. Here's some aspirin. Took Gin to Hugh's. Back later. Q*

She loaded up the car with Gin's belongings and grabbed a manila envelope she had filled earlier, shoving it in her bag. She had to go back for Gin's leash, still looped through the handles of the cabinet from last night. Joe needn't have tied her up; she hadn't moved all night. She was happy to have people keeping her company in the kitchen, where the food was, never mind the hostage situation.

Gin was excited for the car ride, and became overwhelmed with joy when she saw Hugh's house.

As they neared, Quinn worried about how she'd find Hugh this time. Drowning in depression, or pulling himself toward the light? She took a breath and reminded herself, Hugh needed Gin and Gin needed Hugh.

The unlocked and half-opened front door might be a good sign, she thought as they reached the porch. She tried to be optimistic, but left Gin's things in the car, just in case.

She held open the screen door for Gin, who raced inside, and ran down the hall toward Hugh's bedroom. Gin had raced back to the living room before Quinn even saw Hugh sitting on the couch. He wore a robe and had an almost empty plate in front of him on the coffee table, just a few bites of scrambled eggs and toast left next to a mottled brown banana peel.

Gin rushed him, winding herself in between his legs, finally poking her nose a millimeter from the plate.

Hugh laughed and fed her the last few bites. "Don't get used to it. You know what Creighton used to say...people food is for people, not dogs who think they're people."

Gin finished her snack, then licked Hugh's fingers and face.

Quinn thought about telling him what happened last night, but decided to let Rico or someone else do that. Hugh was feeling fine right now and Quinn didn't want to ruin it, talking about Creighton's murderer.

She stood, picking up Hugh's plate.

"You don't have to do that anymore," he said softly. He pushed her hand back down, but in doing so, knocked the banana peel off the plate. It landed on the floor.

Quinn picked it up, the message catching her eye. She read it out loud. "It takes two to mango."

Hugh held out his hand and Quinn gave him the limp peel. He rubbed a languid thumb along it. "That was such a silly game he and Aaron Janikowski used to play. I had to learn to eat a lot of bananas." His eyes got glossy, but no tears fell. "Aaron would sell him these bright green bananas that he poked a message into and Creigh would check them every day to find the hidden messages. He was like a little kid. Then he'd go over to the store and cause mischief in the produce department, always trying to one-up himself. He'd move signs around. Put on a store apron, pretending he worked there, to try to convince people they were using the wrong name for common produce. Once he put all the kiwis under bananas so it looked like a display of genitalia. And, of course, there was always his fallback of asking people to help him weigh his head in the produce scale." He patted the couch next to him. Gin jumped up. "Not you! Quinn." He looked up at Quinn and patted the seat again.

Hugh dropped the banana peel to the empty plate. After she sat, he said, "Thank you for taking care of Gin for me."

"It was no trouble."

"Yes, it was, and I'm grateful. I was in such darkness. I don't know what would have happened to her if you hadn't taken care of her. Of us. But after Virginia brought me that ball yesterday and I refused to play with her, I realized I needed to return to the world."

"Maybe leaving her here would have made you feel better sooner," Quinn said. "I worried about that every day. You do feel better, right?"

"I do."

"Good."

"And thank you for what you did last night."

"You heard?"

"Got a call from a security guy at Buckley Tech. Some guy named Smith." Hugh gave her the side-eye. "Sounds like an alias to me."

"That's what I thought too!"

He nodded. "Seems Creighton had some kind of scheme going on at work. They're not going to ask for any money back or anything, so that's good. His shenanigans didn't cost the company anything, and from what I understand, that guy was excellent at his job. Even though Creigh was just sitting around watching Netflix all day, at least that other fellow was doing the work. It makes sense now that Creigh was so—what's it you kids say? Plugged into culture. I always thought he watched TV after I fell asleep. But he was watching it all day at work."

"I just don't understand why he did it. Why not just do the work himself?"

Hugh shrugged. "He always said he wasn't a great programmer. I never believed that for a minute, and even if he wasn't it wouldn't bother me one bit, but Creighton felt like people—even me—were judging him."

"He was good enough to get that job."

"That's what I told him. But he was obsessive. Once he got his mind fixated on something, he couldn't turn loose of it."

"I can relate," Quinn said dryly.

"That's why it makes perfect sense that he blew up the plan we made for him to retire in a few years. He just decided he couldn't wait. I loved him, but I sure didn't understand him sometimes."

There was a comfortable pause in the conversation, but Quinn still had questions. "Can I ask you something, Hugh? Did you know someone who lived at the old Maynard place?"

Hugh got a far-off look in his eyes. "Oh, I did indeed. James." He stared across the room, a slight smile dancing at the corners of his mouth. "Why?"

Quinn walked into the kitchen and pulled the large envelope from her bag. "My friend Loma is an interior designer, working out there. She and I found these the other day." She handed him the packet of old love letters.

He furrowed his brow as he flipped through them. When he realized what they were, his eyes glistened.

Quinn sat quietly next to him while he read them all.

He placed the pile on his lap, and folded his hands over it. "My secret grand gesture. James might have returned my feelings, but it was the wrong place and time. We couldn't talk about any of that then. I wanted to make it real, though, and felt like this was the only way. Nobody ever found them. Until now, of course, and it's much too late."

"Why in the wall?"

"James told me about his grandmother who dropped coins down there when she quit trusting the banks during the Great Depression. That, combined with my love for archeology and the stories about how they'd be able to re-create a civilization from the contents of firepits, trash piles, even outhouses…well, I just loved the romance of that. It sparked my imagination." He patted her hand. "Maybe someone in the future would find them, maybe not. But by writing those notes, I could make my feelings real, but in a safe place. It was how I came out to myself."

"I totally get that." That's what she had been doing with her OCD. Keeping everything inside like a secret, instead of bringing it all into the open with her therapist.

"A private testament. I guess that's why I showered Creighton with so much affection. It was so nice to love someone in public." His eyes clouded. "Maybe that's why it was so painful to find out Creighton had a family he never told me about."

"Not even a hint?"

"If he gave one, I sure didn't pick up on it." Hugh crossed the room, placed the love notes neatly on the mantle. The *Les Mis* card fluttered to the floor. He picked it up, read it, then replaced it in front of the stack.

Quinn stood. "I have something else to tell you. I found a bunch of money hidden around your house when I was cleaning up." She led him to all the hiding places and helped him make a stack of all the cash. "I think it was the bonus money Joe Macon earned. But I'm wondering why Creighton wouldn't have just put in in the bank?"

Hugh stared, dumbfounded by the pile of cash in his hands. "I don't know. Maybe he didn't want to make a big deal about it and have me start asking questions about his work. Or have me come to the honors banquets. He always went to those alone, said I'd be bored. Maybe he didn't want the potential cross-contamination of his lives." Hugh fanned the bills. "Maybe he always thought he'd get caught by his company. Maybe this was his way of leaving a rainy-day fund for me." Hugh counted the money again. "I've gotta say, Quinn, I'm conflicted about this fellow, Joe Macon. I hate him for taking Creigh from me like this. But I understand desperation."

"There's nothing more dangerous than a desperate man, or so says Silas."

"True. I've been desperate in my life, many times. What would I have done if someone found those love notes when I was young? It would have caused a scandal. My folks couldn't have weathered that, and probably I couldn't have either. Would I have gone after the person who held those letters? Maybe. I don't know."

They both thought about that for a minute, trying to know the unknowable.

"What do you know about this Joe Macon fellow, Quinn?"

"He was in a terrible car accident years ago and has awful pain. He can't get a job because he's addicted to pot, which is the only thing that touches his pain. He has a daughter who's blind. He needed a good-paying job that didn't do any drug testing because she's in a special school. He said he flipped out because Creighton didn't warn him he was going to retire and his job was going to go away. He had a plan to save up a bunch of money over the next few years to pay for the school. Maybe she would have graduated by then."

"Creigh ruined this fellow's retirement plan too." He shook his head. "He did all this because of his daughter?"

"I guess."

Hugh jogged the stack of bills on the table, making them straight. Quinn approved. He dug through a kitchen drawer and snapped a rubber band around it. "Can we get this to the school to pay her tuition? Anonymously?"

Quinn smiled. "I'll get the address."

Hugh picked up the large manila envelope Quinn had left on the table. "Oh, there's more of my old love notes?" Before Quinn could stop him, he'd removed all the unsent cards to Creigh's kids.

"I should have—"

Hugh held up a hand to shush her as he dropped into a chair to read them. "All the birthday cards," he marveled. "Every year." He glanced up at Quinn, eyes glistening again. "Why didn't he tell me? Why didn't he send them?"

Quinn simply shook her head. Another unknowable.

Hugh handed her the cards. "While you're getting addresses...you think you could get these?"

She nodded, now her eyes swimming as well. She blinked hard, then said, "I have one more question for you." She pulled out the final piece of paper from the large envelope: The crossword puzzle Creighton had been working where he wrote the pun in the margin. "Do you know what this means?"

He studied the half-finished puzzle. "It means he hadn't finished the crossword that day."

"No, the pun in the margin." She pointed.

Hugh looked closer at it, then smiled. "I remember this puzzle. It was full of puns, his favorite thing. I remember he giggled the whole time he was doing that one. He thought of this one and scribbled it down. *Spokesperson: who to call when your wheel breaks*. He was going to ask Vera to pass it along to whoever made that puzzle. It would have tickled him so much to see it in one of the crosswords. Do you know who makes them?"

Quinn took the newspaper from him. "Let me see what I can do."

Chicken Pad Thai with Grandma's Dumplings

Makes a big ol' pot with 12–15 dumplings

Stew Ingredients

4 T peanut oil or sesame oil or whatever kind of oil you have around
3 or 4 boneless chicken breasts, cut into bite-sized chunks
1 onion, diced
2 red bell peppers, diced
chopped garlic cloves, as many as you want (I usually use 2)
one-inch knob of ginger, grated (or find the squirty tube in the produce department. Much easier.)
2 T powdered peanut butter, optional, but delish
8-oz. jar pad Thai sauce (or find a recipe and make your own; I never have time for that)
32-oz. chicken broth

Dumpling Ingredients

1 1/2 C flour (whatever kind you like)
2 t baking powder
a shake or two of salt
1 T Chinese Five Spice
1 T powdered peanut butter, again optional, but still delish
2/3 C milk
2 T oil (I like sesame)
1 egg, beaten

I like using my big Dutch oven for this recipe, because it has a large diameter to place the dumplings. You can use whatever pan you want, of course, but choose wisely. If your pan is wide, you get more dumpling surface with a couple of inches of stew underneath. If your pan is tall, you'll have less room for dumplings with a mile of stew underneath.

In your big pan, sauté the chicken, onion, peppers, garlic, and ginger hot and fast in the oil until the chicken is almost done. Take it off the heat for a sec while you mix in the peanut butter powder and the pad Thai sauce. When it's good and mixed up, add the chicken broth and return it to the heat. Bring to a boil.

While you're waiting for it to boil, make the dumplings. In a bowl, mix together the dry ingredients. Then stir in the rest of the ingredients.

When your stew is boiling, drop the dough by tablespoons on top of it. Put the lid on and let it boil for 15 minutes or so, until the dumplings are fluffy and no longer doughy underneath.

The trick to tender dumplings is to make sure the stew is boiling and don't take the lid off to check them. It was risky taking this to Hugh's house, since I could have easily spilled the whole darn thing, but I think it was worth it.

Black Bean Brownies

I borrowed this recipe from a gal named Becky Clark. She wrote a fun cookbook called the Lazy Low-Cal Lifestyle Cookbook. It's full of easy, healthy, portion-controlled recipes. She calls these "Secret Ingredient Brownies," but I say wave your freak-ingredient flag high! If people don't want to eat them because there's beans in there, then great…more for me. She says this recipe makes 16, but I say it makes 9. Maybe it makes 12. You do you.

15-oz. can black beans
2 eggs
1/2 C unsweetened applesauce
2 T baking cocoa
1/4 C white whole wheat flour
1/4 C dry milk
1 T vanilla
2 t cinnamon
1 t baking powder
1/4 C chocolate chips
1/4 C sugar or stevia

Coat an 8 or 9-inch square baking pan with nonstick spray.

Puree the beans in a food processor or mash them real well with a fork or potato masher.

Add the rest of the ingredients and blend thoroughly.

Pour mixture into prepared pan and bake at 350° for 40–45 minutes or until toothpick comes out clean. Cool before cutting.

Acknowledgments

I am deeply grateful to Leslie Karst, Ellen Byron, and Jill Marsal for their thoughtful comments after I threw pages of gibberish at them and asked, "Hey, do you have a minute to take a look at this manuscript?" ... and then the careful guidance of Norma Perez-Hernandez and the gang over at Kensington for turning it all into a beautiful book.

My crossword puzzles would be full of mistakes and nonsense without my supreme posse of testers: Matt Sautter, Bob Clark, Rebecca Rowley, DruAnn Love, Laura Deal, Kirsten Akens, Lori Howard, and Judy Rose. I'm so thrilled you think my puzzles are fun to solve!

And you, dear reader ... thank you so much for loving books. Writers would be nowhere if it weren't for readers.

1 D	2 A	3 C	4 A		5 P	6 E	7 A	8 T		9 D	10 R	11 U	12 M	13 S
14 I	V	A	N		15 O	R	C	A		16 R	A	T	I	O
17 S	O	C	I	18 O	P	A	T	H		19 A	M	E	N	D
20 H	I	T	M	E				21 I	22 A	M		23 S	I	S
	24 D	I	E	D		25 B	26 A	T	M	A	27 N			
					28 T	O	X	I	C		29 E	30 M	31 O	32 S
33 C	34 R	35 E	36 O	37 S	O	T	E			38 S	H	I	V	A
39 L	I	Z	Z	I	E				40 B	O	R	D	E	N
41 A	A	R	O	N			42 P	43 U	R	S	U	I	N	G
44 P	L	A	N		45 H	46 A	R	P	O					
			47 E	48 L	I	T	E	S		49 F	50 A	51 D	52 S	
53 B	54 R	55 A		56 A	P	E				57 B	R	A	I	58 N
59 R	I	V	60 E	R		61 P	62 A	63 T	64 R	I	C	I	D	E
65 A	C	I	N	G		66 O	B	E	Y		67 E	L	L	E
68 D	O	D	G	E		69 I	S	L	E		70 D	Y	E	D

1 J	2 A	3 N	4 I	5 K	O	6 W	7 S	8 K	9 I		10 M	11 I	12 C	13 S
14 A	L	O	N	E		15 A	P	E	D		16 I	G	O	T
17 W	O	N	K	Y		18 I	A	G	O		19 N	I	C	E
20 S	E	E	S		21 I	T	T			22 F	A	V	O	R
				23 A	R	E		24 V	25 A	L	J	E	A	N
26 A	27 S	28 S		29 N	E	D		30 E	L	O				
31 C	H	A	32 N	T			33 O	N	E		34 M	35 A	36 L	37 I
38 H	U	N	T	I	39 N	40 G	L	I	C	41 E	N	S	E	S
42 S	A	S	H		43 O	R	D			44 N	O	K	I	A
				45 I	I	I		46 L	47 E	D		48 S	A	Y
49 M	50 A	51 Y	52 N	A	R	D		53 O	P	S				
54 A	T	E	A	M			55 E	L	I		56 L	57 O	58 M	59 A
60 N	O	A	M		61 T	62 H	A	I		63 P	O	P	I	N
64 I	N	R	E		65 B	E	S	T		66 A	G	E	N	T
67 C	E	S	S		68 D	R	E	A	D	L	O	C	K	S

Printed in the United States
by Baker & Taylor Publisher Services